Amanda

DEBRA
WHITE SMITH

HARVEST HOUSE PUBLISHERS

EUGENE, OREGON

Cover by Koechel Peterson & Associates, Inc., Minneapolis, Minnesota

Cover image © G R Richardson/Robert Harding World Imagery/Getty Images

Debra White Smith: Published in association with the literary agency of *Alive Communications, Inc., 7680 Goddard Street, Suite 200, Colorado Springs, CO 80920.*

AMANDA
Copyright © 2006 by Debra White Smith
Published by Harvest House Publishers
Eugene, Oregon 97402
www.harvesthousepublishers.com

Library of Congress Cataloging-in-Publication Data

Smith, Debra White.
    Amanda / Debra White Smith.
        p. cm. — (The Austen series ; bk. 5)
    ISBN-13: 978-0-7369-0875-7 (pbk.)
    ISBN-10: 0-7369-0875-7
    1. Dating (Social customs)—Fiction. 2. Female friendship—Fiction. 3. Mate selection—Fiction. 4. Australia—Fiction. I. Title. II. Series.
    PS3569.M5178A83 2005
    813'.54—dc22
                                                  2005026893

Printed in the United States of America

07 08 09 10 11 12 / BC-KB / 10 9 8 7 6 5 4 3 2

Dedicated to my wonderful friends, the MacFarlanes.
Thanks for loving me the way I am and
for being our very own "family."
You're the GREATEST!

Cast

Amanda Wood Priebe: Based upon Emma Woodhouse from Jane Austen's *Emma*. Amanda is a witty young heiress of both the Wood and Priebe fortunes. She declares herself wholly devoted to her father and "married" to their prosperous tourist company.

Angie Townsend West: Based upon Anne Taylor. Amanda's former governess, Angie has just married banker Wayne West. Even though her new marriage takes her from the Priebe household, she and Amanda are still the greatest of friends.

Bev Knighton: Based upon Isabella Knightley. Amanda's sister, Bev is happily married to Gordon Knighton. She and Gordon live in Brisbane, Australia, where they are raising their four children.

Betty Cates: Based upon Hetty Bates. The housekeeper at Wood-Priebe International Travels, Betty is a scatterbrained clean freak who never stops talking.

Franklyn West: Based upon Frank Churchill. Son of Wayne West and stepson of Angie Townsend West, Franklyn is the charming newcomer to Highland. His mysterious smile, good looks, and glib remarks attract the attention of many females—including Amanda.

Haley Schmitz: Based upon Harriet Smith. Amanda's dowdy secretary, Haley comes from humble origins and puts ultimate faith in Amanda's judgment.

Harold Priebe: Based upon Henry Woodhouse. Amanda's father and a widower, Harold is the owner of the Wood-Priebe International Travel Agency chain.

Gordon Knighton: Based upon John Knightley. The brother of Nate Knighton, Gordon is married to Amanda's sister, Bev Gordon, and is one of two vice presidents of Knighton's Department Stores.

Janet French: Based upon Jane Fairfax. Betty Cates' adopted niece, Janet usually turns heads in every crowd. An elegant young lady of Asian descent, Janet's good looks and grace could drive even the most accomplished female into a fit of envy.

Mason Eldridge: Based upon Philip Elton. Mason is the minister of music at Highland Metropolitan Church of Tasmania. While his claims indicate his only ambition in life is to be a man of the cloth, his expensive tastes say he's after a wife with money.

Nathanial "Nate" Knighton: Based upon George Knightley. Nate is the brother of Gordon Knighton. Nate, ten years older than Amanda, has watched her grow up. He's a vice president of Knighton's Department Stores.

Roger Miller: Based upon Robert Martin. Roger comes from a hardworking family who owns a dairy farm outside Highland, Tasmania. He is a man of high integrity and good character.

Wayne West: Based upon Mr. Weston. Wayne is Angie Townsend West's new husband.

A Note from the Author

Tasmania, Australia, is a major tourist attraction for all of Australia as well as much of the world, and not without reason. The beauty of its beaches and mountains leave residents and tourists alike breathless. However, if you look on a map of Tasmania, you'll find Highland, Australia, exists as a suburb of Hobart only in the author's imagination...and yours.

One

"Oh hello, Roger!" Haley Schmitz's voice floated through her ajar office door.

Amanda Wood Priebe lifted her fingers off the computer keyboard, scowled at her secretary's door, and waited for the rest of the conversation. *Haley has been seeing that brown-haired baboon for six months. What she sees in the dairy farmer is anybody's guess,* she thought. She had subtly hinted that Haley could do better, but the secretary never wavered in her fixation. Now the guy was calling her at work.

Haley's soft laugh preceded gentle words. Amanda strained to catch the gist of the conversation yet failed. Roger had been out of town for five days, and he'd called Haley every day. What an average Tasmanian farmer needed to go out of town for was a mystery. But absence was making Haley's heart grow fonder.

This is moving to the desperate zone, Amanda told herself and decided to break her staunch rule of never eavesdropping unless absolutely necessary. In the last three months, Amanda could count on one hand the number of times eavesdropping had been necessary—that is, if she counted all five fingers two or three times.

Amanda slipped her feet out of her backless heels and scurried across the wool rug until her toes met the cool tile that stretched into Haley's office. She hovered beside the open door and tried to catch her secretary's every syllable.

"I miss you too, Roger." Haley's rich, Australian coo deepened Amanda's frown.

I've got to get her settled with someone else, Amanda thought, *before she makes the biggest mistake of her life.* Amanda glanced around. The painting of a herd of zebras on the west wall that came from her trip to South Africa. The miniature sculpture of the Leaning Tower of Pisa commanding the corner reminded her of the trip to Italy. Even the woolen rug, in hues of teal and sapphire-blue, was a souvenir shipped back from Asia. All trips had been essential research for the Wood-Priebe International Travel Agency. Wood-Priebe International never recommended a hotel or restaurant that a staff member hadn't experienced personally.

Haley traveled with Amanda on every excursion. Her office told its own story—right down to the ever-burning, ocean breeze candles that scented the office complex and forever whispered of the trip to the Bahamas. The thought of her kind-hearted friend of three years marrying some farmer and being trapped in a cow paddock when she could be exploring the world made Amanda want to scream.

She deserves better! Amanda thought and decided Haley must be taking whatever she thought she could get. Haley had spent half her childhood in foster homes, and Amanda suspected her background had conditioned her to believe no one really wanted her. Amanda crossed her arms, tapped her toes, and decided to take this situation into her own hands. She mentally went through a list of single men who attended her church. None of them seemed a good fit for Haley; none were good enough.

Amanda pulled a package of spearmint gum from her blazer pocket, thoughtfully unwrapped a piece, and inserted it between her teeth. As the strong mint stung her tongue, she thought of the new music minister at Highland Metropolitan Church. Mason Eldridge had a touch of class. He'd traveled extensively. And he seemed broad-minded enough not to harness his wife into a monotonous existence on one continent.

Furiously, Amanda chomped at the gum. *If Haley is so bent upon finding a husband, Mason will be so much better than that baboon.*

But Haley needed to attract Mason first. Presently, there was absolutely no chance of that. The gum popped. Amanda had hinted for months that Haley should update her wardrobe, get a new hairstyle, and learn how to apply some makeup. Despite the encouragement, the 24-year-old secretary arrived daily looking like she always did: drab, tired, and about as stylish as a soggy newspaper. Haley would never attract the likes of Mason Eldridge without a major makeover.

The travel agency CEO touched her shoulder-length hair. Just this morning she'd realized her perm was unraveling into a horrid fit of frazzled, red strings that used to be carefree ringlets. With a calculating smile, Amanda decided the best way to get Haley to update her look was to make her believe her boss needed advice on her own makeover.

An hour ago, Amanda had left a voice mail with Mason about the choir schedule she'd volunteered to put together. She had yet to complete the schedule, even though she was supposed to have e-mailed it to Mason yesterday. Perhaps when he returned her call, she could begin the first stage of her plan.

A light tap preceded the hallway door's opening and Nate Knighton's cheerful voice. "Hello in here!"

Amanda jumped from her post near the other door and pretended to straighten the gold-framed mirror she'd purchased on her last visit to her aunt and uncle's home in America.

"Hello, Nate," Amanda replied. As his footsteps neared, she wondered how one man could always catch her so off guard at the most inopportune moments.

Nate's reflection appeared behind her in the mirror. As usual, her lifelong friend was clad in a fashionable business suit with a red tie and white shirt. Last week Amanda decided the guy had to have the largest collection of red ties in all of Tasmania. The irony was that he was a vice president at his family-owned Knighton's Department Stores. The national store chain featured a menswear section large enough to furnish all of Australia with any color ties they chose.

Amanda feigned the most innocent expression she could muster and wondered why Nate couldn't act like a civilized businessman and make use of the telephone or e-mail.

"Eavesdropping again?" Nate whispered and nodded toward Haley's office.

Haley's hopeful tones underscored Nate's suspicions. "Thanks, Roger. And I'm counting the days until you get home. G'day," she purred, and her phone's faint click accompanied the squeak of her rolling chair.

Amanda widened her eyes and naively observed Nate. "Are you talking to me?" she whispered and laid a graceful hand across her chest.

Nate's dark brows quirked, and he eyed her bare feet.

Amanda curled her toes.

One side of his mouth inched upward, and a dimple formed in his cheek. The gleam in his dark eyes reminded Amanda of the year she'd left Tasmania for college in America. Her aunt's invitation of free room and board during all four years of college had been too good to turn down. So Amanda had applied for Princeton Business School and was accepted. She had spent nearly every summer of her childhood in New Jersey with her mom's sister, so the venture was far from unfamiliar.

Nate had driven her to the airport as he'd done since she was 12 and he was 22. The last thing he'd said before leaving her at the plane's gate was, "You're not a kid any more. I'm not sure American men are ready for an Australian Amazon like you. Stay out of trouble, you hear?" His brown eyes had been just as full of devilry that day as today; so had the dimple.

Amanda was all of six foot two, and that made her only half an inch shorter than Nathaniel Knighton. She gazed into the mirror and didn't flinch from his cheerful mockery.

"Whatever you're up to this time, I say it's best to leave it be," Nate whispered. "Haley's her own woman. Let her make her own choices."

"I'll be glad when you get married and have a dozen kids," Amanda mumbled. "Then maybe you'll be so busy you can take your own advice and do very well to keep your nose out of my business."

"Humph!" Nate said, and Amanda didn't remember one of his "humphs" being so filled with twisted humor. "Then who'd keep you in line, m'dear?"

"Maybe I don't *need* to be kept in line!" Amanda stepped toward Haley's office door. She snapped it shut, smoothed her hand along the side of her knit skirt, and walked toward her desk.

"Tsk, tsk. Let's don't be so testy."

"What are you here for anyway?" Snapping away at her gum, Amanda paused behind the desk piled with paperwork and slipped her feet back into her shoes. She glanced at the big-faced, crystal-studded wristwatch her father had declared obnoxiously ostentatious when she bought it two weeks ago. Nate had agreed. Amanda couldn't have cared less. She liked the sparkle and the large size. Normal-sized jewelry got lost on her towering frame.

The watch said her daily lunch meeting with Nate wasn't for another two hours.

As if reading her thought, Nate said, "I'm not going to be able to do lunch today. I've got another meeting that's come up. I can't get out of it."

"Oh really?" Amanda asked. "Why didn't you just call?"

"I was next door at the bank," he replied. "It was easier to drop by."

When she returned home from college three years ago, their occasional lunch had grown to once a week, then to daily. Amanda hadn't bothered to analyze the pattern and had no plans to start. There was always something more pressing than examining her friendship with good ol' Nate…like planning her attack on Haley. Since Nate was canceling lunch, she would be free to take Haley to Knighton's Department Store. The two of them could spend the afternoon working on Amanda's—and Haley's—new look.

Nate narrowed his eyes and observed Amanda like an elder brother who's gotten too bossy for his own good. "Don't act so sad!" he countered.

"About what?" Amanda asked and picked up the silver-plated pen lying atop a stack of travel agendas she was on the verge of finishing for the only three clients she handled herself—the big boys, as Haley referred to them. Other than these three clients, Amanda's job consisted of overseeing the other 12 satellite travel agencies and personally investigating all new resorts, hotels, and restaurants. She eased her fingers to the end of the cool pen, flipped it, and slid her fingers to the bottom again.

"I just canceled our lunch date…er…meeting," Nate explained without a blink. "Aren't you the least bit disappointed?"

"Oh—you mean that I won't get to look at the great and mighty you over my Caesar salad?"

This time Nate responded with a two-dimple smile.

"I have to admit," Amanda continued, "you *do* look unusually handsome in your suit today." She reached across the desk and straightened his tie. "And I'm *so* surprised to see you coming out of your rut and wearing a *red* tie." She touched her hand to his face as any affectionate sister would.

When she lowered her hand, Nate chuckled and sat sideways on her desk's edge. "You know me, I'd *never* get into a rut." He nudged a pile of papers to create more sitting space and examined her messy desk.

"Of course not," Amanda said and figured their daily lunches were simply another rut Nate had fallen into. There were few men on the planet more methodical than he.

"I'd stake all of Knighton's stock this paperwork has been here since Noah," he teased.

"I know exactly what's here." Amanda laid her flattened palms on top of the mound. "And how long it's been here."

"It looks like your desk is pregnant or something," he added with a wicked laugh.

Amanda narrowed her eyes. "Do you have fever with these fits?"

Nate laughed out loud. "One day, Amanda, one day…" he mused, "…I'm going to have the last word. Just wait." He stood and pulled the tangled paper mass back to its former position.

"Don't hold your breath," she shot back.

"Since I can't do lunch today, let's go to dinner tonight," he said. "I'm not sure I'll make it through the weekend without my Friday Amanda fix."

Amanda sighed. "I can understand your predicament. I really don't know how you survived when I was in college." She fluttered her eyelashes.

"I barely struggled through," Nate responded. "Just barely." He lifted his hand and measured a few centimeters from forefinger to thumb.

"Okay, let's meet at O'Brien's by Knighton's at six. Work for you?"

"Works."

She toyed with the neck of her short-sleeved sweater and eyed the framed wedding photo sitting on the edge of her desk. Her former governess, Angie Townsend, and her new husband, Wayne West, posed at their wedding reception three months ago. That day the happily married couple had profusely thanked her for being their matchmaker.

In Amanda's mind, she superimposed the images of Haley and Mason Eldridge upon the gleeful bride and groom. At Angie and Wayne's wedding, Amanda had wondered who her next match would be. She didn't have to wonder another day.

"Haley will be with me. Is that okay?"

Nate crossed his arms. "Does Haley know about whatever you're planning?"

"No, but—"

"Does she have a choice?"

Chewing the gum like a turbo-charged rodent, Amanda grappled with the best answer and wondered how Nate Knighton always managed to read her mind. The phone's buzz saved her from the burden of an answer.

"See you at six." She picked up the receiver and turned to face the floor-to-ceiling window behind her desk. As she answered the phone and peered onto downtown Highland, Tasmania, her office door clicked shut. She relaxed.

"Amanda," Haley's professional voice floated over the line, "there's a Mason Eldridge on the phone."

"Perfect!" she mouthed and pulled a tissue from the dispenser on the desk's corner.

"He says he needs to talk with you about the church choir schedule. I tried to get him to let me have you call him back, but he said you'd left a voice mail for him this morning. Do you have time to—"

"Yes—yes, by all means," Amanda rushed. She held the tissue to her mouth and released the mint gum into its folds. "Put him through."

As a series of ticks cracked over the line, Amanda's mind spun with schemes. *This couldn't be better timing,* she thought and decided her whole brainstorm was nothing but the hand of God. By the time the minister of music voiced his greeting, Amanda's plans were well laid. All she lacked was the cooperation of those involved. Given her persuasive powers, she figured their compliance was inevitable.

Two

Nate checked his gold watch as he stepped into O'Brien's foyer. The Aussie chain restaurant advertised that they served the best steaks and fish in the world. The staff dressed in black jackets and slacks gave the restaurant a high-class appeal, as did their advertisements. So did the décor—right down to the velvet-covered chairs and rich tapestry drapes. Nate wasn't as impressed with the atmosphere as he was the smell of the food.

He was also five minutes late. Nate scanned the restaurant's crowded entryway in search of Amanda and Haley. His effort was wasted. His expectations of a quick meal plummeted. Not only were the women not present, the waiting list was probably as long as the Tamar River.

The smell of sizzling prawns and somebody's baked potato nearly sent him to his knees. Nate's stomach grumbled. He rubbed his gut, loosened his tie, and decided to go ahead and place his name on the waiting list. Nate glanced toward the empty hostess station. He scowled. At this rate he was going to get grumpy and swiftly.

Out of the corner of his eyes, Nate received the impression of a couple of women watching him from a corner crowded with ceiling-high plants. Curiosity and a load of male interest suggested he should investigate. He'd learned many years ago that numerous single women were interested in tall and lean in a business suit—especially when the suit hinted of tailor-made success.

Nate had also learned that the same women who were interested for those reasons were the ones who usually didn't care to know the real him. They weren't concerned about respecting him for who he was when what he and his family owned was so impressive. By the time he was 28, Nate realized that too many women viewed the vice president and heir of Knighton's Department Stores as an all-expense-paid, lifetime shopping trip.

That's when Nate decided to stop the whole dating game and just wait on God to bring him his future mate. That had been seven years ago. Lately Nate had begun to wonder if God had forgotten he needed a wife.

The pressure of the watching females finally got the best of him. Nate glanced in their direction. Even though the plants cast a shadow across their faces, Nate got a good impression of well-polished and attractive. One was a tall redhead with short, sleek hair and a pair of bronze lips that would probably stop traffic in downtown Hobart. The other was a petite brunette, about half as attractive as the redhead, but dressed in enough high-fashion gear to bless any New York designer. Nate vaguely recognized the redhead's denim jacket and matching skirt as one of the new lines the Knighton's clothing buyer had added to their spring lineup.

The redhead wiggled her fingers at Nate, winked, and blew him a kiss.

As much as Nate wanted to act cool, he couldn't stop his eyes from widening. All sorts of possibilities crashed through his mind. The option that topped the list involved forgetting that he'd sworn off dating.

The brunette mumbled something, the two women giggled, and the redhead moved closer. Once she stepped from behind the plants and merged out of the shadows, Nate recognized her.

"Amanda!" he spouted and didn't know whether to be relieved or disappointed. "I didn't recognize you." As she neared, he dismissed the unexpected zip through his gut as surprise and nothing more.

"No joke," Amanda replied. Her bronze lips curved into a mischievous smile as she stopped at Nate's side and looped her hand through his arm. "You acted like you thought a couple of wild women were after you." The scent of her exotic perfume completed the disconcerting experience.

"Oh, we're wild all right," the brunette drawled as she drew close. "I nearly fell on my face three times in these heels. She looked down at the pointed-toed spikes that perfectly matched her steel-colored, knit skirt.

Nate tilted his head and tried to recall why the gray-eyed woman looked so familiar.

"Allow me to introduce you," Amanda teased. "Nate Knighton meet Haley Schmitz."

"Haley?" Nate wheezed. "Oh my word! I didn't even recognize you!"

"Is there that much difference?" Haley wrinkled her brow and touched her shining hair.

Her head full of tangled frizz had been transformed into shoulder-length straight. Her pale skin glowed with a cosmetic miracle. And Nate guessed somebody must have talked her into replacing her thick glasses with contacts.

"Wow!" he blurted. "You look great!"

"See, I told you," Amanda affirmed as Haley's cheeks grew pinker.

"You don't look so bad yourself, Amanda," Haley encouraged.

"And I'd have to agree," Nate affirmed and touched the end of Amanda's nose.

She wrinkled it. "I guess cute enough to give you a heart attack anyway." She tilted her head back and laughed. "You should have seen your face." She slid him a saucy look out of the corners of her eyes. Those eyes had never looked so green...or so inviting.

Nate glanced down and hoped to hide the sudden attack of embarrassment. Being attracted to Amanda was the same as being attracted to a teenaged cousin. Even though the sensation lasted a few seconds, it was enough to disturb him for hours. The music filtering through the restaurant thumped in sequence with his heart.

He loosened his tie another notch.

"Have you signed us onto the waiting list?" he asked.

"Of course," Amanda answered and looked toward the restaurant door.

"Priebe, party of four," the hostess called.

"Party of four?" Nate glanced from Amanda to Haley.

"I've invited one other...uh...friend," Amanda hedged and glanced at the door again.

Nate narrowed his eyes. His first thoughts included a matchmaking scheme that involved him and some unnamed woman he wouldn't be caught dead with. Amanda was forever trying to marry off the world. During the last two years, she'd been able to claim one successful match out of six tries. Her former governess had been married three months to a man Amanda introduced her to. Amanda hadn't stopped gloating ever since.

Even though she'd never attempted to pair Nate with anyone, she *had* mentioned something about his getting married and having 12 kids earlier today. Nate tensed. He had enough problems when *he* was trying to find a mate. The last thing he needed was the interference of Amanda-the-matchmaker.

Amanda stepped toward the hostess, looked back at Nate and Haley, and then eyed the door again. "Why don't you two go on in. I'll stay here and wait on...I'll just wait."

"Sure," Haley said and cast a curious glance toward Nate.

Deciding he was better off not knowing, he shrugged and turned toward the hostess. *Maybe she's waiting on her dad or something*, he reasoned but wasn't the least bit convinced.

Amanda stood alone in the foyer only two minutes when a lean man with blond, wind-blown hair and pale-blue eyes stepped through the doorway.

"Mason!" she called and strode toward him.

"Hello!" Mason replied and hurried forward like an eager child ready for his first day of school. "The wind is horrible." He smoothed away the irregular spikes in his hair. "Sorry I'm late," he panted and adjusted his sport coat.

"Not a problem," Amanda replied and moved her purse's strap to her shoulder. "We were just getting seated."

"We?" Mason questioned

"Oh, yes, I invited my secretary, Haley Schmitz, and my friend Nate Knighton as well. I thought I told you."

"If you did, I don't remember," Mason said as he gazed up at her. "You look great!"

"Thanks," Amanda replied. *Good thing Haley's short*, she thought and estimated Mason to be no more than 5 feet 5 inches. Haley was about 5 feet 2 inches. *The two will be perfect together,*

Amanda thought as she spotted Haley and Nate sitting near the restaurant's entryway.

"May I help you?" a lithe man questioned from behind the hostess booth. The golden badge on his black jacket read "Zachary Benedict, Host."

"We're with them." Amanda pointed toward Nate and Haley. "I was waiting for my friend. She rested her hand on Mason's shoulder and noticed four menus already lying on the table. "We'll just seat ourselves."

The host nodded and pointed toward the entry.

Mason stepped aside and allowed Amanda to precede him. *Nice touch,* she thought. *He's a gentleman. That should impress Haley.*

The smells of grilling meat and steamed veggies enveloped them as they neared Nate and Haley, who were thick in conversation.

"You know Roger Miller?" Haley's exclamation greeted Amanda.

"Know him?" Nate replied. "He's my third cousin."

"That's absolutely marvelous!" Haley leaned forward, and her smile couldn't have been more ecstatic.

Amanda suppressed a groan. The last thing she needed was Haley to be focused on the baboon when she was being matched with Mason. Nate's being distantly related to Roger only compounded matters.

"Well, we're here," she announced and hurried forward.

"Oh hello," Nate replied, his face tight. He looked past Amanda at Mason, and his features relaxed as Amanda made the appropriate introductions.

"I believe we've met at church, Nate," Mason said.

"Yes, briefly." Nate stood and shook Mason's hand while Amanda nudged Mason toward sitting beside Haley. She scooted over one seat and took her water glass with her. When she placed Mason's water in front of him, he was just taking his seat. His arm nearly brushed the glass, and Haley jerked it away. In the midst of the jerk, the glass leaned toward him and filled his lap with icy liquid.

Amanda, who'd been about to claim the chair across from Haley, groaned, "Oh no."

"Yikes!" Mason squeaked and jumped back up. The ice toppled from his taupe colored slacks and scattered across the short-piled carpet.

"Oh me! I'm so—so sorry!" Haley exclaimed. "Oh my goodness. I cannot believe this happened again." She stood. Armed with her linen napkin, Haley began to dab at Mason's wet trouser legs.

"Again?" Mason croaked.

"Yes, oh yes," Haley muttered. "I seem to be prone to spilling water in restaurants. I think it's some kind of a curse."

Still hunched over, she looked up at Mason, whose face was mere inches from hers.

Amanda held her breath. She wrapped her purse's strap around her knuckles and squeezed. Maybe—just maybe—the sparks were already starting to fly.

A dark-skinned woman wearing a badge that said "Manager" appeared from around the corner. "Oops! Looks like we have a little problem," she cooed.

"A *little* problem?" Nate interjected with a mild grin. "I guess that depends on whether you're the one with the drenched pants."

"We have a hair dryer in the employee lounge," the manager said.

"Great!" Mason said.

"If you'll follow me…"

"I'll go too," Haley insisted and scurried after the two. "I need to find the ladies room!" After several wobbling steps in her spike-heeled sandals, Haley stumbled and yelped. She grabbed Mason's arm to steady herself. He lunged forward and caught himself on an empty chair.

Mason cast a desperate glance over his shoulder. Amanda smothered her laugh until the three disappeared down a hallway.

Nate's chuckle mingled with her own. "We shouldn't laugh," he scolded, yet his words lacked conviction as he scooted out Amanda's chair for her.

She took her seat, deposited her new purse near the chair, and covered her mouth. "I know," she admitted. "But Mason looked like he was worried sick about what Haley might do to him between here and the ladies room."

"That's what got to me too," Nate admitted.

"Oh well, maybe the whole thing will turn into a bonding experience."

"A bonding experience?"

"Well, yes. I was hoping Mason and Haley could make a go of it."

"As in…"

"You know, marriage," Amanda said and sipped her cold water.

"Oh?" Nate's brows arched. "Have you already hired the clergyman?"

Amanda dashed him a sour look. "Oh *please*."

"And what about Roger?" Nate yanked at his tie, loosened the knot more, and whipped off the red strip of silk.

"Roger can go milk his cows," Amanda growled. She pulled the tie from Nate's hands and began folding it.

"But Roger really cares for her." Nate picked up his spoon and tapped the table. The noise added a rhythmic thud to the clink and scrape of patrons' silverware and the hum of their conversations. The restaurant's upbeat music blended with the counter-rhythm.

"How can you be so sure?" Amanda, satisfied with the tie's folds, bent and inserted it into the top of her leather handbag.

"Like I was telling Haley when you walked up, he's my third cousin. We're friends. He mentioned Haley a few weeks ago. Somehow I missed the connection that his Haley was *your* Haley. I think he believes she's the one."

"All the more reason to get her distracted with Mason." A good-looking, dark-haired waiter arrived and placed another tall glass of water at Mason's place. He smiled at Nate. The smile grew warmer when he directed it toward Amanda.

Nate glowered and stopped tapping the spoon. The waiter hurried with mopping up the water out of Mason's seat and cleaning the spill on the floor.

Amanda cleared her throat. "Thanks," she offered.

"Sure. Just let me know when you're ready to order," he added and ignored Nate.

As the waiter hustled away, Amanda cast a furtive glance toward Nate. His straight-nosed profile looked as taut as the uptight energy he was emitting. On top of that, the guy was acting as if he'd eaten a whole truckload of sour apples.

"So what do you have against Roger?" he asked and started drumming the spoon against the table again. "Have you even met him?" The spoon's tempo grew fierce.

"Yes, I've met him." Amanda scowled. "He's a *farmer*. And he doesn't even have the decency to be a *wealthy* farmer. Haley deserves better than that." She picked up the water glass and downed a sizable gulp.

"So Mason's wealthy?" Nate asked.

"No, but at *least* he has class, and he enjoys traveling." She plunked down the glass.

"Well, Roger has high morals, and he's a hard worker. He's even out of town right now, so it's not like he never travels."

"Yes, but for the most part he's stuck on a farm, lacks money, and has no class."

"So good morals and being a hard worker don't count in the face of class and money?"

"Mason has morals. He's a hard worker too!" Amanda countered.

"Well, what if Haley's in love with Roger?"

"She needs to fall *out* of love with him." The water chilled her stomach as intensely as the fear chilling her heart—the fear of her dearest friend saying "I do" to a miserable existence in a trap disguised as a farm.

"Somehow I didn't think you were this shallow, Amanda," Nate mumbled.

"Shallow?" Amanda sputtered.

"Yes. Haley has the opportunity to maybe marry a hard-working, Christian man who adores her. But since he's not good-looking and doesn't have money, he's not good enough for you!" He drove the spoon against the table and released it. The utensil clattered to a stop against his water glass.

Amanda gaped and tried to formulate some retort. All she could think to say was, "How dare you!" Once that was out, more spewed forth. "All I want is what's best for my friend. And I just cannot believe she'll be happy with Roger!" Amanda's voice rose a few decibels, and she balled her fists in her lap. "Even if he had money stuck to his walls, I don't think they're a good match! I really, really don't!"

A woman and man sitting at the next table turned and looked at Amanda.

"Sshhh," Nate said and squeezed her fists. "Sorry there, okay?"

"If I were as shallow as you say, I wouldn't be introducing her to Mason. Like I already said, he doesn't have money either!"

Nate took a lemon wedge from a dish at the table's center and squeezed it over his ice water until his fingers were white and the lemon released its final drop. "Nevertheless," he dropped the wedge into his water, "I really think you should leave her alone. Let her make her own choices."

"I will," Amanda asserted and didn't try to lessen the tension in her voice. In her opinion, Nate Knighton was being the worst kind of judgmental boor. "But at least this way she'll *have* a choice. Before tonight, it was Roger or no one. And quite frankly I believe she was just settling for whoever she could get. She was raised as a foster child, you know."

"No, I didn't know."

"Well, she was. And I really think she's scarred because of it. I don't think she believes she's good enough to attract anyone *but* Roger."

"Just for the record, Roger isn't a 'but Roger.'" Nate drew quotes in the air with his fingers. "There have been more women than Haley after him. He might not be drowning in gold, but his family does own quite a bit of property, and they *are* financially stable, and Roger *is* a good man!"

"And you're not prejudiced, are you."

Nate sighed, placed his elbow on the table, and rested his forehead against his palm. "Just promise me you won't interfere any more, Amanda. *Please*." He lifted his head and stared into her eyes before his gaze jumped to her lips then back to her eyes again.

"Oh, absolutely!" Amanda insisted without a blink. "You know me. I'd *never* interfere." *Influence maybe*, she added to herself, *but never interfere.*

Nate narrowed his eyes. "I mean it, Amanda. I think you need to back off this time."

Amanda's neck stiffened. She yanked the front of her denim jacket. "Maybe *you're* the one who needs to back off!" she snapped.

"Humph," he said. "Why don't you turn all your energies into getting a rich husband yourself?" Nate grumbled before sipping his water.

"I have no intention of ever marrying anyone—rich or poor—and you know it, Nate. But if it's any consolation," she added with a sniff, "I'd choose character over money any day!"

"Glad to hear it," Nate said without bothering to look at her.

"I'm perfectly happy to run the travel agency forever," she said toward his ear. "Besides, Dad couldn't function without me at home. With Bev and Gordon in Brisbane and me married off, he'd probably die of loneliness. I don't think I could ever leave him."

"You're really serious about that?" His forehead wrinkling, Nate peered at her as if she were some weird science experiment.

"Of course I'm serious about it," Amanda affirmed. "I've told you before. Did you think I was lying?" She shifted in her seat and uncrossed her legs.

"No. I just thought you'd eventually change your mind."

"Well, I'm not. Not ever." Her purse flopped against her leg, and Amanda shoved at it with her foot.

"I'm sure dad would transfer Gordon to Highland if the need arose. He doesn't *have* to live in Brisbane."

A waitress passed pushing a cart laden with various desserts. Amanda caught a glimpse of cheesecake topped with strawberries. Her stomach rumbled. Her mouth watered. Nate's attention rested on the tray for several seconds.

"Gordon and Bev could probably find a place close to your dad's," he added. "You could do the same." Nate chuckled and swiveled to face Amanda. "When you couldn't be there, Bev and her four kids could keep him company."

The dessert waitress rounded a corner and Amanda shifted her focus back to the Nate. "Still, there are no guarantees, and I can't see Bev making sure Dad eats right. You know he has diabetes. If I got married, who's to say I wouldn't wind up with six kids. Then how in the world would I take care of Dad? No, I think it's best for me to just stay single and stay put."

"He did just fine while you were in college." Nate lifted his hand.

"Yes, but he didn't have diabetes then." Amanda nodded.

"But your dad's only 65!" Nate argued. "He could live to be 90!"

"So let it be!" She crossed her arms and leaned back. "Mom's gone. Bev's gone. I'm all he has."

"Good grief, Amanda," Nate's face flushed, "this is ridiculous."

"What does it matter to you anyway?" Amanda returned. "You'll probably get married and forget all about me."

"And until that happens, you're going to meddle in everyone else's business and drive me mad? Is that it?" He cut her a glittery-eyed stare.

Amanda's mouth fell open. A flash of heat crawled up her neck, and she studied Nate for a full ten seconds. When he didn't even have the decency to flinch, she shoved back her chair, stood, and stormed from the table. As she maneuvered around the patrons, the heat rushed to her eyes. Amanda blinked against the sting and ducked down a short hallway toward the ladies room.

Three

Two hours later, Haley gaped at herself in her dresser mirror. Even after an evening with her new look, she still couldn't believe the transformation. She went into Knighton's looking like a frizzy-haired lizard and came out a princess. Haley grabbed the snapshot sitting on the edge of her dresser. Roger's sister had taken the photo last month when he'd introduced Haley to his parents. She held the image up to her face, leaned forward, and examined the old Haley in light of the new.

No wonder Nate didn't recognize me, she thought and stroked the side of her silky hair. The beautician had treated her kinky locks with a straightener, and then sold her a whole hair-care regimen that would give her the professional gleam she now enjoyed. When Amanda discovered Haley had a pair of contacts in her purse, she'd insisted she put them in. After a stop at the makeup counter, they'd stumbled into a huge sale and each bought several new outfits. Three pairs of matching spike sandals and warm vanilla body spray had completed the evening.

Haley set the photo back on the dresser. She slipped her feet out of the toe torturers disguised as shoes. The balls of her feet ached with the release of pressure. She groaned and curled her toes into the cottony carpet. Haley longingly looked at the thick-soled slip-ons lying in the room's corner. Amanda said that style was history in 1933, but Haley wondered if her toes would be history after a year of wearing the spikes.

A tap on her door preceded Amanda's looking inside. "Hello in here," her friend called in her American-touched voice. "I thought you were just switching your shoes. Mason is waiting," she continued in a singsong voice. "Did you get lost?"

"No," Haley said. "I was just checking to make sure every-thing was…" she looked back into the mirror, "…still in place."

"You look great," Amanda said and stepped into the room. "At least *Mason* thinks so."

"Do you really think he does?" Haley asked.

"Of course. He could hardly keep his eyes off you all night."

"Right. After I spilled ice water on him."

Amanda walked to the mirror and fluffed her hair. "But he managed to get dried off, and you didn't spill another drop the rest of the night."

"It was nothing short of a miracle." Haley grinned and admitted that even with a complete makeover she couldn't com-pete with Amanda's fiery red hair, long legs, and green eyes. The professional eye makeup made her eyes appear to slant upward. That, plus the chin-length haircut and short bangs reminded Haley of Cleopatra. And she wasn't so obtuse to miss Nate Knighton's being a bit dazzled by the new Amanda—especially when she blew him that kiss.

But something had happened during Haley and Mason's excursion. Amanda arrived in the restroom just as Haley was washing her hands. Without a word, Amanda scurried into a stall. Having noticed Amanda's reddened eyes, Haley had discreetly exited. When the tall redhead had returned, neither Nate nor Amanda were in the best of moods. Shortly after dessert, Nate politely went home and Amanda suggested they all go back to Haley's place. Fortunately, she'd cleaned house last night.

"I need to make a trip to the restroom," Amanda said. "Why don't you entertain Mason for awhile."

Haley glanced toward the photo of her and Roger. Even at 30, his weathered skin showed signs of early aging. Yet his easy smile and thick, curly hair still gave him a boyish appeal. His arm rested around Haley as he pulled her close for the photo. His large nose and high forehead stopped him from being handsome, but he had a heart the size of Australia and a jovial nature that kept Haley laughing.

Over the last few months, their relationship had gradually deepened. During the week of his absence, Haley suspected he might even be on the verge of proposing. She and Roger didn't have an official agreement, but this evening with Mason hadn't seemed quite fair to Roger—even though she wasn't the one who arranged it. Nevertheless, Haley couldn't deny that the spark of male appreciation in Mason's blue eyes had given her much to think about.

"Are you okay, Haley?" Amanda's voice floated from a distant land.

"Sure," Haley said and shifted her attention toward her friend. "I was just thinking about…"

With a sly grin, Amanda turned the photo face down on the oak dresser. "Go on," she said, "enjoy the evening. You aren't married yet, and what Roger doesn't know won't hurt him." She rummaged through the pile of boxes and shopping bags strewn across Haley's oak poster bed and pulled out the bottle of amber-colored body spray. Amanda pulled off the cap and playfully sprayed a mist at Haley. The smell of warm vanilla reminded her of the delightful evening she'd already enjoyed and hinted that more fun was on the way.

Haley thought of Mason waiting in the den. After he recovered from the wet trouser syndrome, he'd been witty, charming, and even made her laugh. Maybe Amanda was right. This might be a good test of whether or not the Roger thing should even be.

"Okay," Haley said and stepped toward the closet. She opened the door and found the new pair of gold sandals she'd purchased on a whim last week. They went great with the long, knit skirt and felt much better than the spike heels. At the time of purchase, Haley wondered what she'd ever wear them with and what possessed her to buy them. Now she knew.

She followed Amanda up the short hallway and turned left into the den when Amanda turned right into the restroom.

Haley blinked hard against the contacts before moving toward Mason. Even though they were soft lenses, she wasn't used to wearing them, and they felt like cellophane in her eyes. After a final blink, Haley smiled and stopped near Mason, who was examining the trio of charcoal drawings hanging on the wall over the sofa. The steel-gray carpet, rich rose furnishings, and dove-gray walls served as the perfect complement for the nature drawings that bore her name in the bottom right corner.

She'd sketched all three pictures while vacationing last year near a wildlife park on Tasmania's northwest coast. One was of a peacock with feathers fully spread. The other featured a Tasmanian devil, nearly hidden by lush river plants. The third drawing captured a koala eating a gum leaf. Most everyone who entered the den was drawn to the images. Haley couldn't deny that seeing Mason studying her art ushered in a rush of pleasure. She timidly linked her fingers behind her back.

He glanced at her, and Haley expected him to express admiration for her talent. Instead he asked, "How long have you known Amanda?"

"Amanda?" Haley repeated. "Three years, I guess. She hired me after she returned from Princeton and took over the travel agency. We became instant friends. Now I'd say we're more like sisters than anything else."

Mason's blue-eyed scrutiny would have left Haley feeling self-conscious were it not for her recent trip to the mirror.

"I thought you two seemed close," he mused.

"Yes. We have a lot in common," Haley continued. "We both even enjoy drawing and painting."

"These are *great!*" Mason said and motioned toward the drawings.

Haley looked down and nudged at the carpet with the toe of her sandal. "Thanks."

"Do you have anything Amanda has done lately?" Mason questioned.

"Well…" Haley hedged and glanced toward the sunroom. She had been teaching Amanda techniques of oil painting as well as charcoal drawings for quite some time. Often Amanda came over and the two of them drew or painted together. Haley was fortunate to have rented a duplex on the outskirts of Highland, a suburb of Hobart. Her large backyard gave her a perfect view of Mt. Wellington. Haley had even coaxed a wounded mother wallaby and her baby to eat the grain she placed on the edge of her yard. Once the injured animal recovered, she regularly returned for more. An oil painting of the wallaby hung in the sunroom.

Amanda, on the other hand, had been trying her skills at portraits in oil. Haley's portrait to be exact. Numerous attempts were scattered around the sunroom in various stages of completion.

"Oh, I see you've noticed Haley's art!" Amanda said from behind.

Haley swiveled to face her friend and was thankful for the reprieve from the awkward moment. She'd have been beyond embarrassed to mention Amanda's latest artwork being portraits of herself. Nothing could sound so pompous.

"Yes, she's quite good. Isn't she?" Mason turned to beam toward Amanda, then he swung an admiring glance at Haley.

Haley's cheeks warmed, and she couldn't quite remember what Roger Miller looked like. Only one impression remained steadfast: Mason was much better looking than Roger. A featherlike ripple fluttered through her midsection.

While Amanda and Mason chatted, something Amanda said during their shopping trip bombarded Haley's mind: *If you're really in love with Roger, then I think it's great for you to marry him. But if you're considering marrying him just because you don't think you can get anyone else, you might want to reconsider. You're a pretty woman. You'll attract many men.*

Maybe Amanda was right on some points, Haley thought. *Perhaps I'm jumping into the relationship with Roger for the wrong reasons.* She contemplated the fact that Roger was the first man who had really pursued her. *Am I just settling for who I can get without really knowing my own heart?*

Mason seemed to have noticed her. And if he noticed, maybe other men would too. That is, if she could remember how to pull off this look again. She touched the edge of her hair, blinked against the contacts, and rubbed her glossy lips together.

"Haley says you draw too. Is any of your work here?" Mason's question invaded Haley's musings as he gazed around the house.

"Well as a matter of fact, it is!" Amanda exclaimed. "Some of my oil paintings are, that is." She looped her arm through Haley's and knowingly smiled at her friend.

"Oh no!" Haley babbled. "That's quite all right. Amanda has some wonderful drawings in our travel agency. You'll have to notice them the next time you go there."

"Come on, Haley," Amanda pressured and repeatedly winked in an exaggerated manner that left Haley beyond mortified. "Don't be so modest. Let's show Mason what we've been up to, shall we?" Amanda tugged Haley toward the open doorway that led to the sunroom.

"Please, no," Haley argued. "I don't think—"

"I'm *dying* to see what this is now," Mason countered as he strode beside Amanda.

"Actually, it's some rough beginnings on a portrait of Haley. Oh," she said and stopped. "But that was before..." She looked at Haley, tilted her head, and nodded. "Yes, I think we need to begin a new portrait now. One without the glasses and with your new hairdo."

"I'm interested in seeing whatever you have." Mason hurried forward.

Amanda directed another wink toward Haley, released her arm, and rushed after Mason. Her spiked heels clicked against the sunroom tile as Mason cried, "Wow! These are *great!*"

Haley's fingers shook. She covered her face with her hands and didn't quite know whether to run after the two or melt.

"She looks great!" Mason continued.

Amanda was right! she thought. *Mason really is interested in me!*

"I think that's a wonderful idea!" Amanda's exclamation sent a jolt through Haley. Somehow, she suspected this "wonderful idea" might involve her. She lowered her hands and waited.

"Haley! Come here! Mason's had a brilliant idea."

After a bolstering breath, Haley stepped from the carpet onto the tile that led into the sunroom. She hesitated on the edge of the room filled with wicker and plants, easels and canvasses. The faint smell of paint tinged the air and brought comfort to her soul. This was her domain—a place where even Amanda, as brilliant and beautiful as she was, could not compete.

"There you are!" Mason exclaimed. "I was just suggesting that Amanda should start the new sitting with you tonight. Perhaps I could help her with some angles or the lighting."

"You mean of—of me?" Haley stammered and laid her hand on her chest.

"Of course you!" Amanda crowed. "Who else is there!" She rested her hands on her hips, and the assured angle of her chin only added to her appeal. When Haley compared herself to her friend, she wondered why Mason wasn't asking for a portrait of *Amanda.*

"Come on!" Amanda grabbed her hands and tugged her forward. "Don't be shy." She leaned down and whispered, "You're scoring big! Play it for all it's worth, girlfriend." Amanda nudged Haley onto the stool they'd used many times during the protégé's learning process.

Mason's broad smile revealed teeth whiter than Roger's and appeared to be all for Haley. Like Nate Knighton, he also had dimples. Her fingers as unsteady as her heartbeat, Haley picked at the rings in her chain-link belt.

If I'm really in love with Roger, would I be so unnerved by Mason? she pondered.

Mason lifted a strand of Haley's hair away from her face, his fingers brushed her temple, and he smiled. A shower of tingles started at her temple and engulfed Haley as she returned his smile. His eyes were like a kaleidoscope of pale blue that the evening shadows enhanced to the fullest.

Nevertheless Haley maintained a serene aura that she hoped hid her quivering reaction. With the last rays of Tasmanian sunshine seeping over the peaks of the mountains, she straightened her shoulders and relaxed her hands in her lap while Mason fussed with adjusting the spotlights and consulted Amanda about her satisfaction.

At last Mason pronounced the lighting and pose perfect. Amanda secured the easel in front of her. The two stood side by side behind the easel and studied Haley.

"I need some herbal tea," Amanda said and turned to Mason. "I always sip tea when I paint. Haley usually keeps a pitcher of mango tea in the refrigerator." She glanced back at Haley. "Do you have some now?"

"Absolutely," Haley assured.

"You drink your tea cold?" Mason asked.

"Sure!" Amanda nodded.

"How enchanting," Mason replied. He crossed his arms and included Haley in his endearment.

His glowing approval prompted Haley to explain. "We learned how to make it during a trip to the southern United States last year. We both brought home a huge supply, and we've been drinking it ever since."

"Would you like some too?" Amanda questioned and put her brush on the easel.

"Sure!" Mason agreed.

"I'll get it," Haley said and started to stand.

"No!" Amanda and Mason said in unison.

"You'll mess up your pose," Mason continued and slipped off his sports coat. "You couldn't be closer to perfect right now." He dropped the coat on the back of a wicker chair, positioned his hands as if holding a camera, and focused solely upon Haley.

She lowered her gaze to the golden sandals.

"I'll be only a minute," Amanda promised as she walked toward the door to the kitchen. "You two entertain each other until I get back." She wrinkled her nose, wiggled her fingers, and directed another discreet wink toward Haley.

"I'll come help you," Mason said and hurried toward Amanda.

"No, no, no!" She placed a restraining hand upon Mason's shoulder and shifted her index finger from side to side. "You stay here and make sure Haley doesn't move a muscle."

The rhinestones on her denim jacket shimmered in the diminishing sunlight as did the bronze lip gloss. Haley was certain the whole effect had nearly given Nate a heart attack... along with several other men on their short trek from Knighton's to O'Brien's Restaurant.

"Well, if you insist," Mason hedged.

"Absolutely!" Amanda enthused. "Believe me, talking to Haley is ten times more exciting than pouring tea."

She hustled from the sunroom before Mason had a chance to protest again.

"Well!" he said and sat on the wicker love seat nearest Haley. "I guess it's just you and me."

"Yes." Haley averted her gaze to the mountains, now dark against an indigo sky streaked with pink and gold and azure.

Mason shifted. The wicker creaked. Haley detected a faint whiff of his masculine cologne. The sporty scent reminded her of the ocean and sand and sun and brought back memories of her trip to the Bahamas last year.

Haley hadn't been seeing Roger then. A faint worry trickled through her soul. She pressed her thumb against her fingers and held her breath.

Mason cleared his throat. "So you and Amanda have known each other three years."

"Yes, three." Haley lowered her head and cast him a sideways glance. His stylish blond hair, square jaw, and straight nose chased away thoughts of Roger.

"She seems to have some promise as an artist, don't you think?" He observed Haley with that steady-eyed gaze that suggested she was the only woman in the world.

"Absolutely," Haley agreed. "But she's such a perfectionist." She waved toward the four unfinished portraits propped against the far wall. "In the past, she's only gotten so far. She'll be doing fine, then she decides she doesn't like something. So she scratches the whole thing and starts over."

"Maybe this time will be different," Mason asserted. "She probably just needs a little encouragement. I'll be that for her." He laid his hand on the love seat's armrest. "I've got a good friend who owns an art gallery in Melbourne. I was thinking it might encourage her—and you as well, of course—if I send the portrait off to be professionally framed once it's finished."

"Wow! You'd do that?" Haley leaned forward.

"Of course." Mason shrugged and blasted her with another white-toothed grin. "That's what friends are for."

Four

With a cool pitcher of tea in hand, Amanda hovered near the refrigerator and peered over the beverage bar that served both the sunroom and kitchen. She couldn't decipher what Mason just said, but Haley's ready smile suggested he was charming her into a purring fit. Amanda giggled and hurried toward the cabinet holding the tall tumblers.

Roger doesn't have a chance, she thought before setting the pitcher on the counter. She nearly broke into merry whistling as she took three glasses from the cabinet. Another giggle gurgled up her throat.

This couldn't be more perfect! she thought and decided the wedding must happen by fall. *That's just six months away.* Amanda imagined a modest wedding with herself marching down the aisle as maid of honor. She was wearing a tea-length dress in rich apricot, a perfect accent for her hair.

When she stepped back to the refrigerator for the ice, memories of Nate-the-grouch blotted out the wedding plans. Amanda glared at the refrigerator, whipped open the freezer, and yanked out the ice bucket. The cool plastic chilling her palms was nothing compared to the icy knot in her heart.

After suppressing a good cry in the restaurant's ladies room, Amanda had walked back to the table and said nothing of the barbed exchange between her and Nate. He'd been coldly polite to everyone. Once he swallowed the last bite of his strawberry cheesecake, Nate mumbled something about needing to go home and left. Amanda had been so embarrassed by his curt behavior, she'd stammered for something to say until she suggested they all go to Haley's place. Thankfully Haley agreed with her usual ease.

"Too bad other people can't be that easy to get along with," Amanda complained as she plopped the ice bucket on the counter. She dropped several pieces of ice in each tumbler. With each clink of ice on glass, she struggled to make sense of Nate's odd behavior. She could understand his wanting to look out for his cousin's best interest—just as she wanted to look out for Haley's.

"What I simply cannot understand," she whispered and focused on the eyelet curtains above the sink, "is his bizarre interest in whether or not I get married and his dreadful remark about my driving him mad."

He's never been so rude to me. Never!

Her eyes stung anew. Her lips trembled. Amanda grabbed the ice bucket, stomped toward the refrigerator, yanked open the freezer door, and slung the bucket inside. It crashed against a tub of ice cream with a clunk and jiggle of ice. Amanda shoved the door closed, rested her forehead against the refrigerator, and closed her eyes.

Mason's rich laugh reminded her she had an important project underway. She squeezed her eyes tight until twin drops of moisture oozed from the corners. Amanda swiped at the tears with unsteady fingers, lifted her head, released the freezer handle, and straightened her shoulders.

There'll be time for crying later, she decided. *I've got Haley's future to think about now.*

⌒ ⌒

"Heeeelllllllo! Heeeelllllllo! G'day, mate!"

The parrot's shrill voice drifted from the living room and pierced Nate's fitful sleep. He moaned and covered his head. The smell of fresh linens attested that today was Saturday. His cleaning lady, Betty Cates, came every Friday. She changed the sheets, dusted everything in and out of sight, swept, mopped, and did all sorts of other things Nate didn't even want to think about.

"Here kitty, kitty, kitty, kitty! Heeeeeeeeeere kitty! Meow! Meow! Meow!"

Gary's morning calls normally made Nate smile. But today he was in no mood to be awakened by a parrot with a wild vocabulary fueled by Amanda's twisted American humor.

"Cock-a-doodle-do!" Gary bellowed. "I said, cock-a-doodle-do, man!"

Nate grabbed the pillow and crammed it against his ear. Seven o'clock was no time to be waking up when a person had barely slept all night. Nate didn't have to look at the clock to see what time it was. Gary was better than any alarm clock and as predictable as the sun.

"Amanda! Amaaaaaaaaaaannnda! Where's Amanda?" Gary slid into a laugh that duplicated Amanda's carefree giggle.

"That's it!" Nate growled. He slung back the covers, swung his feet out of bed, and stood. Frowning, he stomped across the polished wooden floor toward the door that opened onto the living room. In dawn's shadows, he slammed the door.

Gary shrieked but soon recovered. "Cock-a-doodle-dooooo!" he squawked.

Nate stepped to the room's corner and fumbled with the knob on a portable fan. He twisted the knob, and the fan hummed into the highest rotation. Gary's routine was drowned out by the drone.

"Thank goodness," Nate grumbled, then grimaced at the pasty taste in his mouth. He languidly scratched his chest, stretched, and tugged at his pajama bottoms while walking back toward the bed. Nate glowered at the open drapes, which were allowing the weak morning sun to seep into the room. As usual, the Tasman Sea rolled toward the white beach, the sunlight hitting the waves that sparkled with droplets of gold.

A new day. A new sun. A new ocean. Nate's normal morning chant spun through his mind and was as welcomed as Gary's annoying mantra.

"I need sleep," he groused and yanked on the curtain cord. The drapes swished forward and blotted out the maddening light. Only a faint remnant bled around the edges.

He rolled onto the bed, covered his head, and squeezed his eyes shut. But his ragged mind began repeating part of Gary's routine: *Amanda! Amaaaaaaaaaaannnda! Where's Amanda?*

Soon the clean sheets took on an imagined aroma of whatever that fragrance was Amanda wore last night. Nate uncovered his head. "The sheets smell like laundry soap, not Amanda," he said through gritted teeth. Nate flopped onto his stomach, punched the pillow, and buried his face into the soft folds.

His mind churned with the events of the past 24 hours. He'd gone from being charmed by Amanda's usual eavesdropping in the office to being duped into believing she was some flirting

Cleopatra with inviting, bronze lips. From there, the evening grew worse while his temperature increased.

Before it was over, Nate had argued with Amanda, not only about her interfering in Haley and Roger's relationship, but also about her decision not to marry. Nate couldn't determine which issue aggravated him more. He rolled over, opened his eyes, and stared at the ceiling.

Through the years Amanda had repeatedly proven herself to be nosy, strong willed, and beyond reason when she made up her mind, but never had she been more exasperating. *And last night she had the audacity to show up looking like...like...* Nate flopped his arm across his forehead.

"Like some 25-year-old woman!" he complained aloud and admitted that he could have cheerfully smacked that waiter for ogling her. Nate rubbed his gritty eyes, scrubbed his face with his palms, and finally admitted the truth he'd fought all night.

I was attracted to her and jealous of that waiter!

He propped himself up on his elbow and stared at the closed curtains. Gradually he understood the problem. Until last night he'd viewed Amanda as the Princeton-bound teenager he'd dropped off at the airport seven years ago. From that vantage, Nate had made a career of teasing her senseless, indulging her like he was an elder brother, and...

"And flirting with her," he confessed and considered their daily lunch meetings. Yesterday he'd called them dates. "Are they dates?" He attempted to analyze the situation. When all logic failed, he thought, *Whatever they are, they've got to stop!*

Nate's attention slowly slid to the charcoal drawing hanging on the wall near the foot of his bed. Amanda had drawn the ocean from the deck that stretched half the length of his home.

His focus shifted to the pile of clothing lying where he'd dropped them last night—a jogging suit Amanda had picked out.

He stroked the elastic waistband of his pajama pants that featured the Warner Brothers' Tasmanian Devil character. Amanda had given them to him three birthdays ago. She laughed like a schoolgirl when he opened them. He'd worn them ever since.

"Oh boy...oh boy, oh boy, oh boy," Nate mumbled and scrambled out of the bed.

"I am not!" he argued with himself.

"I will not!" he added.

"I cannot! I refuse to let this happen! It's...it's...insane!" Nate nodded. "It's worse than insane!" he yelled at himself. "She said she's not getting married!" He rubbed his face again and tried to recall any romantic attachment in Amanda's life since she'd arrived home from college. The list was a short one. As in there were no names.

She's serious about not getting married!

"I've got to stop this, and stop it now!"

He walked toward Amanda's drawing, removed it from the wall, and brainstormed for a place to put the thing so it would be out of sight. He marched to the hallway that connected his bedroom to the guest room. The closet was the perfect place for the drawing. Betty Cates was a cleaning machine who organized every inch of Nate's home. That meant this closet actually had spare space.

He opened the door, flipped on the light, and eyed the empty top shelf. "Perfect!" he proclaimed and prepared to put the framed art out of sight.

But he made the mistake of glancing at it one last time. Nate touched the glass. *She put hours into this,* he thought and recalled sitting on his deck while she stroked the paper with charcoal. They'd shared lemonade, some laughs, and a beggar seagull that wouldn't quit until they threw him bread.

Nate's fingers tightened upon the frame. The longer he held the drawing, the closer he felt to Amanda. The closer he felt, the more he knew he needed to make a clean break before he got more ensnared than he already was.

Tightening his jaw, Nate slid the drawing onto the top shelf and hurried back into his room. His next stop was the jogging suit. He swept the suit off the wooden floor, wadded it into a ball, and walked to the closet. The suit was his favorite because Amanda perfectly understood his taste.

He looked at the ball of cloth and remembered her saying she'd gone to four shops trying to find the right jogging suit. As a result, Nate had worn the suit more than any other. Amanda teasingly referred to it as his uniform. Nate deliberated over releasing his uniform as much as he had the drawing. Finally he opened the door, tossed the suit inside, then shut the door before his resolve weakened. Knowing his mind was too shocked to sleep for hours, he flipped off the fan.

"Amanda! Amaaaaaaaaaannnda! Where's Amanda?" Gary's raspy voice made Nate consider placing the parrot in the closet as well.

"Can't do that," he told himself and eyed the Tasmanian Devil pajama bottoms, clinging to his hips. "These have got to go," he decided.

Soon he was dressed in a pair of sweats, a T-shirt, and running shoes, all which Amanda had nothing to do with. His mouth was minty fresh. His stomach was pleasingly full of cool water.

And the pajamas were on the closet's top shelf with the drawing.

The only thing left to do before his morning jog was feed Gary. Once he had his fresh bird food along with a few carrot and apple slices, the parrot usually stopped the spiel and settled for a while.

Even though Nate's eyes felt like they were full of sand, he had never been more alert. As he hurried from his bedroom into the beach home's expansive living area, he began developing his plan. Nate's father had taught both his sons that the best way to stay on track in business was to develop a solid strategy and stick with it. Using that method, Knighton Sr. had expanded one Hobart department store into a national chain with offices in Brisbane and Sydney and new stores opening in Europe.

Nate figured if that method worked in business, it would work in his personal life as well. His plan would be simple. He would avoid Amanda and remove anything connected with her from his life.

Unfortunately, Amanda isn't business, he told himself. *And avoiding her will be like avoiding myself. How simple is that?*

"But what else am I going to do?" He lifted both hands and imagined himself dissolving into a big glob of jelly the next time he saw her. That was exactly the way she made him feel last night.

Rubbing his forehead, Nate stepped passed the leather sofa and approached his parrot, who had the best vantage in the whole room. The cage sat in the middle of the large window that offered a full view of Nate's private stretch of the Tasmanian coast.

"Good morning, Gary!" he proclaimed and detected the faint odor of feathers and seeds. "You old buzzard, you woke me up, didn't you?"

"Here kitty, kitty, kitty, kitty!" Gary replied. The bright-blue bird jumped from the side of the cage to the swing in the middle.

"Amanda! Amaaaaaaaaaannnda! Where's Amanda?" Gary bobbed his head up and down and mimicked Amanda's laugh.

Nate flinched. The bird was one thing he could not give up. The parrot had been with him for 10 years. Many birds like Gary lived to be 40 or 50. Nate had made the commitment to Gary. He could not abandon him because of his vocabulary.

But he's the only exception to the plan, Nate thought. *I've got to at least try to avoid her. That's the only way to get her out of my blood.*

He checked the brass clock sitting on the mantel. The pendulum forever swung with ease and grace, and the clock declared the time to be seven thirty.

The timepiece also had the unfortunate fate of being given to Nate by none other than Amanda—last Christmas, to be exact. Nate recalled the way she'd plopped the box in his lap and said, "Here. Open this. You desperately need it." Then, when he struggled to remove the ribbon, Amanda wound up unwrapping the gift for him. The whole time she pulled the brass clock from the box, she was explaining that he should put the piece on his mantel.

Nate smiled. At times Amanda could be as cute as an impulsive child. But that childlike quality, coupled with this new awareness of her womanhood, sent Nate into a fresh panic.

Nate pointed at the clock. "It's in the closet for you," he said as the phone belted out a ring.

While he strode toward the cordless phone sitting on the corner computer desk, he deduced that the caller was probably his elder brother, Gordon. The guy always had a way of phoning at odd times. A week ago, he woke Nate out of a deep sleep at one o'clock in the morning because he was wide awake with his six-month-old baby and in the mood to talk. It never occurred to Gordon that Nate wouldn't be awake at one.

Seconds after he picked up the receiver, Nate's assumption was proved correct. After the usual pleasantries, Gordon got to the point.

"Bev and I are planning a trip to Highland early November. Bev was wanting to get away with Amanda and do some Christmas shopping. She's talking about leaving us with all four kids while she and Amanda shop. Then we're supposed to find some brave babysitter and take Amanda and Bev out to dinner. As far as I'm concerned," Gordon continued in an elevated tone, "these Priebe women act like they *own* the world since they've toured it."

A suspicious giggle tottered over the line as Gordon fell silent. *Oh brother,* Nate thought and looked toward the ceiling.

"What do you think you're doing?" Gordon's yelp was followed by a full-fledged female laugh that resembled Amanda's. "Get away from me, you wild woman!"

Nate grimaced and pulled the phone from his ear. The last thing he needed was being privy to his brother's marital celebration. He'd watched those two flirt for 15 years. The way they acted, their marriage grew more fun every day.

I'm glad somebody's got a good marriage! Nate dropped into the rolling chair, and the wheels whispered against the mat beneath them.

"So what do you say?" Gordon said through a thick chuckle.

Nate jabbed his fingers against his forehead. "Has Amanda already agreed to this?"

"Agreed to it?" Gordon laughed. "The whole thing was her idea! By last Wednesday, she and Bev had everything arranged— right down to what they're going to wear. I told Bev last night we ought to call you just to make sure you've got it on your calendar."

"That figures," Nate grumbled. "She never even bothered to tell me."

"What?"

"I said it figures." He placed his elbow on the desk, rested his face in his hand, and stared at the neat pile of bills on the shelf underneath the computer screen.

"What's the matter? Did you have a bad night or something?" Gordon asked.

"You could say that," Nate replied and wondered if it was even possible to avoid Amanda when his brother was married to her sister.

Five

Within two weeks, Amanda could not have been more pleased. In Roger's absence and Mason's presence, Haley had blossomed. While Haley had not relinquished all reticence, she was at least learning how to recreate her new look. She was also walking with the assurance and grace of a woman who knows who she is. In all the years Amanda had known Haley, she had never acted so much like she belonged...*really belonged*. It was as if the orphan was fading away and the assured woman was finally budding forth. Mason had been so good for her.

In the last two weeks, Haley had decided to skip the church she and Roger attended and go to services with Amanda. Every service Amanda made certain Mason spent ample time talking with Haley. Amanda had also invited Mason and Haley to her home four times. The three played board games, ate together, and chatted with her father. They'd also landed at Haley's place five times for Amanda to work on the portrait, which was now complete.

"The plan is working," Amanda mumbled under her breath as she bent to retrieve a disposable cup. She placed the cup under the cooler's water spout and pressed the lever that released a flow of cold water.

"Good morning, Miss Amanda!" Betty Cates' merry voice accompanied the crash and rumble of a mop bucket.

Amanda turned to face the scrawny housekeeper who serviced Wood-Priebe International Travel as well as her father's home and Nate's beach house.

"Good morning, Betty," Amanda called.

The housekeeper wrestled the industrial-sized mop bucket down the hallway and shoved at the thick glasses that magnified her soft-brown eyes. "I told that woman at the bank this morning my arthritis was acting up so I knew it was going to rain today. But did she believe me? No!"

Betty stopped and studied Amanda. At this closer vantage, Amanda detected a fine mist frosting the hairnet harnessing Betty's scraggly, gray curls.

The housekeeper's gaze shifted to Amanda's neck and the irritation diminished. "Love your jewelry," Betty said.

Amanda touched the thick strand of red glass beads Nate bought for her last year in Paris. Before she could express her thanks, Betty resumed her ranting.

"She said it was too sunny to rain. I told her that didn't matter; I felt it in my bones. 'Specially my backbone." She rubbed at her lower back. "And there you are." She gestured toward the front of the travel agency. A low rumble of thunder supported her claims.

"When it comes to weather, you're usually right, Betty." Amanda smiled and sipped the cold water.

"That's what I told that clerk. But she persisted in arguing. I've never met such. She's *new,*" Betty said wrinkling her nose.

Like a captain steering his ship, she passed Amanda and rolled the aluminum mop bucket down the hallway. The weak aroma of arthritis rub wafted in her wake.

"I don't think she'll last long unless somebody tells her you don't argue with customers," Betty continued. "I've got to remember to buy some Swiss cheese at the market," she added, and bent to scratch at her shin. One leg of her slacks was caught in her knee-high stocking, which was marred with holes.

Amanda tuned out Betty and began a mental list of the things she needed to do this morning. Hiring the tour guide for the group of Canadian retirees who arrived next week topped her list. She calculated where the tour guide's number was in the mile-high mix on her desk and drank the rest of her cold water. The liquid left an icy path down her throat and sent a short-lived ache between her eyes.

"And another thing," Betty added and paused, "that Nate Knighton has started doing some strange things."

Amanda sputtered, coughed, and lowered the disposable cup. A spray of water showered her black jacket and trickled down the front of her matching slacks. Amanda hacked over the moisture lodged in her throat, stroked at the droplets on her clothing, and honed her focus on Betty.

"When I say strange, I mean strange." Betty nodded and picked at the front of her floral smock.

"Oh really?" Amanda queried and stopped herself from stepping forward. No sense appearing too interested.

Amanda hadn't heard one word from Nate in two weeks—except one terse e-mail stating he wouldn't be able to make lunch for a while. He hadn't even bothered to call and end their lunches. He'd just sent that one-line e-mail. The thing was so frigid it nearly froze her inbox. At the end of last week, she finally realized the man was purposefully avoiding her. Amanda wadded the paper cup into a tight ball.

"He's turning into a slob, I guess. That's the best I can decide." Betty dug her hand into her smock's pocket.

"A slob?" Amanda wheezed and tried to imagine Nate in such a mode. The man was the personification of organization.

"Yes." Betty nodded. "Last week I found all sorts of things crammed in his hall closet. She lifted her hand out of her pocket. "Well, would you look at that!" Betty exclaimed. "I've been looking for that pen for a week. And there it was all the time." She pulled open her pocket and peered inside.

Amanda stepped forward. "Exactly what was in his closet?" she queried and knotted her fingers.

"You should have seen what fell out at me when I opened the door to hang up the leather jacket I found in the linen closet— the linen closet, mind you!" She extended her arm as if she were a Sunday-morning preacher on a tear. "Can you believe he'd shove something that nice under a stack of sheets in the linen closet?" Betty blinked.

"No," Amanda rasped and pressed her thumb against the crumpled cup. The paper wad bit into her palm. She'd bought Nate a leather jacket the year before last for his thirty-third birthday. He said it was his best present that year.

"Did it have a lamb's wool—"

"And you wouldn't believe what else I found in the closet even if I told you," Betty continued. Then she touched her temple and stared into space. "I've also got to remember to buy some mutton," she said and turned back to her bucket. "I'm going to do the floors in the kitchen and bathrooms as usual. Let me know if there's anything extra you want me to do, Miss. Otherwise, I'll just clean as usual."

"Uh, Betty…" Amanda tossed the crumpled cup into the lined trash can and hustled toward the retreating housekeeper. She put her hand on Betty's shoulder and hid her aching curiosity behind a mask of concern.

"You mentioned something falling out on you in the hall closet. Did you get hurt?"

"Nearly! A crystal candy dish the size of…" she extended her hands to the dimensions of a large saucer, "…fell out and almost hit me smack on the noggin. I knocked my glasses off just trying to get out of the way." She adjusted the wire-rimmed glasses. "And it's a good thing I moved quick because a basketball fell out next. Landed on my foot."

"The basketball," Amanda asked, her throat tightening, "was it autographed?"

"Who knows!" Betty said. "I was so aggravated I just threw the thing back in." Her bottom lip protruded. "It's enough to make a housekeeper quit. I think being a cobra trainer would be less dangerous."

"And was the candy dish shaped like a leaf?"

"I guess," Betty grumbled and shifted the pen back to her smock pocket. "I was still too disgusted over the broken picture frame. *That* happened by accident when I tried to put the candy dish on the top shelf. Crack! There the picture was. You know, the one that's usually in his room?" Betty turned up the hall, paused, and looked back at Amanda. "I think it's your drawin'." She jerked her thumb toward the hall wall where four sketches of Nate's parrot hang.

"Was the sketch damaged?" Amanda panted.

"No. Just the frame was broken. One corner had come apart and the glass was chipped. Best I could tell, the crazy man had also rammed a brass clock into it." Betty shook her head, bent, scratched her shin, and mumbled, "I need to remember to get some body lotion too. My legs are so dry, they look like they're covered in feathers." Betty shoved at the mop bucket. .

Amanda crossed her arms, hunched her shoulders, and hovered against the wall.

The housekeeper stopped her trek and pivoted back to face Amanda. "Don't forget about Janet coming next week."

"Janet?" Amanda raised her brows.

"Yes, remember? My niece Janet French. I told you last week she'd be here next week." The housekeeper abandoned her bucket and stepped closer.

"No, I didn't remember." Amanda plucked at the large beads around her neck. *That's all I need right now,* she thought and didn't even bother to deny that being next to the petite Janet French made her feel like a gawking giant.

"You don't look so well, Miss Amanda." Betty stopped a few inches away, placed her hands on her hips, and angled her head to one side.

At this close range Amanda realized that Betty's pearl earrings didn't match. One was a flat button; the other a cluster of seed pearls. Amanda, in need of some emotional release, nearly laughed out loud.

"Are you getting ill?" the housekeeper questioned. "Because if you are, I've got some—"

"No. No, that's fine. Perfectly fine." All temptation toward humor vanished. Amanda held up both hands and edged down the hallway. The last time Betty tried to cure her of an ailment, the concoction put her in bed with intestine problems for two days.

"I'm—I'm okay," Amanda stuttered. "I was just—just thinking. That's all. Don't worry."

"Good. Because I'd hate for Janet to get sick. You *know* how much she likes you. I'm sure she's going to want to see you as much as possible." Betty raised her index finger for emphasis and ambled back toward her mop bucket, then through the kitchen doorway.

"Great," Amanda groaned and covered her eyes. All she could see were images of a dark-eyed Asian beauty with satin hair that flowed down her back and a size-three figure. Amanda struggled to like that woman from the first time she ever saw her. Janet's pending visit, added to Nate's odd behavior, was enough to make Amanda plan a trip to Mars.

Each of Nate's things Betty mentioned were gifts from Amanda—right down to the basketball autographed by Michael Jordan. Amanda strained for a logical explanation for Nate's odd behavior. Finally she deduced that he might be romantically involved with someone who was jealous of other women in his life. *That would also explain his not having lunch with me,* Amanda decided.

"He's probably having lunch with *her,*" she pouted and imagined the imposter looking much like Janet French. After all, Nate had mentioned how pretty Janet was the first time he met her.

Amanda pressed the heel of her hand against her forehead and slid her fingers into her hair, only to encounter her sunglasses. They had been riding there since she arrived an hour ago. The sunglasses toppled from her head, and Amanda juggled the thick-framed, polka-dotted specimens before finally capturing them.

She looked at the gaudy glasses and sighed. When she bought them, she and Nate had been investigating the new resort on Tasmania's northwest coast. Nate playfully told her if she ever wore the fuchsia-and-navy glasses, he'd pretend he didn't know her. Amanda had immediately put the glasses on and didn't take them off the rest of the day.

Her chin quivered. She'd never had an older brother, and Nate was as close as she'd come. Thoughts of losing him to some wife-sort really cramped Amanda's agenda. *If this unnamed Janet look-alike is causing Nate to hide all my gifts, I doubt the woman will tolerate his traveling with me.*

"Well, great, Nate," she grumbled under her breath and stomped toward her office. "Go ahead, just get married, then, and don't even ask me! Of all the nerve!"

Amanda stormed into her office, tossed the polka-dotted sunglasses onto the window ledge, and attacked the mountain of papers on her desk. Layers of paid bills, old grocery lists, and a sprinkle of receipts had slid to the floor by the time Amanda got to the "Noah level." And that's where she found the business card of the new Tasmanian tour group.

Refusing to think of Nate and the dreadful things he was doing to her gifts, Amanda reached for the telephone and prepared to take care of business. She had the receiver halfway to her ear when a gasp from across the office stopped her. She looked up.

Haley stood in the doorway that connected the two offices. Even the rose blusher couldn't camouflage her ashen complexion. She gripped a piece of paper and observed Amanda like a child who lost her mother in the market.

"You've—you've got a terrible mess," Haley stammered and glanced from the desk to the paper-covered floor and back to the desk.

"So I do," Amanda replied, "but I found it!" She held up the business card. "This is the phone number for Tasmanian Tours— that new group I was telling you about a couple of months ago."

"Why didn't you just call information and save yourself the headache?" Haley walked closer, and Amanda noticed her thick-soled shoes. The atrocities looked like something Betty Cates would reject and did nothing for the secretary's new classy pantsuit.

She stopped herself from blurting an admonishment and decided to just answer Haley's question. "It wouldn't have been the same," Amanda explained and kicked off the spike heels that would have made Marilyn Monroe wince. "I knew I had the card, and I wanted to find it. It would have driven me crazy for weeks just knowing I lost it."

"Oh," Haley replied, her eyes narrowing, "I see...I guess," she added and focused on the paper in her hands. Her pallid face tensed.

"What's the problem?" Amanda asked. Fully expecting some issue with the business, Amanda imagined all sorts of catastrophes. A fire in the Woltongong office. Flooding in the Newcastle branch. Her churning mind stopped just short of a space alien invasion.

"Here!" Haley shoved the message into Amanda's hands and stumbled toward the overstuffed love seat.

Amanda glanced at the e-mail printout and immediately dismissed any professional disaster. The note was from Roger Miller. Amanda looked back at Haley, who was hunched forward with her face in her hands.

"What am I going to do?" Haley begged.

"Uh..." Amanda read the brief e-mail and tried to absorb every detail as swiftly as possible:

Dear Haley,

I'm back on the farm. The trip was very profitable. Father and I have ordered some new equipment. It was all very expensive, but we hope it will be worth the investment.

But that's not the reason I'm e-mailing. I've debated a thousand different ways to ask you what I'm about to ask. I don't know if I'm doing this by e-mail because I'm a coward—too afraid of being rejected in person—or because I just can't wait another hour.

Haley, will you marry me?

Forever yours,
Roger

"For Pete's sake!" Amanda exclaimed. "I can't believe this!"

"Neither can I," Haley moaned.

Amanda tossed the message onto the middle of her desk. "This is about as romantic as reading the back of a cat food box."

"I didn't even notice that," Haley rasped. "I was just too over-taken by—"

"You aren't actually considering him, are you?" Amanda prompted.

"Well, I..."

"Oh Haley, Haley, Haley." Amanda hurried toward her friend and knelt in front of her. She wrapped her fingers around Haley's unsteady fingers and looked into her rounded eyes.

"I'd *never* interfere. You know that," Amanda insisted.

"Of course." Haley nodded. "But I desperately need to know what you think."

"I think..." Amanda looked past Haley to the collage of photos covering the wall. Each shot was taken at a different place on the globe. Many of them included both Haley and Amanda. The one that held her attention the longest was an 8 x 10 of Amanda, Haley, and Nate. They were sitting at an outdoor café in Paris. Last year, Nate had been traveling to Paris for the grand opening of Knighton's first European store. Amanda and Haley had decided to plan their trip to Paris to coordinate with Nate's. He'd bought the red beads she now wore for her at Knighton's, Paris. The two of them had been the jewelry counter's first customers.

"You think…" Haley prompted.

Amanda stroked the beads and returned her focus to Haley, who looked like a lost puppy. Nate couldn't remain single forever. Even if he didn't marry this new mystery woman, he'd undoubtedly marry soon enough. If Nate was married and Haley was harnessed to the farm and Roger, Amanda would be left with no one. She pinched at the beads.

"I think…" she repeated and reminded herself she needed to focus on what was best for *Haley*. Amanda envisioned her kind friend being consumed by the responsibilities of farm life. She saw her working in the fields like a slave with no hope for deliverance. She could never believe the gentle-spirited soul would ever be happy with such an existence.

"Roger…I do—do believe he r–r–eally cares for me," Haley stammered.

"But so does Mason," Amanda replied.

"Oh no!" Haley rubbed her temples with her fingertips. "I forgot all about him. What would I ever tell *him*. This has all gotten so complicated!"

"Well, if you aren't certain…" Amanda paused.

"If I'm not certain," Haley opened her eyes and shook her head from side to side, "I should…"

Amanda always prided herself on never telling people what to do unless they absolutely forced her to the point. This was undoubtedly one of those situations. She would simply have to tell Haley she should not marry Roger and be done with it.

"You should—" A telephone's ringing stopped Amanda and sent Haley to her feet.

"That's my phone," Haley said and stepped toward her office.

"No." Amanda nudged her secretary back to the couch. "You stay here. I'll answer it this time."

"But—"

"Whatever it is, I can handle it," Amanda asserted and wagged her index finger from side to side.

Haley's face relaxed. She once again claimed her perch on the love seat's edge and continued with her worried staring.

Amanda stepped to the phone on her desk, picked up the receiver, and pressed the blinking button that connected her to Haley's line. "Wood-Priebe International," she said while never taking her concerned gaze from Haley.

"Amanda!" Mason Eldridge's voice floated over the line. "I didn't expect you to answer."

Six

~ ~

"You were expecting Haley, I assume?" Amanda questioned.

Haley jerked her attention toward Amanda. "Is that Roger?" she whispered, her face tightening.

"No—Mason," Amanda mouthed and wiggled her eyebrows for effect.

"Mason!" Haley silently replied with no change in her stressed demeanor.

"Haley's right here. Did you want to speak with her?" Amanda prompted and hoped Mason's voice might influence Haley to make the final and correct choice.

"No. That's perfectly fine," Mason replied. "I really called to talk with you."

"With me? Whatever for?" Amanda laid her hand on her chest and exchanged a curious glance with Haley.

"Well…" Mason began, "I have a big surprise for you."

"For me?"

"And for Haley too, I guess," Mason added.

"A surprise for *Haley?*" Amanda returned and directed a thumbs-up to her friend.

"I was wondering if you were going to be home this evening," Mason hurried.

"Yes. As a matter of fact I am," Amanda replied. "We're going to be having dinner guests, but as always, you're welcome to join us, Mason. I can make certain Haley comes too."

"Perfect!" Mason exclaimed. "What time?"

"Does six o'clock work for you?"

"Absolutely!" Mason replied. "I'll be counting the hours."

"Good," Amanda said. "I'm sure *someone else* will be doing the same," she finished in a singsong voice.

"And you have no idea how *good* that makes me feel," Mason replied before bidding adieu.

Amanda hung up the telephone and grinned from ear to ear. "Mason has a surprise for *you!*" she cried before rushing to Haley's side. She plopped onto the sofa beside her friend, laid her arm along Haley's shoulders, and squeezed.

"For me?" Haley echoed.

"Absolutely! And he said he was counting the hours until six tonight when he'll be at my house to give you the surprise."

"He really said that?" Haley gasped.

"Yes! Upon my honor, he said it." Amanda lifted her right hand. "Now all you have to do is decide what you're going to wear! What about that cobalt-blue number with the short jacket and skirt and…" she glanced at Haley's horrid clogs, "…*shoes* to match. He hasn't seen you in that outfit, has he?"

"I haven't worn that one yet at all," Haley replied and stared into space. "I've been saving that one for…for…R–Roger."

"Roger? Who's he?" Amanda quipped.

Haley snapped her gaze back to Amanda.

"Oh yes, I remember him." Amanda tapped her temple with her index finger. "He's the boring guy who proposed by e-mail, and who wouldn't know a surprise if it bit him on the nose."

Haley giggled. "I guess you're right." She sighed. "Mason is so much more…well, he's better looking, and he's…uh…"

"A *much* better match for you!" Amanda patted Haley's arm.

Haley nodded. "Maybe you're right. I guess I'll just e-mail Roger and politely decline."

Smiling, Amanda toyed with her crystal watch's clasp and thanked heaven she never had to tell Haley to reject Roger's proposal.

"Oh!" Haley rapidly blinked. "I won't be intruding on your dinner guests tonight will I?"

Amanda stood. "Absolutely not!" she assured. "It's just going to be Angie and Wayne West. They'll be *thrilled* to see you!"

⌒ ⌒

Nate steered his Mercedes convertible along Highland Beach's scenic drive. The cold wind whipped at his face while the evening sun simmered toward the mountainous, western horizon and promised a bejeweled setting. When Nate had lowered the convertible's top, he'd hoped the white sand and October's nippy air would calm his temper. So far the plan had failed.

The smell of saltwater that stretched to the base of the northward mountains brought to mind the water's icy embrace. Despite his shiver, he gripped the leather-wrapped steering wheel, gritted his teeth, and pressed the accelerator. Not even thinking of the frigid water could cool his temper. The vehicle jumped to his command. The contemporary Christian music thumping over the speakers beat in sequence with his increasing pulse.

Nate hadn't been this riled in years. And he'd *never* been so angry with Amanda. Looking back, he couldn't ever remember being incensed with her, for that matter. Any mild irritations had always been wrapped in big brother indulgence.

This afternoon when he called her to talk about the issue, she'd been distant and claimed she didn't have time to chat due to dinner guests on the way. So Nate had told her to set another plate for dinner. He was coming, and they needed to talk.

"Whether you want to or not, Missy," Nate mumbled while navigating a curve in the road.

He slowed the vehicle and turned into the twisting lane that began the Wood-Priebe Estate. Amanda's grandparents, the Woods and Priebes, were once coastal neighbors. They had shared the neighborhood and had also been business partners; they founded Wood-Priebe International Travel when their children were young. When the Wood daughter married the Priebe son, they linked the Wood and Priebe estates, fortunes, and the international travel group where Amanda now served as CEO.

The statewide magazine, *Tasmania Today*, had even featured an article on Amanda last year. She was supposed to be the youngest CEO in Australia these days. The article's author had commented on her level of maturity and her solid business knowledge. Of course, Amanda had cleaned her desk before letting that guy come for the interview—if you could call cramming all the clutter into a box and stuffing it into the coat closet "cleaning her desk."

Nate had caught her in the act and laughed the whole time he helped her shove the closet door shut. But not even *that* memory could lessen his irritation today. All he could think about was poor Roger and his broken heart. *How in the world Amanda has time to serve as CEO when she's meddling in everyone else's business has to be a national enigma!*

He rounded the last curve and accelerated for the final stretch. The massive stucco home that came into view sat on the peak of a rocky point that overlooked the Tasman Sea and offered an unforgettable view. Nate drove the Mercedes around the circular drive, lined in ferns, and parked behind a Lamborghini he recognized. Apparently Angie West, Amanda's former governess, and her new husband were the dinner guests. A Honda Eclipse Nate had never seen sat in front of the Lamborghini.

He scanned the horizon for any signs of an evening storm and saw no clouds. Nate turned off the ignition without raising the car's roof, opened the door, and climbed out. He wrestled with the knot in his tie, whipped off the tie, and tossed it into the passenger seat. After checking his gold watch, Nate unbuttoned his shirt's top button and slipped out of the sports coat. He welcomed the chilly coastal breeze that penetrated his sweater vest and decided to put the coat back on only if the other guests were so dressed. The tie wasn't going to happen under any circumstances. He needed the breathing room.

Nate strode up the brick passage, canopied in hemlock trees. When he was mere feet from the home's front door, he glimpsed movement out of the corner of his eyes. A threatening growl and hiss suggested the presence of his archenemy, Cuddles. Nate glanced toward the cat as she streaked to the front door to protect her territory. The Siamese blinked a threat before hissing again.

"Oh no," Nate groaned, "not you." The last time Nate came to the Wood-Priebe Estate this cat had wrapped herself around his leg and inflicted some serious scratches that took two weeks to heal.

Amanda had found the poor creature on the side of the road. Nate vowed the thing was emotionally marred and needed a psychiatrist. Amanda, however, had bonded beautifully with the creature and teasingly told Nate *he* was the one with the problem. She always had been a fool for strays.

The cat lowered her ears and snarled. Nate backed up and raised both hands.

"Okay, mate," he soothed, his anger with Amanda swiftly replaced with the primal need to survive. "I'm not here to cause any problems. Just let me ring the doorbell, you hear?"

The knob clinked, and the massive door sighed inward. Amanda's strained smile greeted Nate. "I've been watching for you," she explained. "The table is set, and we're all waiting."

"Just trying to get past the welcoming committee," Nate explained, glancing from the cat, to Amanda, and back to the cat. Experience had taught Nate Cuddles had some fast moves that would put a few mongooses to shame.

Her tail hair standing out, the Siamese scurried into the house.

"Oh no, you," Amanda fussed and lunged for the cat. Before Cuddles darted up the stairs, Amanda captured her. Securing her in a tight hold, Amanda turned back to Nate.

"I've got her. I won't let her down until you come in."

Cuddles glared at her enemy.

Nate waved and smiled his victory. "I won this time, ol' girl," he taunted as he entered the home's entryway.

The cat arrogantly lifted her nose and appeared less than impressed. Amanda released her outside and swiftly closed the door.

When she turned back toward Nate, he realized what he hadn't noticed in the middle of the cat threat. Amanda looked as good tonight as she had two weeks ago when she'd impishly thrown him that kiss from the shadows. Her "Cleopatra" hair swung near her chin like burnished copper. Her green eyes and creamy skin couldn't have been more exotic in the sun's evening rays pouring through the window. And she smelled as good as she had in O'Brien's.

Nate's irritation wavered in the face of a blatant attraction that started in his gut and consumed his mind to the point that he forgot why he was even here.

"Are you okay?" Amanda queried. She leaned toward him and scrutinized his face like a researcher examining a rare form of fungus.

Nate jerked away and stumbled into the banister. The pain shooting up his spine jolted him back to the reason for the visit—not to admire Amanda, but to chastise her.

"Actually, I'm *not* okay!" Nate snapped and doubted the wisdom of jumping into the subject so early in the evening. He'd actually planned to have a discreetly quiet, yet intense, conversation with Amanda after dinner.

Amanda's face stiffened. She backed away and crossed her arms. "What—"

"Nate! Great to see you!" Angie West's melodious voice cut off Amanda's question. "I thought that was you I heard!" Angie, a petite blonde with more energy than three men, bounded toward him. She clasped Nate in a platonic hug that peeled away the years and ushered in many memories.

Angie, who became Amanda's governess 22 years ago, had been more of a doting, older sister than a mother figure for both Nate and Amanda. She'd set aside her own aspirations of a home and husband and been better to Amanda than three moms. Now at the age of 45 she had finally found matrimonial happiness.

As the hug ended, Nate said, "You've never looked better," and clasped both of Angie's hands. "Looks like married life is agreeing with you."

"Oh absolutely!" Angie enthused, her blue eyes taking on the violet hue of her pantsuit. "You should try it! Maybe Amanda could fix *you* up too! I can't thank her enough for introducing me to Wayne!"

Amanda sputtered over a cough, and Nate tried to ignore her.

Angie moved to Amanda's side and placed her arm along her waist. "Amanda seems to know what's best for all of us," she bragged.

Nate fleetingly wondered if Angie's doting was part of Amanda's problems now. After her mother's tragic drowning, her father had overindulged her and had plenty of support from Angie in the endeavor. The result was a young woman who didn't know when she'd crossed personal boundaries.

A very beautiful young woman, Nate added and wondered exactly how long Amanda had been this beautiful. *How long have I been so blind?*

"Well, let's all eat, then, shall we?" Amanda questioned as if she were reading out of a book of manners.

Nate felt as awkward as Amanda looked. Nevertheless he followed her and Angie down the hallway of the home that had been modeled after the European villa Amanda's parents spent their honeymoon at. The nineteenth-century antiques, stylish yet simple, completed the home's romantic appeal. And Nate idly pondered if it was any wonder that Amanda was such a matchmaker. She'd grown up in a home that looked like the setting for the best in romantic drama.

Their heels tapping along the Italian tile, Nate noted the casual cut of the women's big-legged pantsuits and decided he could safely hang his sport coat on the coat tree at the corridor's end. With that chore complete, he stepped into the dining room, replete with a table that seated 20. Amanda called for the other guests in the great room.

The smells of Sarah's specialty—baked cod in lemon sauce—sent a rumble through Nate's stomach. Even his dilemma with Amanda paled in the wake of his sudden hunger. He'd skipped lunch more often than not in the last couple of weeks, working through that "Amanda hour" like a mad man. His loosening slacks suggested he should enjoy a double portion at tonight's meal. Nate salivated over the steaming asparagus and dinner rolls the cook was adding to the antique sideboard. Even though he heard the other guests shuffling into the room, his attention was fixed upon what his stomach dictated.

"Great to see you again, Nate!" A vaguely familiar male voice broke through Nate's salivating and jostled his memory. He turned to offer a greeting toward the man, but his smile stiffened as he recognized Mason Eldridge. While Nate acted the part of the polite acquaintance and shook Mason's hand, he noticed Haley standing close, but chatting with Amanda. For once Haley looked nearly as lovely as Amanda in a bright-blue suit that matched the ocean and brought out the blonde highlights in her brunette hair.

Mason, dressed in a flashy sport coat and slacks, wasted no time on Nate. As soon as the polite greeting was finished, he wedged himself between Amanda and Haley like the cream in a sandwich cookie. And no cream had ever looked so ecstatic. Mason first gazed at Amanda, then Haley, then back to Amanda. At this vantage, Nate was hard-pressed to determine which woman interested Mason most.

Furthermore, the masculine hunger in the music minister's eyes raised Nate's hackles. His suspicions from the O'Brien's meal were confirmed. A primeval male intuition insisted this was not a person Nate would want dating his sister.

What is Amanda thinking? Nate asked, then answered himself, *She's not thinking!*

From there, Nate pieced together the whole scenario. This little dinner party was nothing more than another opportunity for Amanda to push Haley into Mason's lap and out of Roger's heart. With Mason absorbing every nuance of Haley and Amanda's words, Nate gripped the back of the high-backed dining chair and forced himself to project a calm persona.

He and Roger had been more than cousins; they'd been good friends since childhood. In some ways, Nate was closer to Roger than to his own brother. Roger had been so blasted by Haley's e-mailed rejection this afternoon, the poor man had called Nate and cried. Nate had never seen Roger cry—not even at a family funeral. The man was made of stone, or so it seemed…until now.

Nate was thoroughly convinced that Roger loved Haley—the real Haley—not the polished new dame settling into the chair beside that smooth-talking Mason Eldridge.

After adjusting Haley's chair for her, Mason made a monumental task of pulling out Amanda's chair and even placing her napkin in her lap like a tuxedoed waiter at an upscale restaurant.

"What a gentleman," Amanda cooed. "Don't you think so, Haley?"

"Yes," Haley demurely responded.

Nate jerked out his chair and dropped into it.

"What do you think, Nate?" Harold asked.

He peered toward Harold Priebe's commanding voice. The Priebe patriarch stared back, his bushy brows raised in query. While some guests had taken the party seriously enough to dress up, Harold wore his usual retirement uniform—a pair of cotton pants and a casual shirt splattered with flowers.

"I'm sorry," Nate replied. "I didn't catch that."

"I was saying our dinner will be much better now that we can see the coast." He motioned toward the massive window that spanned the dining room. Another window just like it claimed the living room's east wall.

"Oh yes, of course," Nate agreed and blinked toward the azure ocean, kissed by twilight, that rolled toward the rocky cliffs.

"Are you feeling okay, m' boy?" Harold questioned.

Nate looked back at the man who'd been like a second father to him. He wanted to say something like "Everything's fine," but he couldn't get the half-truth past his lips. Nate made a purpose of never lying. He figured if he even tried, Harold Priebe, of all people, would spot his lack of sincerity within a second—two at the most. So instead of answering, Nate just blankly stared at him.

The room fell silent, and Nate sensed all eyes on him. Harold's keen gaze, as green as Amanda's, shifted to his daughter at the end of the table, then back to Nate. "If I didn't know any better, I'd say you two were quarreling like an old married couple," Harold drawled. "Amanda hasn't said your name for a week, and now that you *are* here, the two of you are barely speaking."

Nate grabbed his water glass and gulped the liquid while Amanda gasped, "Dad! Why would you say something like—"

"It's amazing to me why people want to get married anyway," Harold continued and mischievously eyed Angie and Wayne, who were sitting in the chairs across from Nate. "On top of the fighting, it ruins your social life."

"Speak for yourself!" Wayne jovially responded. The middle-aged banker rested his arm along Angie's shoulders and gave her an endearing squeeze. Angie gazed at him with the adoration of a new bride. "Angie and I have been married more than four months and haven't fought yet! And we're more socially active than before we got married. We're here, aren't we?"

The whole group burst into laughter—everyone, that is, except Nate.

"Of course everything's perfect with you two," Amanda quipped. "What do you expect? *I'm* the one who matched you up." She fluttered her eyelashes.

"And a good matchmaker you are, I say." Wayne lifted his water glass. "I propose a toast to Amanda. May she live long, and may she see many more successful matches."

"Here. Here." Angie agreed as she and Wayne touched the tops of their glasses.

Amanda lifted her water glass toward Wayne and Angie. Then, with a daring smirk, she shifted it toward Haley and Mason. Beaming, Mason touched his glass to Amanda's. Haley ducked her head while Amanda drank some water and looked over the edge with calculating certainty that she was about to make another successful match.

Nate didn't even bother to hide his scowl. When Amanda's gaze slid toward him, her impish smile faded. She lowered the water glass, darted a defiant glance back at Nate, and set down the glass.

Harold cleared his throat with enough meaning to alert the whole party to the undercurrents between Amanda and Nate.

This could turn into a long night, Nate thought and doubted his wisdom in coming.

Seven

~~

"How are you feeling?" Amanda sidled next to Haley, who was helping herself to an after-dinner cup of tea.

"Fine." Never lifting her gaze from her task, Haley finished filling her cup from the silver water urn and dunked the tea bag with a spoon.

"I'm assuming you never heard back from Roger?"

"No. Nothing." Haley sipped her steaming tea and gazed out the dining room's window toward the dark ocean.

During the throes of an afternoon brainstorm, Amanda had arranged for Mason to pick up Haley on his way to the Priebe villa. She hadn't been free to talk with Haley since she arrived.

"Well, I'm sure it's for the best," Amanda replied and patted Haley's arm. "You would have never been happy with him. You're just too special to be stuck on a farm all the time."

Haley smiled into her friend's eyes. "You always make me feel like a queen," she claimed. "You're better to me than all the sisters I never had."

"I *am* the sister you never had," Amanda declared and looped her arm through Haley's. Amanda leaned closer. "Did Mason say anything about his surprise on your ride here?"

"Not a word," Haley said with an expectant grin. "I've been dying of curiosity all evening."

"Here you two are," Mason exclaimed from the edge of the dining room. "I wondered where my two favorite ladies were hiding."

Amanda moved away from Haley and hoped she didn't look like a guilty conspirator.

"I was in need of some tea." Haley lifted her cup from its saucer as naturally as if she and Amanda had been discussing the beverage and nothing else. "It's been a long day," she said and stifled a yawn.

"Would you care for some tea, Amanda?" Mason questioned and reached for a cup sitting on the sideboard.

"No, that's quite all right." Amanda shook her head.

"Are you sure?"

"Absolutely," she assured and smiled at Haley. "Such a gentleman."

Mason's grin couldn't have been broader. "I was thinking now might be a good time for me to share my surprise."

"What surprise?" Amanda questioned with a knowing grin. "We forgot all about your surprise. Was there to be a surprise?"

Haley giggled.

"So I've kept you guessing, have I?" Mason teased, his blue eyes sparkling with an attraction Amanda knew Haley couldn't miss.

"Maybe a little," Haley admitted.

"Well, come back into the great room then," Mason encouraged and motioned toward the sunken room where Angie, Wayne, Harold, and Nate sat in conversation. "I'll go out to my car and bring it in for everyone to see."

As Mason hurried down the hallway, Amanda whispered, "It's been in his car this whole time. Did you see it on your way here?"

"No," Haley replied. "Maybe it was in the trunk."

"I can't stand it any longer," Amanda said and toyed with the collar of her casual jacket. She couldn't possibly imagine that Mason was ready to propose to Haley and offer her a ring, but the idea wouldn't be quieted. Before she and Haley entered the great room, Amanda strained for a last glimpse of Mason as he exited the home.

"Whatever he's up to, he seems to have planned it well," Haley said.

Amanda looked at her friend who, like her, was staring up the hallway. "*Absolutely*," she agreed. "And it's all for you." She squeezed Haley's hand.

Haley's gray eyes twinkled. "I like a man with a plan."

"What woman doesn't?" The two snickered.

"Excuse me, Amanda," Nate's voice sliced through their feminine revelry.

Amanda's neck stiffened as she looked Nate eye to eye. She'd stopped having to look up at Nate by the time she was 18. With so many men shorter than she, Amanda liked the effect of looking one straight in the eyes—even if he was only Nate Knighton.

"I'm about to leave," Nate explained with no hint of kindness, or any other emotion, for that matter. "I'd like to speak with you before I do."

"Well…" Amanda hedged and eyed the villa's hallway. "Uh…Mason is…is…"

Nate moved closer and whispered, "Blast Mason. We need to talk." His warm breath brushed her neck and sent a rash of prickles in its wake. Amanda detected a trace of mint tea on his breath. When she backed away, she recognized more than a trace of ire in his eyes.

"I'll be in the great room," Haley said and shuffled away with the clink of her teacup and saucer. "Whoops!" she bleated.

Amanda peered at her friend, who offered a silent apology then observed the drops of tea pelting the wooden floor.

"Not to worry," Amanda soothed.

"I'll get a napkin for it," Haley offered and scurried back into the dining room.

"Let's go into the kitchen." Loosely gripping her upper arm, Nate pulled Amanda toward the swinging door near the sideboard.

"What if I'm not in the mood for the kitchen?" Amanda retorted.

Nate's dark-eyed glower began a slow tremble at Amanda's knees.

He'd called her shortly after she arrived home and abruptly told her he wanted to talk about Roger and Haley. No pleasant greeting. No inquiries about how she'd been the last two weeks. Just a blunt demand that they discuss his third cousin and her friend. Amanda thought she was going to deter him with claims of the dinner party...until he invited himself.

"And what if I'm not in the mood to talk?" she continued and prayed he didn't detect that the knee trembles had now swept to her eyelids.

"Well, *I am* in the mood to talk," Nate insisted.

Her heart thudding, Amanda stood fast and grappled with how to deal with this new version of her old friend. Nate had never been so confrontational, not even two weeks ago in O'Brien's.

Silently she glared at him until a trickle of common sense insisted she let him have his say. The sooner he delivered his spiel, the sooner he'd leave. *And good riddance,* Amanda thought. *Who wants to be around anybody when he's acting like this?*

Amanda brushed past him and smacked the kitchen's swinging door. It flopped open with a thud that elicited a yelp from the gray-haired Sarah. She dropped the saucepan she'd been drying and exclaimed, "You scared me batty, Miss Amanda!"

"Sorry, Sarah," Amanda said and marched past the cook to the kitchen's outside door.

"I wasn't thinking about Sarah still being here," Nate mumbled.

"Most men forget the cook once their stomachs are full," Amanda shot back and couldn't imagine what had prompted that sexist remark.

"Humph," Nate responded and Amanda wished he wouldn't "humph" her at a time like this.

She didn't risk another reply. Instead, Amanda attacked the outside door with the same force she'd used on the kitchen door. The Tasman Sea greeted them with the smell of salt and the swish and pounding of waves against worn rocks and white sand. The full moon rising in the east offered a luminous shimmer upon the heaving ocean. The cold breeze sent a shiver through Amanda, but she feigned indifference. Instinct insisted this was not the time to show any signs of weakness.

As Nate clicked the door shut, Amanda walked across the miniature balcony, and it pleasantly creaked beneath her step. She placed her hands on her hips and observed Nate in the balcony's lighting.

"So talk," she said.

A frown line formed between Nate's brows. "I guess you know Haley rejected Roger's proposal today?"

Amanda crossed her arms. "Yes, I know."

He squinted. "You told her to, didn't you?"

"Haley made her own decision," Amanda defended as a gust of wind swished her hair across her cheeks.

"Oh, I'm sure she did." Nate raised his hand. "After you talked her into falling in love with Mason."

Amanda gaped, and a strand of hair smacked into her mouth. "I'd never interfere to such a level." She jerked the hair away from her lips.

"Of course you wouldn't," Nate mocked. "You…you…" His face darkened. He worked his lips. Then he turned and marched to the edge of the balcony. His back to her, Nate gripped the railing.

Amanda, now fiercely trembling, hugged her torso and considered running. She'd never had to deal with this side of Nate and pitied anyone who did. She'd also never noticed how broad the man's shoulders were…or how the moonlight dusted his hair with as much gold as it did the sea. A perverse voice suggested his mystery woman saw all this and more long ago. Shaking her head, Amanda crept backward and stopped when she bumped the balcony rail.

Nate whirled around and moved in for more. "Amanda, you cannot spend the rest of your life arranging other people's lives for them."

"Whatever makes you think I'm interested in doing that?" She raised her chin. "Just because I don't think Roger is a good match for Haley—"

"Why didn't you let Haley decide that by herself?"

"She did!" Amanda stomped her foot. "And if she was so committed to Roger, do you think I or anyone else could have done anything to persuade her?"

Nate jerked his head back and blinked.

Sensing she'd scored a point, Amanda continued, "It's better for her to find out how she really feels now, rather than after the wedding, don't you think?"

Nate tugged his earlobe and stared toward the horizon.

"I think she and Mason are really starting to fall for each other. Maybe they're meant to be. You know, like Angie and Wayne."

"That idiot?" Nate erupted. "Mason Eldridge doesn't have one thought for Haley Schmitz."

"But *of course* he does!" Amanda argued. "He even brought her a surprise tonight. He's gone out to the car to get it."

Nate shook his head. "Mark my word," he insisted, "he's nothing but a wolf in sheep's clothing. And it's not Haley he's after. It's *you!*"

"*Me!*" Amanda squeaked and decided Nate Knighton was going daft. *No, he's already gone daft,* she thought. "Mason's nearly a foot shorter than I am! What would he want with *me?*"

"What indeed?" Nate mumbled and swept a pointed gaze from her feet to her head.

Amanda balled her hands at her sides and considered a dozen retorts, only to say nothing.

He turned for the balcony again and grabbed onto the rail as if he were afraid of falling off. "I watched him all evening, Amanda. You had to have noticed. He hardly took his eyes off you. He's just being nice to Haley because she's part of the Amanda package. And besides all that, he's not someone I'd want my sister—or any woman I care about—getting involved with."

"This is insane!" Amanda insisted. "He's a *minister!* How can you say something so—"

"Because it's the truth." Nate whipped back around. "Look at me, Amanda. I'm a *man!* I'm *not* one of your girlfriends. I'm a guy!" He pressed his fingertips against his chest and leveled her a stare that bordered on desperation. "I can read other men. I *know* what Mason Eldridge is thinking. It doesn't have a thing to do with Haley and has everything to do with *you!* And if you've somehow convinced Haley he's after her and that she should dump Roger because of it, you've royally botched her life—and Roger's!"

With a huff, Amanda marched past Nate and gripped the kitchen doorknob. "I don't have to listen to another syllable of this—this—of whatever this is you've cooked up in your—your wild imagination." Amanda paused long enough to realize the bad analogy. Nate Knighton did not equate and had never equated with "wild imagination."

Until tonight, she thought and decided there was no reasoning with the man. "If you've said all you wanted to say, I'm going back to the dinner party. Mason has a surprise for Haley."

She lifted her nose like the Siamese she-devil who'd nearly attacked Nate when he arrived, stepped through the doorway, and didn't look back. Nate rubbed his face and groaned. The whole conversation had gone like he'd presumed—only worse. He fully expected Amanda to defend Haley's rejection of Roger. But for some unknown reason, Nate had believed Amanda would see the truth about Mason.

"How can she be such a good businesswoman and be so naïve when it comes to men?" Nate mumbled, shook his head, and rubbed his chin. *It's like she has no concept of the power of her own beauty,* he thought. *She's so busy matchmaking, she doesn't notice when a guy wants to make a match with her.*

"Like me, for instance," Nate said. He stepped back to the railing, looked toward the infinite waters, lifted his face to the heavens, and closed his eyes. His cheeks stung with the air drifting from Antarctica. Likewise his mind stung with the reality of his own folly.

He shouldn't be too hard on Amanda and her naïveté when he'd been just as thoughtless in his friendship with her. This whole attraction had somehow sneaked up on him, then bitten him like a venomous sea snake he'd swam with because he was fool enough to believe it harmless.

A woman of Amanda's caliber wouldn't be harmless to the most stoic of saints. And Mason Eldridge was far from a stoic saint. The awe-stricken guy had absorbed Amanda's every word. Poor Haley didn't stand a chance with Amanda in the room.

Except with Roger, he thought. Nate opened his eyes. His jaw tightened.

"I'm going to have to get over this," he told himself.

Amanda had made one good point. If Haley really was in love with Roger, she wouldn't be so easily swayed by Mason. And, like Amanda said, it was better for Roger to know she wasn't completely committed now, rather than waiting until after the marriage.

But that doesn't stop Roger's pain. Nate sighed and thanked God he had stopped himself from making Roger's mistake.

Fortunately, Nate had recognized his inclinations toward Amanda before he fell in love with her. Currently his heart was not involved. His masculinity was intrigued. That was all.

He further deduced that if Amanda was so clueless about all of Mason's ogling, she must be oblivious to Nate's hidden attraction.

All I need to do now is make sure I stay away from her, Nate thought and wasn't fool enough to imagine he was immune to falling in love if he didn't keep his distance.

Not that he'd be opposed to the idea of love, of course, if Amanda were so inclined. But that was the problem. She wasn't inclined. End of story.

Nate stepped toward the short flight of stairs that led from the balcony to the yard. Then he remembered his jacket on the coat tree.

"Fabulous," he sarcastically mumbled. Lowering his head, Nate reentered the villa with plans to slip into the hallway, retrieve his sports coat, and exit without anyone detecting him.

The white kitchen still smelled of cod and lemon sauce, and

Nate was tempted to ask Sarah for any leftovers. On his way past her, he offered the cook a tight smile. She returned his grin and resumed her task of wiping down the counters.

Amanda's comment about men forgetting the cook bit into his conscience. "Great dinner," Nate said. "I could have eaten all night."

Sarah's cheeks flushed, and she attacked the cabinet with renewed fervor. In all the years Nate had known Sarah, she said little.

He pushed open the dining room's swinging door, stepped onto the Italian tile, and glanced toward the great room. Nate held his breath, tiptoed around the long dining table, and arrived in the hallway. He sighed, retrieved his jacket, and headed for the front door.

"I can't believe it. It's gorgeous!" Amanda's exclamation halted Nate.

He looked over his shoulder and was tempted to investigate the cause of Amanda's elation. Whatever Mason had surprised them with certainly had impressed her. After a scowl, Nate decided he'd rather not know.

Eight

Haley's teacup shook into a rhythmic clatter, and she set it down on the nearest table lest she dribble the whole cup all over the area rug. While Amanda exclaimed over the surprise, Haley sat on the edge of the sofa. Mason had said he was going to have the portrait framed, but neither she nor Amanda had expected it so soon.

Hand in hand Angie and Wayne stood beside Harold and joined Amanda in her praise. "Look at the mat and frame," Angie said.

"I was about to say the same thing." Wayne touched the frame that Mason held with pride. "They're a perfect match for her suit and hair, aren't they?"

Haley couldn't agree more. Amanda had painted her in a cinnamon-colored suit. The mat coordinated with the suit while the dark frame matched Haley's brunette hair. The brass chandelier emitted a velvety glow that immersed the painting in a surreal aura. Haley's smile took on a classic appeal, and Amanda's art-work had never appeared so accomplished.

"Wonderful job, m' dear!" Harold encircled Amanda's shoulders with his arm and gave her an approving squeeze along with a loving smile. "You get better with every piece." He motioned toward the oil painting Haley had tutored Amanda through last summer. While the seascape hanging on the west wall above Amanda's piano was notable, it paled in comparison to the level of skill the portrait revealed.

Mason propped the painting on the faux fireplace's marble mantel. "I couldn't be prouder if I'd painted it myself," he said and backed away for an admiring assessment.

"So what do you think, Haley?" Amanda questioned.

All attention rested on her.

As Haley searched for something to say, her gaze shifted from Amanda's portly father to Angie and Wayne, then to Amanda, before she focused upon Mason.

"I think it's lovely," she said and stroked the seam in the striped sofa. "Absolutely lovely."

Mason's emphatic nod underscored the affection Amanda insisted he must be feeling for Haley. "I was thinking we'd share the work," he said.

Amanda tilted her head. "Share it?"

"Yes. It really belongs to all three of us," Mason claimed. "Me, you, and Haley, of course." The gold buttons on his sport coat twinkled as he motioned toward Haley—as did his eyes when he gazed at her.

Haley began to suspect that she and Mason must be moving from mere surface attraction to something deeper. Her hands steadying, she dared to hold the cup of tea once more. After picking it up, she enjoyed a sip of warmth. The smooth, sweet liquid oozed down her throat and bolstered her courage.

"I was thinking we'd take turns having it at our homes," Mason explained. "You know, maybe each of us could keep it four months out of the year. But…" he hesitated and again glanced toward Haley, then Amanda, "I was wondering if you'd mind if I keep it at my place first. I think the work is, well, exquisite and I'd like to show it off to my family."

Amanda's grin was all for Haley; so was her sly wink. "Haley, would you mind?"

"Of course not," Haley breathed. She absorbed Mason's approving smile and knew beyond all doubt that Amanda was right about everything. Mason really was enamored with her. His wanting her portrait first spoke volumes.

"I'd be honored," she added.

"Fantastic!" Mason exclaimed like a small child who's been given prime choice from the cookie platter.

Wayne moved in for a closer examination of the portrait. The fine cut of his banker's suit affirmed that while Angie's marriage was based on love, it wasn't without financial security.

"My word, Amanda, you *are* getting to be quite an artist," Wayne said.

"I agree!" Mason said. "I was impressed with it before it was framed, but now it's…it's a masterpiece. My mother and sister are coming next week. I want to make sure they see it. That's why I wanted the first rotation in my home." He smiled at Haley. "I'm sure you understand."

"Oh, we *all* understand." Amanda laid her hand on Mason's shoulder, and her chin-length hair swayed with her nodding. "We understand *completely*."

Mason's grin couldn't have been more meaningful. Harold cleared his throat, lifted his bushy brow, and examined first his daughter, then Haley.

No telling what he's thinking! Haley fretted. Her cheeks warming, she avoided looking at Angie and Wayne or Mr. Priebe for fear they would see what *she* was thinking. She focused on her steaming tea and allowed her hair to shield her expression as the liquid's sweet aroma enticed her to another sip.

Mason had never even offered to hold her hand, but his claim on the portrait spoke more than any sign of affection. The e-mail ordeal with Roger faded to the back of Haley's mind. Even though Haley hadn't told Amanda, she *had* worried about rejecting his proposal. Haley hated hurting poor Roger, especially when she knew how deeply his feelings ran.

But Amanda just didn't think they were suited, and her friend was so insightful. For Haley, Amanda was like a sister and mother all rolled into one. She'd connected with Amanda as she never connected with any of her foster families. And Haley had learned from experience that Amanda was right more often than not. Angie and Wayne's lovers' glances alone were enough to convince Haley that Amanda's guidance should be heeded.

Mason's being enamored with the portrait underscored her every assumption and convinced Haley she'd done the right thing regarding the proposal. Roger had never been as demonstrative as Mason over anything. Mason would obviously care for her more than Roger ever did.

And I will learn to care for him just as deeply, Haley decided and wondered if Mason might at least hold her hand on the journey home.

"You know my son Franklyn will be in town next month." Wayne's comment ended the elongated silence. "Amanda, we should get you to paint us."

"Yes! That's a *wonderful* idea!" Angie exclaimed and snapped her fingers. "A father–son portrait. That would be perfect!" She moved to Amanda's side and clasped her arm. "Amanda has already seen pictures of Franklyn. Would you consider doing the portrait?"

"Well, I…" Amanda peered at Haley like a protégé asking for guidance. While the prospect of painting the handsome Englishman held definite appeal, no one in the room knew that Haley had assisted Amanda on her own portrait. Many times, Haley had guided Amanda's hands in the proper strokes that produced the desired effect.

"Of course she'll do the portrait!" Mason assured and placed his hand in the small of her back. "I'm her agent. I'll arrange the whole thing!"

The group laughed.

"Whatever happened to Sarah and her apple pie?" Harold queried and meandered past the oak coffee table toward the dining room.

"Oh, Daddy," Amanda complained. "How can you think about pie when I'm starting my new career?" She followed her father, paused at his side, and lovingly patted his protruding stomach. "Go sit down in your chair." She motioned toward an overstuffed recliner, replete with a TV remote lying on the hand rest. "I'll go see about your pie. Do you want coffee or tea with it?"

"Decaf coffee," Harold said with a satisfied grin.

"I don't think there's ever been a lapdog more pampered," Angie teased. Her big-legged pants swishing around her ankles, she strode to Amanda's side and shooed Harold toward his recliner. "We'll take care of your every wish, as usual."

"Don't forget about poor ol' me, here," Wayne called. "I like pie and coffee too."

"So you do," Angie retorted and crooked her finger at her new husband. "And you're the perfect choice to help us load the service tray." She threw in a flirtatious wink.

"Well, if you put it like that…" Wayne said and hustled to his wife's side.

The three of them disappeared into the dining room, and their steps mingled with Amanda's satisfied snickers.

"I do believe my daughter thinks she's Cupid." Harold Priebe, quite the obedient father, relaxed into his recliner just as his daughter had prescribed. "I wonder who her next victims will be," he added, his intelligent gaze taking in both Haley and Mason.

"I don't think it takes a rocket scientist to figure that one out," Mason replied with a satisfied grin that said he was thrilled to be Amanda's victim. "What do you think, Haley?" He settled onto the end of the couch and cut her a sly glance.

Her teacup quivered, and Haley gulped another mouthful in preference for answering the obvious question. From that moment forth she decided Roger Miller was a thing of the past and nothing more.

Nine

A month later Amanda glared at the strand of hair that insisted upon flipping out instead of under. No matter how many times she tugged it under with her hair brush, the strip stuck out like a sideways horn. The smell of the salon hairspray sitting on the decorative table beneath the mirror attested that Amanda had pulled out every weapon she possessed to combat the problem. Six weeks had lapsed since she got the new haircut, and Amanda couldn't put off a trip to the hairdresser's another week. Of course, that didn't help her tonight.

Tonight of all nights she'd wanted to look as close to perfect as possible. In half an hour her office building's spacious foyer was going to be crowded with a reception especially for Betty Cate's niece, Janet French. Looking back, Amanda *still* didn't know how she was talked into this event. One day Betty was telling her Janet was going to be arriving. And the next week, Amanda heard herself agree to host a "Welcome to Highland" party for the Asian beauty.

Now she and Haley were expecting 20 people in a matter of 30 minutes, and Amanda had horn-hair extraordinaire! No doubt Janet would arrive with every hair perfectly in place and looking like the Queen of Korea.

That ought to give Nate plenty to stare at! Amanda fumed and pulled on the hair-horn. *That is, if he doesn't have the mystery woman with him.*

He'd used a cryptic e-mail last week to invite himself to the party once he heard his brother and Amanda's sister were on the guest list. Amanda hadn't seen him since that crazy night at the villa a month ago. The very idea that Nate could think Mason Eldridge was after her was even more bizarre now than it had been a month ago.

Because of Nate's increasingly odd behavior, Amanda hoped Gordon and Bev weren't still planning to have dinner with her and Nate tomorrow evening. Weeks ago, she'd made plans to go shopping with Bev tomorrow, then afterward have dinner with Nate and Gordon and Bev. She hadn't mentioned the plans to Nate and hoped Gordon and Bev hadn't either.

Her relationship with Nate was rocky at best. Thoughts of losing his friendship only made her dread the evening with Janet all the more. If Nate brought the vixen who made him stuff all Amanda's gifts in his closet, she would be hard pressed not to leave her own party.

She slapped at her hair again. "Haley! I need help!" Her bare toes tapped along the cool tile floor as she strode toward the doorway that connected her office to Haley's. "Didn't you say you bought a flat iron?" Amanda looked up in time to see Haley before the two smacked into each other.

"Oh, sorry there," Amanda said as Haley did the two-step to stop from being run over.

"Quite all right," Haley replied. She handed Amanda the flat iron and grimaced at the hair-horn. "I had just unplugged it. I think we need new haircuts. My hair wouldn't do a *thing!*"

"It looks great!" Amanda examined Haley's straight hair, shimmering and swaying just above her shoulders.

"It ought to," Haley fumed. "I just spent 20 minutes making it behave!" She pointed to the flat iron. "You should go ahead and plug it in now. It's still warm and won't take as long to heat up."

"Thanks." Amanda heeded Haley's advice and traipsed back into her office. "You look scrumptious, by the way," she called over her shoulder and stole another glimpse of Haley's red sundress. "Too bad Mason couldn't make the party."

"Yes." The hesitant drag in Haley's voice stopped Amanda's journey.

She pivoted to face her friend. "Is something wrong?"

"Well…" Haley placed her fingertips upon her desk, wiggled her bare toes, and looked downward. "He's just so…um…it's not that I want him to make a move in a wrong way or anything but well, he's…I guess he's just a really slow mover," Haley finally said.

"Oh, so he hasn't even kissed you yet and you can't wait?" Amanda teased.

Haley jerked up her head. "N–no! Nothing like that." She worked her fingers. "I'm not after any kisses necessarily. It's just that—that…um…it wouldn't hurt if he tried to hold my hand or something. Anything, just to let me know—"

"That you've still got him?" Amanda questioned.

"Well, I don't necessarily mean it *that* way!" Haley huffed through a smile. "Why do you always do this to me?"

Amanda laughed. "Don't worry, lady! I guarantee Mason's all yours. He'll probably propose by Christmas."

"Do you really think so?" Haley asked.

"Absolutely! You need to get ready." She wagged her index finger from side to side. "That's only about six weeks away." As October had slid into November, the temperatures rose nicely into the 70s. Summer was nearly in full swing, which meant Christmas planning was almost upon them.

"I'm having high hopes for the church Christmas party," Amanda said. "Angie just told me last night she's volunteered to host it at her place. You haven't seen their house yet, have you?"

"No," Haley answered.

"It's to die for!"

"Have you met Wayne's son yet?" Haley asked. "What's his name?"

"Franklyn."

"Oh yes, Franklyn."

"I haven't met him. He only arrived two days ago. So far I've only seen his pictures." Amanda paused, glanced down, and brushed a piece of lint from her little black dress. "Angie says he's very handsome," she added.

"Oh she does, does she?" Haley teased.

"He's supposed to be here tonight," Amanda continued and never acknowledged Haley's speculations or her heightening interest over his arrival. He was indeed as handsome as Angie claimed. Furthermore, he was every bit as tall as Amanda, as blond as Mason, and, from what Angie said, much kinder than Nate these days.

She hid a scowl and determined to likewise hide that she'd been tempted to at least consider a romantic involvement—despite her commitment to her father.

"I'm just glad for Wayne's sake that Franklyn's here for a while. From what Angie says, he and his father haven't been close for years. He's only 28. Sad, isn't it?"

"Oh, I don't know," Haley said without a blink, "I'll be 28 in 4 years, and I'm not thinking it's all that sad."

"No, silly!" Amanda waved the flat iron. "It's sad that Wayne and Franklyn aren't close."

"Oh!" Haley said and laughed. "I was wondering why 28 was all of a sudden so sad."

Amanda rolled her eyes.

"Why aren't they close?" Haley said through a final chortle.

"Well, when Franklyn's mother died, Wayne's sister and her husband wound up taking care of Franklyn a lot. He was only five."

"Wow! That sounds a little like your story." Haley blinked.

"Yes, I guess it does," Amanda said. "And I guess a little like yours too." Both women fell silent. Amanda gazed toward the tile floor and scrounged through the closets of her memory for recollections of her mother. The painful wound that might have festered had long been healed through Angie's unconditional love…and that of her heavenly Father's.

"Anyway," Amanda continued, "Angie says Wayne was devastated when his wife died. He went into this horrid depression." Amanda crossed her arms and rested the warm flat iron along her upper arm. "Once Wayne recovered, his son had seriously bonded to his sister. He didn't feel right about taking him away from her. When the international banking job came open, he took it. That meant a lot of travel, of course." Amanda uncrossed her arms. "Now that Angie and he are married and he's not traveling as much, she's trying to get Wayne to work on the relationship with Franklyn."

"I think it's great," Haley affirmed. "Especially for you," she added in a cunning voice.

"Oh no!" Amanda held up her free hand. "I'm not available, remember? I've got a dad to spoil." She waved the flat iron before

Haley could jump to any more conclusions. "I need to get busy or I'll be late for my own party," she called while scurrying back toward her office's mirror.

As she plugged in the flat iron, Amanda purposed to be less obvious in her thoughts regarding Franklyn. If Haley was detecting her growing interest, everyone else might clearly see it as well.

Amanda straightened from the plug and gazed at herself in the mirror. "You haven't even met him yet," she mouthed and gave herself a level stare that invited no arguments. "And don't forget," she added and pointed at her reflection, "you've got your dad to think of!" Satisfied with her self-lecture, Amanda nodded and decided a romance with Franklyn West was about as logical as one with Nate Knighton.

Ten

Nate planned to be late to Amanda's little party, and he was. He figured the entry would be less of an upheaval if the room were already full. Nate eased into the sizable lobby and hovered near the wall.

Designed for corporate entertainment, the area looked like a small ballroom at an exquisite hotel. Along the south wall, a 200-gallon saltwater aquarium offered a sampling of the ocean's most striking occupants, including an imposing lion fish, a gaudy orange sea anemone, and two clown fish entertaining their audience with water aerobics. Two waiters, laden with silver-trayed delicacies, circled the room while a harpist dressed in cream-colored silk plucked out a melody intended to sooth the soul. But the effect was lost on Nate—all the way lost.

He was too agitated at the thought of being with Amanda for his soul to be soothed. He hadn't seen her in a month—not since that upheaval over Mason Eldridge. And that's the reason he'd invited himself to this gathering. Nate had stayed away as long as he could. The day had come for an Amanda fix, and there was nothing he could do to stop himself. He hadn't even tried.

His heart thumped in rapid cadence as he caught site of her trailing from one guest to another. She was wearing a straight black dress that demurely stopped just above her knees. Her black spiked heels probably placed her a full inch taller than him. She towered over the whole group like a larger-than-life goddess with flaming hair.

Nate swallowed hard. He didn't remember Amanda ever looking more beautiful…or his experiencing this melting sensation in the center of his soul. His palms moistened, and Nate blasted himself for being so weak.

This has nothing to do with love, Nate told himself, just as he'd told himself a dozen times during the last month. *It's just an irrational attraction, that's all,* he reasoned. *Like a cold,* he added. *I'll recover soon and be done with it. Amanda won't ever have to know.*

Finally she stopped near Angie and Wayne West. Beside them stood a tall, blond guy dressed in a tuxedo and looking like he just stepped off a high-dollar yacht. Nate glanced down at his usual navy suit and the ever-present red tie. This one was peppered with bronze golf clubs. Amanda's comment about his predictable red ties made him wonder if he was like wallpaper in her life—forever present but never seen.

His mouth tightened as he observed Amanda again. When she returned the yacht king's smile with enough warmth to ignite the whole outback, he grimaced and meandered toward the beverage table with all the nonchalance he could feign. The smell of coffee did nothing to tempt his dry mouth. Nate needed wet and cold. Heavy on the cold. He spotted several bottles of club soda nestled in a bowl of ice and was deciding he might drink all of them when he noticed a bronze-skinned beauty near the table.

He didn't need a second look to recognize Janet French. The only other time he'd been with Janet, Nate had been tempted to get her phone number. But after prayerful consideration he did not sense that was the best move. He quickly reconsidered that whole decision, as well as Janet's petite figure in a simple-yet-elegant fuchsia suit. Nate couldn't deny the prospect was tempting. Nevertheless, he knew in his heart the decision from a year ago must remain firm. Janet French, while highly appealing, simply was not the woman for him.

A baby's familiar cry rippled from behind, and Nate swiveled to peer across the room. As he presumed, the cry belonged to none other than his nephew, Matthew Gordon Knighton. Matt's mother, Bev, stood near the entry, jostling the seven-month-old while scanning the crowd.

With an indulgent smile he couldn't deny, Nate momentarily abandoned the club soda pursuit and strode toward his redheaded sister-in-law. While there was no questioning her relation to Amanda, Bev lacked Amanda's height, the stun-gun effect of brilliant green eyes, and the knock-'em-dead smile. Of course, that was in Nate's opinion. He was sure Gordon would disagree.

Whatever, Nate thought as he approached his nephew, *those two have something most married couples would die for.* He could only pray God would be as good to him one day.

He was mere feet from Matt when the dark-haired child spotted him. He smiled and lurched forward with enough gusto to challenge Bev's grip and her balance. "Aaahhh!" she exclaimed as Nate hurried to her rescue.

The baby squealed and welcomed Nate's opened arms. "How's my champ?" he asked and settled Matt near his heart.

"I'm surprised he's going to you like this!" Bev exclaimed while adjusting the neck of her cotton sweater. "He hasn't seen you in nearly two months. I didn't think he'd recognize you."

Still smiling, Matt reached for Nate's face. But the child's eyes widened. He held his breath, then jerked his head back and released a scream that hushed the whole crowd.

The harpist's fluid cords and the quiet gurgle of fish tank bubbles were all that filled the breathless silence.

"What'd I do?" Nate squawked.

Bev laughed and accepted Matt as he scrambled back into her arms. Still crying, he latched on to Bev's neck and stared at Nate as if he were the Loch Ness Monster.

"I think he thought you were Gordon," Bev explained as the guests resumed their chatting. "Then when he got a good look at you, he realized he'd made a mistake."

"Well, hey there little guy." Nate patted the baby's back. "I'm just your old Uncle Nate. I wouldn't hurt you. No I wouldn't."

"What are you doing to my son, you old buzzard?" Gordon's jovial voice floated from behind.

Smiling, Nate turned toward Gordon. The elder Knighton son was two inches shorter than Nate, 20 pounds heavier, and showed more signs of gray hair every time Nate saw him.

"Looks like I've scared him out of a year's growth," Nate explained.

Gordon reached for his son. The baby settled into his father's arms and laid his head on his shoulder.

"I couldn't get him to go to sleep," Bev explained. "We left the girls with Dad, but Matt wouldn't have any of that. So we decided to just bring him with us. I was in Amanda's office, trying to get him to sleep so I could enjoy the party. But..." she shook her head, "he kept crying for 'Da, Da, Da, Da.'"

"I guess that's what you get for being such a good pop!" Nate slapped Gordon on the back, squeezed his shoulder, and for the first time experienced a twinge of envy for his older brother.

All these years Nate had relished his freedom. Even though thoughts of a wife had been highly inviting for quite some time, Nate still enjoyed his untethered status. He could come and go as he pleased, with whom he pleased, when he pleased. Presently, it would be highly pleasing to come and go with his own little tyke.

"Ah well, Bev," Gordon said. "I'll just manage him while you get a snack." He nodded toward a waiter laden with a tray full of goodies. "Those bacon things are too good."

"Amanda always comes up with something so good you want to stuff your pockets full and take them home for later," Nate quipped and wondered about the possibilities of stuffing Amanda in his pocket and taking her home…forever. He blinked and shook his head.

She'd never fit in my pocket, Nate reasoned, but his mind didn't seem to register the logic.

"Well, hello there, lil Matt," Amanda's distinct voice floated from nearby, and Nate couldn't stop himself from stiffening. This is what he'd come here for—his Amanda fix. He eyed her as she stooped to look into her nephew's face. All the while, Nate searched for something to say.

"Be careful," he drawled. "He's got a scream that shatters glass."

"So I've heard," Amanda replied without looking at Nate. Matt lifted his head and observed his aunt.

"Want to come to Aunt Amanda?" she encouraged and patted her hands together. "If I can get him to come to me, maybe you two can have some time together," she mumbled from the side of her mouth.

"Don't tell us that," Gordon joked, "we might leave for hours."

"Oh, Gordon." Bev slapped at his arm.

"Well, maybe you could at least enjoy a bottle of club soda together," Nate offered and was reminded of his own thirst as Matt extended his arms toward Amanda.

She took the baby and turned him toward Nate. "See there. There's your Uncle Nate again." Amanda waved Bev and Gordon away while Nate cringed.

"Not sure that's such a good idea," Nate said. "The last time we got close, he shut down the party."

"Oh, he's okay," Amanda crooned as the baby focused on the red beads clasped upon her neck. He wrapped his chubby fingers around the expensive new toy and tugged.

"Yikes," Nate whispered, "he's got your beads. Those things didn't come cheap either."

"Who cares," Amanda mumbled under her breath, "he's quiet. And besides all that, you owned the store in the first place. You probably turned in the receipt for a company voucher."

While Nate could have done exactly that, he hadn't. He never did on the Amanda gifts. He always wanted them to cost him something—even if bought from Knighton's. Nate had never examined his reason for this, but tonight he suspected the motives might involve this chemistry that had sprung between them. Or at least had sprung upon Nate. Amanda, completely focused upon her nephew, didn't appear to be sprung upon whatsoever.

Nate loosened his tie a bit and wondered if anyone else in the room were having problems breathing.

When Matt lowered his mouth toward the pretty red playthings around Amanda's neck, Nate said, "Now he's going for the chew."

"That won't work," Amanda agreed. "Quick. Do you have something else he can play with?"

Nate shrugged. "I…I…"

"Quick!" Amanda repeated while trying to discourage Matt from chomping at her beads. "I'm afraid if I have to break his hold he's going to scream again." She looked toward Nate's tie. Before he understood her intent, Amanda was waving the red strip of silk under Matt's nose.

"Here," she offered, "you can chew on this. It's pretty and red too."

"But that's my *tie!*" Nate squeaked as Matt grabbed the tie and shoved the end into his mouth.

"Don't worry." Amanda waved aside his concerns. "You've got 40 dozen red ties at home. You won't ever miss this one." She slid him a saucy look much like the one she'd hooked him with at O'Brien's, and Nate forgot all about the tie…or what day of the week it was.

"So what have you been doing with yourself these days?" Nate asked as Matt continued gnawing.

"Oh this and that," Amanda replied. "You know, all the usual." She glanced past him, then back to the baby. "And you?"

"The usual," Nate repeated and grappled for something brilliant to say. But the smell of her perfume blocked all brain activity. "You smell great," he said. The second the compliment popped out of his mouth, Nate was tempted to jerk the tie from the baby and stuff it in to *his* mouth.

"Thanks," Amanda said as casually as if he'd just mentioned the weather forecast. "It's Jasmine. I think you gave it to me two Christmases ago."

"I did?" Nate blurted and recalled telling his secretary to pick out some perfume for Amanda and his sister and mother. He'd never even bothered smelling the stuff, but had been pleased when Amanda was delighted with the gift.

"Yes." She peered smack into his eyes. "I still have all your Christmas presents." The admission took on a challenging edge.

Nate, confused by her hidden message, observed Matt, who was still in the tie-devouring business. Finally he said, "Well, I guess I still have all yours too."

They're just in my closet, that's all, Nate thought and that whole ordeal took on a ridiculous twist. The purpose in "Operation Closet" had been to rid himself of Amanda stuff and, therefore, Amanda thoughts. But the closet was filled, and Nate was more consumed with Amanda than ever.

Now his spirit was more thirsty than his body, and the only "drink" that would satisfy was Amanda. While she focused on the baby, Nate allowed himself the indulgence of perusing her features and shamelessly absorbing the delicious effect.

When she looked directly at him, Nate glanced away, only to encounter the blond yacht king nearing them. Interestingly enough, Janet French approached from the other side, and Nate realized his time alone with Amanda was over.

Just as well, he thought, *before I compliment something beside her perfume.*

"There you are, Amanda," the yacht king said. "I was wondering where you got off to."

"Just doing some babysitting," Amanda said as Matt abandoned the tie for a hard stare at the newcomer.

"Nate," Amanda asked, "have you met Franklyn West? He's Wayne West's son—Angie's stepson."

"No, we haven't met." Nate extended his hand for a shake and experienced the odd sensation of meeting a male who was both taller and broader-shouldered than he. The guy's tousled blond hair, straight nose, and engaging smile placed him on Nate's "it doesn't matter if I never meet him again" list. He grappled with the unusual sensation of somehow being outdone.

"So nice to meet you," Franklyn said, his voice laced with a British tone. He glanced toward Janet, who was demurely approaching. "And I believe I remember you from the last time I visited. You were at Dad's house helping your aunt clean, weren't you?"

Janet nodded and smiled.

"You've visited before, Franklyn?" Amanda asked.

"Yes, six months ago, actually," he said.

"Why didn't we meet then?" She widened her eyes.

"Wasn't that when we were in Paris?" Nate asked.

"Ah yes. I believe that's right." Amanda shifted Matt and touched the beads, and Nate wondered if her memories of the trip were as fond as his.

"So it looks like I missed a beautiful part of Tasmania then," Franklyn said with a meaningful smile.

"You'll have to forgive his accent," Amanda teased and winked at Janet. "He spent a lot of his childhood in Britain with his aunt and uncle. His uncle's family are from there. I told him earlier we'd try to teach him to talk while he's here."

"Don't take lessons from the likes of her," Nate grumbled. "She's spent one too many days in America. It's ruined her but good."

"I guess we're the only ones who talk like true Aussies then, Nate," Janet's soft addition to the conversation drew Amanda's focus. She looked down at Janet, and Nate thought he detected a slight swell of dislike. But the impression was so short-lived he dismissed it. Amanda had never been prone to disliking people. She was usually quite the opposite—friendly to everyone. Besides, she was the one throwing the party for Janet.

A resounding crash sent baby Matt into a leap and prompted his crumpled-faced crying.

"Oh no! How did *that* happen?" Haley wailed, and Nate spotted her at the end of the drink table. A large, stainless steel bowl lay on the floor. Ice was scattered like marbles in all directions. Haley held a small bottle of soda and gazed at the mess near her feet.

"Haley strikes again," Amanda moaned. "I don't know how she always does this." She extended Matt toward Nate. "Here. You take the baby. I'll go help her."

"Oh no," Nate said and lifted his hands, palms outward. "The last time I held him, he gave me ear drum damage for life. *I'll* help her. You just keep Matt happy." He directed a vague, "I'm outta here" smile toward the yacht king and Miss French and strode to Haley's rescue.

Eleven

Haley gazed at the wet, cold mess near her feet. She'd been leaning across the table to retrieve a soda when her backless spike heels failed her. Her ankle turned. And she plunged into the ice bowl. The metal bowl sloshed water on her and plummeted off the end of the table. Now she had streaks of water down the front of her sundress, her toes were cold and wet, and ice and soft drink bottles were everywhere.

Helplessly, she looked up to see if someone might take pity on her mishap, only to encounter half the crowd gazing at her. Harold Priebe's bushy brows had never appeared so domineering. Angie West's eyes bugged like the lion fish's in Amanda's tank. Betty Cates, that eternal scatterbrain, observed the whole mess with a "How did you manage that?" look on her face. Her neck warming, Haley figured this act must have transcended even Betty's abilities.

In the face of Amanda's perseverance, Haley had agreed to the regular addition of spike heels to her wardrobe. "You'll get used to them," Amanda had insisted. Haley was now wondering if Amanda's prediction was an impossibility. So far the results had been far from fashionable. She'd twisted her ankle twice, rubbed blisters on her little toes, and nearly fallen on her face so many times she'd lost count.

If God wanted all women to wear mile-high, toothpick heels, then why did He inspire people to create flats? she thought and shook her head.

Haley placed her soda on the table, knelt beside the bowl, and turned it over. She cupped her hands and scooped up some of the ice.

"Here, let me help," a considerate male voice said.

She looked up to encounter Nate Knighton's gaze, full of kindness and compassion...and a trace of humor. Haley glanced around the room to discover all guests had lost interest in her latest escapade. The bushy brows, fish eyes, and Betty's astonishment were otherwise occupied. Haley's face cooled, and an unexpected giggle escaped her.

Nate chuckled and knelt beside her.

"They say everyone has a special talent," Haley chirped. "I guess mine is spilling things."

"Well, it could happen to the best of us," Nate soothed as he retrieved the sodas and began placing them into the bowl.

A pair of polished black shoes appeared near the ice's edge. Haley gazed up the length of long, black slacks, a white jacket, and a smiling waiter. "I'll take over from here," he offered.

"Oh sure," Haley said and stood.

"Would you believe it?" Nate whispered, "This bowl of ice jumped out at Haley and tried to bite her." He looked from one side to the other as if he were a spy. "If you don't get some control on these things, I'm going to have to report you to headquarters."

The waiter laughed outright, and Haley giggled. Nate threw in a relaxed smile and reached for Haley's arm. He respectfully guided her away from the scene of the crime and said, "Are you okay?"

"Fine," Haley said and remembered her soda. "Whoops! I forgot my Coke," she exclaimed and abruptly turned back the direction she came. She stepped on something that nearly knocked her off balance again.

"Yikes!" the waiter squealed. "You got my finger."

"Oh no!" Haley wailed. "I'm sorry. I am *so, so sorry!* I didn't mean to do that."

The sandy-haired waiter shook his hand, then looked at his reddened index finger.

Haley stooped toward him. "Are you okay? Are you going to be okay?" she worried.

"Yes, I think so," he mumbled and drew away from her.

"I was just getting my Coke. I left it here." She picked up the bottled beverage. "And I didn't see you down there." She shook her head from side to side.

"It's okay," the man said and rubbed at his finger.

"Are you sure? I could go get something for you. Maybe some ice?"

"No, I think you've already taken care of the ice," he said through a dry smile.

"Yes, I guess so," Haley fretted and twisted open the bottle cap. A hiss of air escaped the bottle. "Well, I guess I'll just move along then."

"Please do…I mean—" The waiter shook his head. "That's fine."

"Well, okay then." Haley edged away from him. She stopped near Nate, sipped the sweet liquid, and relished the sting on her tongue.

While Nate's face was impassive, his eyes danced with new humor. He retrieved a bottle of club soda from the bowl on the table's other end and unscrewed the cap.

Haley sighed. "I'm tempted to go change into the pair of slip-ons I keep in my office. I'm beginning to think spike heels just weren't meant for me."

Nate looked at her feet before downing a fourth of the bottle.

"I nearly fell off them," Haley continued. "That's why I knocked the ice bowl crazy. I'm just surprised stepping on his finger didn't make me topple."

Nate lowered the bottle and winced through his final swallow. "But they look so good with your dress."

"Now you're starting to sound like Amanda," she countered and couldn't stop the rush of pleasure over Nate's compliment.

Up until she met Roger, Haley had been smitten with Nate. Amanda had never suspected. Neither did Nate. But from the first time she saw him strolling into the travel agency, Haley thought he was the most handsome man she'd ever seen.

That day when she'd asked him if she could help, Nate had said he'd come to see Amanda. Haley immediately assumed Amanda and Nate must be a couple. When Amanda treated him like a brother she took for granted, Haley had been astounded. How any woman could gaze upon the likes of Nate Knighton and not see all his masculine glory was beyond Haley.

Then she'd met Roger and recognized her interest in Nate for what it was—a young woman's appreciation for a fine masculine specimen. While Haley believed her attraction could have grown into love, she was also rational enough to understand it had not. She'd never felt for Nate what had grown between her and Roger. Even now, she thought fondly of Roger—when she wasn't with Mason.

Haley disciplined herself not to dwell on Roger or worry about what he thought. That chapter in her life was closed. *Mason* was the one who cared so much he asked for her portrait. A pleasant tremor raced through Haley. Mason was enamored enough to hang her image in his home and share it with his mother and sister. It was as if she finally belonged to someone… to a family.

She smiled up at Nate. "Thanks for your help."

"Any time," Nate responded and returned her grin. "I make it a habit to always assist women who spill things."

"Well, there are days you could make a full-time job of helping me."

"Humph," Nate said and patted her shoulder. "Don't be so hard on yourself."

Haley beamed up at him. Even now she appreciated the kind-hearted man beneath the external appeal. Nate didn't have to help her with the spill. Any other person in the room could have aided. But no one else offered, and *he* did. The vice president and heir of Knighton's Department Stores never hesitated at lowering his knee to assist a mere secretary.

Haley came within a breath of sighing like an adolescent pining over a photo of her favorite movie star. Nate's being so completely unaware of her thoughts only sweetened the moment. Haley never imagined the likes of Nate Knighton would ever be romantically interested in her—a child-orphan turned secretary. But the old daydreams beckoned Haley to immerse her mind anew in "what ifs."

"Would you care for an hors d'ouevre?" he politely inquired as he indulged in another long drink.

"Sure," Haley replied and disciplined her mind not to go to "what if" land. Reminding herself she had Mason to consider, Haley wondered if Amanda would ever wake up.

As Nate motioned for a waiter, he cleared his throat. "Um," he hesitated, "I didn't know if I'd get the chance to tell you or not, but since we're here…"

Haley leaned toward him and tried to fathom what he could be leading to. "Yes?" she prompted.

"Well, Roger told me to tell you hello." Nate scrutinized Haley, and she decided the rug needed to be examined.

"Uh…well…um…thanks—thanks for telling me," she stammered and could not deny the heightened interest. "How is he these days?" she asked.

"Fine. A little lonely," Nate hinted, "but fine."

Haley nodded and peered at Amanda, who was still holding baby Matt while talking to Franklyn West. Haley had only briefly met Franklyn at the beginning of the party. He'd chatted with Amanda off and on ever since then. She wished her friend could rush over and give her something to say about the whole Roger business. Haley could conjure nothing appropriate—or inappropriate either, for that matter.

Her attention flicked to the saltwater aquarium spanning the south wall. Neither the colorful fish nor coral provided inspiration.

The waiter approached, much to Haley's relief, and saved her the misery of dissolving into a heap of inadequate verbiage.

"Why don't you just leave the whole tray with me?" Nate joked as he chose four morsels rolled in bacon, and Haley joined the two men in their laughing.

Twelve

❧ ❧

"Do you mind my saying you're every bit as beautiful as Angie said you were," Franklyn's cultured voice blended with the harpist's fluid chords and washed over Amanda.

"I don't mind in the least," Amanda returned and smiled into eyes the color of the Tasman Sea. Her agitation at seeing Nate dimmed in the light of Franklyn's appeal.

"All right then," Franklyn said, "you're every bit as beautiful as Angie said you were." Franklyn's charming grin matched his fluid words and warmed Amanda to the point that she put the Nate issues on hold for later. Nate was acting odder than ever tonight. Who knew why.

"Thanks," Amanda said through a chuckle and touched the side of her hair where the horn had been only 45 minutes ago. All was smooth.

Baby Matt followed her lead and grasped for her hair.

"No, no," Amanda crooned and moved the baby to her right hip. If her hair were baptized in baby spit, she wasn't sure what it would morph into. She shifted her weight to her right foot and allowed her aching left toes some relief. High heels certainly were not the shoes for hauling a baby around.

"He's cute. Is he yours?" Franklyn glanced toward her ring finger.

"No!" Amanda shook her head and stroked Matt's velvet soft hair with her left hand to clearly reveal no signs of a wedding band. "He's my sister's." She kissed Matt's soft forehead and enjoyed the smell of baby shampoo.

"Ah." Franklyn nodded. "I thought I recognized a resemblance, but I also thought I remembered Angie saying you were single."

Amanda nodded and nearly allowed her smile to enter the flirtatious zone. She stopped just short of coy and said, "You're right. I've never been married. And you?"

"No." Franklyn shook his head. "But I'm not necessarily *against* the idea." He leaned forward as if they were sharing the sincerest of secrets, and Amanda wasn't expecting the tiny thrill that zipped through her tummy.

She lowered her gaze to his tuxedo's bow tie and swallowed hard. Even though she was as dedicated to her father as ever, Amanda decided a lighthearted attachment couldn't hurt a thing, especially not with someone as attractive as Franklyn West. Like Nate, he was tall, broad-shouldered, and witty. She was already adept at dealing with the likes and enjoyed looking Franklyn eye to eye nearly as much as she did Nate.

Maybe more, she thought.

"My dad and Angie say you might paint a portrait of Dad and me," Franklyn said.

"If we can find time," Amanda said, "I'll be glad to."

"I think we'd both like that. We're trying to get to know each other better, you know."

"So I've heard," Amanda said. "Would you say it's going well?"

"Very." Franklyn nodded. "And I'm wild about Angie."

"Who isn't?"

"Amanda, thank you so much for all of this," Betty Cates' shrill voice broke into their conversation.

Amanda turned to the housekeeper who became part of the Wood-Priebe family many years ago. She'd been cleaning the villa and office as long as Amanda could remember. Amanda thought of her more as an aunt than an employee. She'd do anything for Betty—even throw a party for the niece who made Amanda feel oversized and dowdy.

"You're welcome, Betty," Amanda said. "If it weren't for you, my whole life would look like the top of my desk, and there'd be an inch of dust on everything I own. The least I can do is welcome your niece to town."

In a glance, Amanda noted Betty's earrings matched this time. They were both pearl buttons. And she'd somehow managed to don a silky two-piece dress in blue with a pair of shoes that matched the dress…and each other.

Betty toyed with her long strand of faux pearls, then pushed her "binocular" glasses up her nose. "And who are you?" she asked while peering up at Franklyn.

"This is Franklyn West," Amanda explained. "He's Wayne's son. Angie's stepson."

"How do you do?" Franklyn said, and Amanda couldn't help but admire the suave British lilt to his voice. "I believe we met briefly at church when I was in town six months ago."

"Yes!" Betty nodded. "I remember you now. Just had to get my eyes lined up."

Baby Matt gurgled and reached for Betty's pearls.

"Oh no you don't," Amanda crooned and wondered when Nate and his tie would be back—despite the fact that these days he was as hard to read as Chinese. His tie had really captured Matt. Or better yet, Matt had captured his tie.

While Betty interrogated Franklyn, Amanda scanned the crowd. She spotted Nate still near the beverage table with Haley. But now Janet had joined them. Shortly after Nate left to help Haley, Janet had excused herself on the grounds of needing a drink. Nate chuckled at something Janet said and gazed at her with blatant male appreciation that had nothing to do with Janet's "personality."

Amanda told herself not to react. Her face tightened anyway. *If Nate's going to throw himself at some woman,* she fumed, *the least he can do is find one who isn't so petite and bronze and charming.*

Then Amanda considered Nate's mystery woman—that ever-elusive feminine entity who forced him to shove all her Christmas presents in his closet. *I wonder what she'd think about Nate ogling Janet French?* Then another idea barged through her mind. *Maybe Janet is the mystery woman!* Amanda's growing frown only deepened.

And at that moment Nate looked past Janet and straight at Amanda. With a one-dimpled smile, he raised his bottle of club soda toward her like a wordless toast. Amanda snapped her attention back to Betty. Sensing Nate's observation, she tried to dissolve the frown and look as casual as possible.

Betty lowered her voice and leaned closer to Franklyn. "Janet doesn't know it, but I'm looking for a husband for her," she explained. "That's part of the reason I asked Amanda to have this party. I just knew there'd be some single men here who might do the trick." She snapped her fingers and nodded. "I've just added you to my list." She toyed with the fringe of hair at her neck.

"Me?" Franklyn blanched.

"Yes, you. What do you do for a living anyway?"

"I'm finishing medical school," he wheezed.

"Good. That's a good profession." She nodded.

And Amanda wondered if Betty would act like someone buying a horse and ask to examine Franklyn's teeth next.

"I'm not sure how long I'll be here or—or if I'll have time for a wedding." His chuckle sounded about as sincere as a drowning man asking for a drink of water. "My aunt is ill, you know. My dad's sister. She's like my mother. Or should I say, she *is* my mother. She raised me. I'll be going back home soon—back to London."

"That's okay." Betty shook her finger at him and wrinkled her nose. "You don't have to marry her this week. Next year might do just fine."

"Well, I…" Franklyn lowered his head and looked from side to side.

Amanda stifled a groan and wondered if Betty would ever learn to refrain from saying exactly what she was thinking at every given moment. "Betty—" she began, only to be cut off by the housekeeper's exclamation.

"Don't tell me! Amanda, look here in the back of my hair." Betty whipped around. "Is there a curler back there, or am I imagining things?"

Amanda pulled her face away from Matt's chubby fingers as he groped at her mouth. While grappling with the baby, she struggled to focus on Betty's hairline. Sure enough, a pink curler peeked from the depths of Betty's frizzy hair. Amanda's chortle preceded her nod.

"Yes, there's a curler," she affirmed.

"I can't believe this. I just can't!" Betty fretted and tugged at the curler. "And I can't get it out either. No wonder I missed it. I guess it's stuck!"

"Here, let me help," Franklyn offered with a good-natured smile.

Amanda touched Matt's nose and said, "Boo!" in an attempt to cover her mortification. Even Matt's delightful smile couldn't smother her embarrassment. Betty Cates had reduced the most eligible bachelor in the room to removing a curler. And on top of that, Betty had just added him to her "Janet's Husband" list.

Can't Betty see those two would never *fit each other?* Amanda wondered.

She glanced back at Nate. He leaned closer to Janet as if he were pining for her every word. Amanda wondered if Betty had placed Nate on her list as well.

If she doesn't, Amanda huffed, *he'll probably beg to be on it by midnight!*

Amanda recalled what he'd said outside the villa a month ago. *Look at me, Amanda. I'm a* man! *I'm not* one of your girlfriends. *I'm a guy!"* She narrowed her eyes and scrutinized the person who'd been her friend since her sister married his brother. They'd met when Gordon and Bev started dating. He'd been 20. She was 10. By the time Amanda was 12, she was the founding member of the Nate Knighton fan club. Her adolescent hero worship had grown into a reasonable friendship.

Even though Nate had mercilessly teased her, he'd eventually been like a comfortable sweater, warm and cozy and just the right fit. Now nothing about Nate was comfortable or cozy. If anything, he was as uncomfortable as an old sweater, worn out and outgrown.

To add to her misery, Amanda realized with a jolt that Nate had been right. He *was* a guy! He wasn't just her friend or brother, he was a *man!* At least, that's what Janet's expression said. So did Haley's for that matter. And so did some feminine instinct deep within Amanda.

Baby Matt's insistent whine snared Amanda's attention, and she focused on pacifying the infant. But all the while she wondered how long Nate had been so *much* of a man.

"Do you want me to find his mom?" Franklyn asked while handing Betty the curler he'd pulled from her hair.

"I see her right there." Still fussing with her locks, Betty pointed across the room where Bev and Gordon had found a corner of their own.

Amanda sighed and bounced baby Matt. "That's okay. Those two need their time together." Gordon and Bev were so in love it was enough to tempt Amanda ever closer to the prospect herself. Given the fact that tall and blond and available was within reach, the option was nearly too tempting to reject.

"Maybe he'd like the fish tank," Franklyn said.

"Great idea!" Amanda didn't even wait for anyone to follow. She hustled straight to the saltwater aquarium and prayed this would be the answer to all of Matt's restlessness.

As soon as the baby spotted the clown fish, he was hooked. His tears ceased. He placed his chubby hand against the tank and began to babble as if he were speaking some language only the fish would understand.

"It worked!" Franklyn said.

"Looks that way," Amanda said and smiled up at tall and blond and available.

He didn't bother to hide his male appreciation. "So what are you doing after the party?" he asked.

"You mean, after—after *this* party?" Amanda stammered and sensed she was about to be asked out on a date.

"Yes. After *this* party," Franklyn repeated.

"I...well, I'm probably going to have to do some cleaning up," she said and hoped Franklyn understood she was sincere and not trying to get out of a date. She gazed across the reception room. The trash can was overflowing. Crumbs dotted the carpet. And whatever the caterers left would have to be refrigerated. Normally Amanda relied on Betty Cates to take care of party cleanups. But the etiquette of a big-hearted woman wouldn't dream of allowing Betty to clean up after her niece's party. It was unthinkable.

Amanda's attention shifted to Nate. Even though he was still talking with Janet, his gaze skipped toward Amanda, then Franklyn. And Amanda received the vague impression that Nate wasn't happy about something specifically to do with her. Confused, Amanda tried to focus on what Franklyn was saying but somehow missed the whole gist.

"I'm sorry," she said. "I was sizing up the mess and missed what you were saying."

"I was going to ask you out for coffee or a late movie or something, but since you've got all this, I thought maybe you could use some help," Franklyn repeated.

Amanda, stricken with his warmth and willingness, silently gaped at him.

"As in me," he added and leaned toward her. "I'm offering to help."

"Absolutely. That's superb!" Amanda replied. "I'll take all the help I can get."

"It's the least I can do since you've agreed to paint my father's and my portrait. I'm sure your work will become our family heirloom."

"Maybe you should wait before you jump to any rash conclusions." Amanda patted Matt's back and eyed the baby's rapt expression.

"I've heard nothing but wonderful things about your art...and you," Franklyn added. "My stepmother has so praised you, I fully expected a halo." He examined the top of her head. "And I do believe I see one."

"You do know how to flatter a woman, don't you?" Amanda asked and didn't bother to hide that she was shamelessly enjoying the flirtation.

"Who said this was flattery?" Franklyn parried.

Amanda looked down and couldn't deny the quiver in her stomach. While she'd expected Wayne's son to be terribly good-looking and suave, she'd never expected to be met with such silver-tongued, blatant charm. And never had Amanda enjoyed it so much. Franklyn was everything Angie said he was and more.

Baby Matt squealed and slapped the fish tank. The lion fish jerked as if it had been zapped with an electric shock.

"Oh no!" Amanda shifted Matt out of reach of the glass. "I didn't see that coming."

"That can't be good for the fish," Franklyn said.

"It's not," Amanda said. "The man who helps me maintain the tank says the fish can kill themselves running into the glass and just tapping on the tank can make them sick."

Matt gurgled in fish talk again and pointed at the eel that slithered along the tank's bottom while the lion fish retired to the other end of the tank, toward Franklyn, where life was less eventful.

"There you are old boy," Franklyn crooned at the fish. "I certainly know how you feel. I wasn't expecting to be hit tonight either," he said and slid a wink toward Amanda.

Thirteen

Several weeks later, Amanda sprinkled the food flakes into the aquarium and watched as the brightly colored fish devoured their meal. Streaks of blue and red and orange zipped through the tank as the fish darted to fill their tummies. The pump's gurgling cheered them on.

The lion fish continued to fascinate Amanda the most with his tawny and white stripes and plethora of fins. She watched the king of the tank gracefully float to the top, gobble some flakes, and move to the next patch of food.

She dropped another pinch of food onto the water and rubbed her fingers together. They now smelled like shrimp, and Amanda made plans to wash her hands as usual. Despite the urge to feed the fish another big pinch of food, she put the lid back on the flake canister. The expert who serviced her tank warned against overfeeding her finned pets.

She touched Baby Matt's fingerprints, still smudging the tank's glass. Amanda had told Betty Cates not to clean off the infant's marks. They were a perpetual reminder of his sweet presence and his aunt's doting admiration. The smudges also continually connected Amanda to the memory of the man who was standing beside her when Matt was touching the tank. That night had proven to be the beginning of a budding relationship with Franklyn West.

The sigh of the agency's front door prompted her to turn around and investigate.

"Flowers for Miss Priebe?" a young man called from the entryway as he walked toward the agency's lobby.

"Yes, I'm Amanda Priebe," she affirmed. Amanda set the fish food in the opened cabinet over the tank and hurried from the aquarium.

"Good." The dark-skinned man held a huge bouquet of red roses in one hand and a corsage box in the other. "Looks like somebody wants to wish you a merry Christmas," he said with a broad smile.

"I guess so!" Amanda exclaimed and accepted the offerings. "Thanks so much," she called as the man hurried back into the warm sunshine as quickly as he'd arrived.

Amanda moved near the enormous Christmas tree in the room's corner and made use of the row of straight-backed chairs lining the wall. She set both the corsage box and the bouquet on the chairs and knelt beside them. The smell of roses blotted out the whiff of fish food on her fingers as Amanda fumbled with the card that read, "Wood-Priebe International."

Secretly she hoped the bouquet was from Franklyn. Over the last month they had become very pleasant friends, to say the least. Franklyn had never said a word about romance or even tried to hold her hand, but he'd been her companion for many lunch dates and had even sat with her in church. He also remained more complimentary than any man Amanda had ever known.

As she'd promised, Amanda had painted a portrait of him and Wayne and allowed Haley to offer more than her share of input. Given all the time she'd spent with him, Amanda was as close as she'd ever been to forming a romantic attachment, and the prospect was growing more appealing by the day.

At last she withdrew the card from the tiny envelope and eagerly read the message: "All my love, Mason Eldridge."

"Mason?" Amanda exclaimed.

She reached for the corsage box, ripped out the card, and read the same inscription. Squinting, Amanda read the envelopes again and affirmed they said, "Wood-Priebe International." There was no person's name, although the delivery man had specifically asked for her. Amanda stood.

The memory of Nate's suppositions left her face cold. *Mason Eldridge doesn't have one thought for Haley Schmitz....Mark my word, it's not Haley he's after. It's you!*

"No," Amanda whispered. "It can't be." Lowering herself onto a chair, she stared at the card. *Nate can't be right. I won't let him...because he's not right!*

"There's been some mistake," she whispered and fingered the textured linen paper.

Last night, Amanda had sent an e-mail to Mason, telling him Haley would not be at the church Christmas party tonight due to a dreadful upper respiratory infection. The doctor had put her to bed yesterday and said Haley would probably be in bed several more days.

When Mason hadn't responded to the e-mail or even called Haley, Amanda had been a bit offended. Of course, she'd not allowed Haley to detect her irritation when she went by her flat this morning and played nurse. Nevertheless, she'd been on the verge of thinking Mason self-centered and insensitive.

Suddenly the truth broke through to Amanda. *These flowers aren't for me! They're for Haley!"* She pressed the heel of her hand against her forehead and leaned back. "Of course!" Amanda re-examined the envelope and affirmed that her name was not to be found—only Wood-Priebe International. It all made perfect sense now. Mason wanted her to give the flowers to Haley. This was his response to her e-mail.

Amanda checked her watch and decided lunch was close enough for her to take her break. She'd promised Haley she'd come back to her apartment and make some chicken soup at noon. But Amanda would be offering much more than chicken soup. Smiling, she buried her face in the roses, relished their velvety softness and delightful smell.

Haley's head had never hurt so bad. While she'd experienced upper respiratory infections in her days, she'd never felt like the whole back of her head was exploding. The doctor mentioned that the infection was also in her sinuses. Her eyes half closed, Haley stirred in bed, moaned, and thought about getting up and watching TV for a while. But she just couldn't get her body to cooperate.

Her eyes stinging had nothing to do with the December sun erupting upon the room and everything to do with the lump in her throat. Amanda told her she would e-mail Mason with the news of her illness last night. This morning Amanda confirmed that she had sent the message, but so far he hadn't even phoned.

Haley eyed the silent phone sitting on the nightstand near the digital clock. Amanda made certain the phone was within reach before she left. But the effort was wasted. No one had called. No one.

Roger would have already called. Last spring when Haley sprained her ankle, Roger arrived within two hours of her call. He'd had his sister, Esther, with him. After fussing around Haley like a doting grandfather, he'd left Esther with Haley all night and gotten a nearby hotel room for himself.

Haley sighed and wiped at the tear seeping from the corner of her eye. She sat on the side of the bed and reached for the unscented hand lotion Amanda brought to her last night. Upon slathering on a layer of the cream, Haley replaced the tube and picked up her bottle of antibiotics. She read the blurry label and comprehended something about every four hours. After trying to remember the last time she'd taken the medication, Haley decided she ought to down another.

Amanda had also left a tray with a pitcher of water on the nightstand. Haley poured a cupful of water and swallowed her antibiotic. It stuck at the back of her throat, then slipped down in the river of cool liquid. With another sigh, Haley stood and planned to hobble toward the restroom when the doorbell chimed.

She glanced at the clock to see the noon hour near. *Probably Amanda,* she thought. *She'll let herself in.* Amanda had promised she'd be back to make Haley eat chicken soup. The very thought left her queasy. Her head's severe pounding supported her stomach's complaint.

Haley was inching closer to the restroom when Amanda's cheerful voice erupted against her hurting brain.

"How are we doing this afternoon?" she called.

Leaning against the wall, Haley groaned. "Why does she have to talk so loud?" she complained.

"I've got a surprise for you," Amanda called in a singsong voice.

Haley lolled her head against the wall, clutched at her cotton nightshirt, and slid a glance toward the hall's entry.

Amanda appeared with a massive bouquet of roses. And all Haley could conjure for an expression was a slight twitch of her brows.

"You shouldn't have done that," she breathed.

"Oh, but I didn't!" Amanda exclaimed and bounded forward. "Mason did! They're from Mason especially for *you!* All my love, Mason," she said. "That's exactly what the cards say. Look!" She held up a box. "There's a corsage too."

Haley couldn't stop the pool of tears trickling down her cheeks. "He remembered me," she whimpered.

"Of course he did, sweetie!" Amanda crooned. "Oh Haley, don't cry."

She sniffled, and her sinuses hurt all the more. "It's just that—that I thought he didn't even care."

"He cares! Look! I'll show you!" Haley pivoted and watched Amanda as she hurried into the bedroom, placed the roses and corsage on the dresser, and removed the cards from the envelopes. "See!" Amanda hurried back to Haley's side and lifted the cards to her face. "All my love, Mason," she read.

Haley grasped the cards and held them to her heart. "He loves me," she cried.

"Of course he does!" She wrapped her arms around Haley and patted her back.

Trembling, Haley rested her head on Amanda's shoulder and couldn't ever remember feeling so weak. "I wish so b–b–bad I could go to the—to the party tonight," she rasped. "I want to see Angie's new house. And Mason might—might even k–k–kiss me!"

Amanda's hug tightened. "Haley, I'm so sorry you're sick. It's just awful!"

"I feel awful too," Haley croaked. The smell of Amanda's jasmine perfume made her nose sting.

"Of *course* you do!" Amanda crooned. "Go on and get back into bed. I'll pin the corsage on you. It will make you feel all better. Then I'll fix you a nice big bowl of chicken soup."

"Okay, but I've got to go to the restroom first," Haley said and pulled away. "I won't be long."

"Take your time." Amanda patted her back again and said, "I'll go fluff up your pillows. Do you want me to fix you some juice or anything to drink while the soup is warming?"

"Yes." Haley frowned and tried to remember the juice she wanted. "The kind that's orange," she finally said.

Fourteen

Amanda strode up the step's of Angie's new home. Her father had dubbed it a mansion, and Amanda hadn't argued with him. Neither had anyone else in town. The enormous, two-story home featured the latest in architectural design and had been the talk of the town for months. Sitting on the edge of Highland, the brick home appeared to hover over the neighborhood like a sentinel forever guarding the city's entrance.

She couldn't have been happier for her former governess. Angie deserved everything she got and then some. She had sacrificed her youth to be at Amanda's side. Now that she was in her mid-forties and Amanda was all grown up, she warranted God's every blessing.

Balancing two platters of goodies along with her red purse, Amanda paused on the porch and debated how she was going to ring the doorbell. She examined the platter of cookies and tray full of candies. She'd gone to the deli and bought the best-looking cookies and candy they had, then placed them on decorative dishes. Maybe somebody would think she actually made them from scratch, but that would be her little secret.

The summer sun, sinking toward the western horizon, produced beads of perspiration along her neck. Amanda had taken extra care with her appearance tonight, and she still wondered if she wore way too much red for her hair color. On top of being a redhead in red, the last thing Amanda needed was going into the party profusely sweating.

Finally she decided to set the platter of cookies on the wrought-iron porch table. Then she was able to push the doorbell. A man wearing a black suit and a long face opened the door.

Amanda started to smile at Joe, but decided not to waste the effort. She realized months ago Angie's doorman was born smileless. "Do you mind taking one of these platters?" she asked.

"Of course not," Joe said, his saggy mouth never losing the droop.

"I'll take them both and place them with the other food. There's enough in there to feed all of Highland. I can't imagine anyone bringing more." He peered past Amanda.

She turned to examine the car-lined curb. A Hummer purred past the house but didn't stop. Amanda figured she was the last guest. She'd stopped by Haley's on the way here and was 15 minutes late. The visit had done Haley good. She'd even wrote Mason a thank-you note, and Amanda was now anxious to deliver it. She had planned on Mason being closer to proposing by now and began to hope for a fall proposal and wedding in early winter.

"I guess I'm the last one here," Amanda stated as she stepped past Joe and into the chandeliered entryway.

He nodded and walked ahead of her toward a bright room filled with the drone of voices, laughter, and music. Amanda maneuvered the marble entryway in her new shoes and wondered at the wisdom in wearing three-and-a-half-inch heels on the glasslike surface. By the time she reached the carpeted party room, Amanda feared she was going to act like Haley and twist her ankle.

Thoughts of Haley brought to mind her special note once more. As Amanda scanned the crowd, she checked the outside pocket of her evening bag. When her index finger touched the corner, deep in the pocket, she was assured the note was still in place.

Tonight's Christmas party consisted of the Young Adult Bible Study class taught by Angie and Wayne. Already the room was full of people in the 20- to-40-year-old range, all dressed in their Christmas finest. The smell of warm apple cider mingled with the aroma of fresh-baked goodies and reminded Amanda she'd eaten nothing but a bowl of chicken noodle soup for lunch.

"There you are, Amanda!" Mason's exuberant voice floated from her right.

She paused and turned a smile his way.

"I didn't think you'd ever get here," he said as his eyes widened. "Wow! You look *great!*"

"Thanks," Amanda said and looked down the length of her brick-red dress. "I wondered if this was all too much with my hair. I was afraid I looked like a big candy cane."

"No way!" Mason said, his blue eyes a bit too warm for a man who's girlfriend was sick in bed.

"Did you get the corsage and flowers?" he asked and glanced toward her shoulder.

"Oh yes! Yes, we got them. I took them to Haley today at noon. She was so thrilled."

"Oh really? That was nice of you," Mason said and tilted his head to the right for an odd staring session.

Fully expecting Mason to ask about Haley, Amanda paused to allow him that opportunity while she reached into her purse for the note.

"Did you bring the candy and cookies I saw Joe carrying in?" Mason asked.

"Yes," Amanda replied while scrounging for the note.

"So not only are you beautiful, you're also a chef!" Mason cheered.

"No," Amanda vigorously shook her head, "not by any means. I bought those things at the deli." She pointed at Joe as he entered the service bar area. Then she resumed the note pursuit.

"And if you think *I* look good, you should have seen what Haley was going to wear tonight. It was this black silk number that—"

"Listen, did you know you're on the list to play the piano for us tonight?"

"I am?" Amanda blurted and forgot the note.

"Yes." Mason crossed his arms, and his sport coat's gold buttons flashed in the chandelier's light. "You're the most talented woman I know," he bragged as if he were a child and she were his newest toy.

Even though she couldn't deny that Mason was acting rather peculiar, Amanda dismissed his comments in preference for worrying about her pending performance. While she often played for her father at night, Amanda considered herself far from an accomplished musician. She certainly didn't want to perform when she wasn't prepared.

"I bet Angie's the one who did this to me," Amanda mused and peered around the room in search of her surrogate mother. She caught a glimpse of the petite blonde behind the service bar. Her attention was on the assortment of food lining the bar. As

Joe handed her Amanda's platters, she didn't even bother to look for Amanda.

Amanda narrowed her eyes. The last time Angie did this to her was at her father's birthday party three years ago. She'd slipped Amanda's name in as part of the entertainment, and no one even told her until it was time to play.

"I know why she didn't tell me," Amanda complained. "She's always trying to get me to play and knows I'll weasel out of it if I find out. I played at last year's party and told her then I'd take this year off."

"You and Janet French are both on the list," Mason said.

"Janet's here?" She scanned the crowd of 35 and spotted Janet near the grand piano with none other than Nate Knighton chatting her up. She forgot about the pending performance.

While Amanda had never considered herself the most beautiful woman in the world, she had at least felt pretty tonight. Until now. In the face of Janet's smoldering Asian eyes and deep-green dress, Amanda really did feel like an oversized candy cane—and a gaudy one at that. In a fleeting fit of exasperation, she considered hanging herself on the Christmas tree as an ornament. *Not even the red baubles on the ten-foot tree commanding the corner can touch my garish appearance,* Amanda moaned to herself.

Ducking her head, she hovered near Mason and thought, *If Nate was any kind of friend at all, he wouldn't even look at that woman.*

But is he even my friend any more? she questioned and began the lecture she'd delivered to herself on the way to the party. *If Nate's there, pretend he's not. Don't worry about what he is or isn't doing or who he is or isn't seeing or what's in his closet! He hasn't even called to wish you merry Christmas. Apparently, he's tired of you and is trying to say your friendship is over, in so many words—or lack of them.*

Last night her father had even commented on Nate's absence these days. Amanda had pretended she didn't care and changed the subject. But the pretense was swiftly growing thin. Whether she wanted to admit it or not, she missed Nate. Aside from Haley, he'd been her best friend for many, many years. In some ways, she felt like a little sister ignored by an elder brother who now thought he was too advanced for her.

Amanda glanced toward Mason and saw his mouth moving but had no idea what he was saying. She convinced herself it must have something to do with Haley. *Or at least it should,* she thought and realized Mason hadn't even asked about Haley.

As though powerless to stop herself, Amanda cast another glance toward Nate. That's when she noticed the portrait of Franklyn and Wayne hanging over the piano. Amanda gasped. Never had she dreamed anything she painted, even with Haley's help, would project such aristocratic ambiance. The straight-nosed subjects appeared near royalty in their tuxedoes and fine poses. A glow filled her soul. She would have never been able to finish the work without Haley, but she *had* finished and finished nicely.

"Is that your work?" Mason exclaimed.

"Yes." Amanda breathed.

"Wow! That's even better than Haley's portrait. Good job!" He placed his hand in the small of her back and gave her a sideways hug. "Like I said, the most talented woman I know! And I *love* talented women!"

Fifteen

During the next hour, Nate and everyone else stuffed themselves on innumerable holiday morsels. *At this rate,* he thought as he popped the final bite of fudge in his mouth, *I'm going to gain back every pound I've lost.*

He eyed Amanda, sitting on the sofa between Mason and Franklyn. She sure was drawing the male interest these days. *And well she should,* Nate admitted. He never remembered Amanda so stunning.

The only one of the two men who bothered him was Franklyn. Amanda had flirted with him all evening. If the guy didn't recognize her silent invitation, then he was as thick-skulled as a gorilla. The whole ordeal particularly rankled because Amanda told Nate she absolutely was not going to get married.

Maybe she's finally met the man who made her reconsider, he thought. A stab of regret pained his heart and snatched his breath. While Amanda could look him straight in the eyes and never find reason to forsake her vow to remain single, she apparently found something in Franklyn that challenged her decision. This only added feelings of inadequacy to Nate's growing anxiety.

Because of all this, Nate couldn't deny his increasing dislike for Wayne's son. His rational side insisted he was being unfair to Franklyn, but Nate couldn't seem to talk himself out of it. He disliked everything about him, including that portrait hanging over the piano. The portrait had the unfortunate fate of being painted by Amanda. Tonight Angie had bragged on her surrogate daughter—the artist, the pianist, the CEO—to anyone who would listen.

And the whole time all Nate could think was, *Why hasn't Amanda ever offered to paint my portrait?* Every time the thought crossed his mind, Nate felt more and more like a petty, spoiled child. Nevertheless, the empty, neglected feeling wouldn't quit. And Nate sensed he was losing all chances with Amanda—and losing fast.

Mason leaned closer to Amanda and cut Franklyn a cold stare that nearly made Nate laugh out loud. While Franklyn gave Nate fits, Mason offered a humorous diversion. All night he'd stayed by Amanda's side like a koala hugging a eucalyptus tree. Nate had silently watched her exasperation grow and wondered if she was finally realizing he was right about who Mason was *really* after.

All the irritation with Franklyn and the humor regarding Mason paled when he once again focused on Amanda. Like a connoisseur of great art soaking up every nuance of a masterpiece, Nate allowed himself to absorb the essence of Amanda. He stopped just short of a sigh.

Roger Miller moved to his side and elbowed his ribs. "You're looking a little obvious, old man," he warned. "Cool it."

Nate focused on the champagne-colored carpet and didn't say anything. Roger was the only person on the planet who knew what was going on. He'd convinced Roger to attend the party for moral support. Nate needed someone to help him keep his balance. Otherwise this growing attraction would take him under. Of course, Roger had required no encouragement when he discovered Haley was going to be present. He'd nearly dissolved into the carpet when he learned of her illness.

"I think she gets better-looking every time I see her." Nate toyed with the end of his tie, peered into his punch cup, then cut Roger a sideways look.

The poor guy had dark circles under his eyes. He said he hadn't slept at all last night. He nursed his third cup of coffee, and Nate figured the mellow brew was what was keeping him awake. Roger also looked like he hadn't eaten anything in weeks. His white dress shirt hung loosely in places it used to fit. His pants were a bit baggy. And his cheeks had taken on a hollow quality. Not that Roger was emaciated, but he looked like his appetite was about as bad as Nate's these days.

Lifting his cup to his lips, Roger mumbled against the edge, "I still say you're in love with her."

"No." Nate shook his head and tugged at his shirt cuff peeking beneath his suit sleeve. "It can't be." He couldn't admit what Roger had supposed last night. "I'm just going through some kind of a phase," he added with a nod. "It'll blow over."

He stole another glance at Amanda as Angie moved to the monstrous grand piano near the room's fireplace. "It's time for music!" Angie exclaimed with all the eagerness of a child who's unwrapping her first Christmas present.

Nate finished his sparkling punch and stepped toward the group of folding chairs he and Roger had helped Harold set up minutes before.

"If you'll all gather to the chairs we've placed over here…" Angie pointed toward the 40 or so chairs. The annual Christmas

music usually involved solos, sing-alongs, and special performances by numerous musicians.

Soon the group was settled in their chairs. Somehow Janet
French landed on one side of Nate while Roger claimed the chair
on the other. Nate smiled at Janet and detected the same flowery
scent he'd noticed when they were talking earlier. Janet couldn't
even touch Amanda tonight, despite her exotic appeal and sweet
perfume.

Amanda sat between Franklyn and Mason and looked like a
cornered female if there ever was one. Nate hid a smile and tried
to focus on a ladies trio finishing a touching rendition of "Away
in a Manger."

After the crowd's polite applause, Angie stood and grinned
toward Amanda. Angie's blonde ringlets and chic, off-white
pantsuit made her look 10 years younger than her 45 years.

Nate glanced at Wayne, who sat near the front of the crowd.
The balding man appeared as stricken over his new wife as Nate
was with Amanda.

"Now, for a performance from one of my very own students—
Amanda Wood Priebe," Angie said and motioned toward
Amanda. "I have to admit, though, that I'm pushing a little to
get Amanda to play. If I don't, she won't." Angie shrugged. "But
how else will I show off my teaching abilities?"

A chuckle rippled from the group.

"And while she's coming, I've also got to add that Amanda is
the artist who painted this portrait of my husband and stepson.
I'm very, very proud of her."

The group's applause accompanied Amanda's embarrassed
smile. When Mason whistled, Amanda ducked her head, scurried to the grand piano, and sat down.

"I have no idea what I'm going to play," she admitted and glanced toward Angie. "You'll have to give me a minute or two to get focused here."

"Whatever you need, dear," Angie said and patted Amanda on the back with the maternal love of a thousand moms.

Nate hadn't thought Amanda could look any more beautiful until she settled on the bench. Her red dress, vibrant hair, and meticulous makeup were a perfect complement for the glossy black instrument.

"I haven't practiced a thing for Christmas," she admitted to the group, eager for her offering.

"You'll do fine, Amanda," Mason encouraged from the front row of chairs.

Amanda placed her hands on the keyboard, cut Nate a panicked glance, ducked her head, and waited. Taking his cue, Nate scooted to the edge of his seat and prepared to stand. Last year, they'd practiced extensively before the party, then sang a duet while she played. Their cheerful performance of "We Wish You a Merry Christmas" had reaped a standing ovation.

"I have a request," a British voice called from near Mason.

Nate stifled a groan. Franklyn West was beating him to the mark. The blond imposter was already striding toward the piano.

The pianist lifted her head and welcomed her new friend with a grin she'd never used on Nate. He scooted back in his seat and watched as Franklyn paused beside Amanda, smiled into her eyes, and bent to whisper something in her ear. She nodded. And never had a nod held such glee. Nate had never worked so hard to look so disinterested.

When Amanda crashed into the chords of "God Save the Queen" and Franklyn bellowed forth the first words, the whole group whooped and clapped and cheered them on. Even Nate couldn't stop a burst of humor.

"Talk about the unexpected!" Janet said.

"Exactly!" Nate agreed and ignored Franklyn for the rest of the song.

When the final note was sung, the last chord played, the rowdy crowd stood in an applause that swelled with more gusto than what Nate and Amanda's performance had earned a year ago.

Franklyn bowed low, then stood to the side and extended his arms to Amanda. She bowed as well before the two relinquished the spotlight.

"I believe I'm next," Janet said.

"Oh?" Nate lifted his brows and observed her. "I didn't know you played."

"Yes. Whether I want to or not. My parents made me take lessons." Janet chuckled.

"You and Amanda could join the same therapy group," Nate teased.

Sixteen

Amanda strolled from the piano, passed Mason, and headed straight out of the room. The restroom was on the other side of the marbled entryway, and Amanda planned to hide there awhile—at least until Janet finished her number and Mason found another focal point.

Fully expecting Mason to be on her trail, she glanced over her shoulder as she began the "glass floor" journey to the restroom. A crashing eruption of piano expertise flowed from behind, and Amanda admitted what she'd already suspected. Janet French could eat up the piano and make anything she did sound like child's play.

Amanda ducked her head and scurried toward the restroom. Thankfully she remained alone. She slipped into the bathroom, locked the door, and peered into the mirror at the redhead wearing red.

She looked like a wallaby staring into headlights. Those unfortunate animals were always getting hit by cars and left for dead. Right now Amanda felt as if she'd already been hit by a car.

All evening she'd been plagued about the true state of Mason's affections. Nate's claims were gradually taking on more credence. Mason hadn't even hinted about Haley or her absence or even her health. He'd been too focused on making certain Amanda had every morsel she wanted and that her punch glass remained full.

All Amanda could think now was *Poor Haley! Poor, poor Haley!*

She removed her evening bag from her shoulder, plopped it on the side of the sink, and stared at the floral wallpaper as her mind churned with the evidence. *If Mason is after me, that would explain why he's never even held her hand,* she thought.

"How could I have been so clueless?" Amanda whispered.

And the flowers! she wailed to herself. *Did he really mean those for me?* That would validate why he'd acted a bit odd when she reported giving them to Haley.

Her friend's note, penned in love, floated to the surface of her thoughts. Amanda dug deeply into her purse's side pocket and pulled out the note. Carefully she slipped her polished fingernail beneath the seal and lifted it with little resistance. Her fingers trembling, she pulled the note from its haven and read the words, written in Haley's plump letters.

My Dear Mason,

You have no idea how much I appreciate the flowers and your sending your love. Please accept this letter as a token of my love. I hope you have a great time at the party. I'll be home, missing you.

Yours truly,
Haley

"Oh no!" Amanda squeaked, her worst fears founded. Haley really had fallen for Mason. *What are we going to do now?* she fretted and reread the note. Her first impression remained. There had been a horrid mistake! Amanda's pulse pounded behind her eyes as she studied the note until she'd almost memorized it.

How perfectly dreadful! she wailed to herself, then turned to the only source of help she could—her heavenly Father.

Oh Lord, Amanda prayed, her eyes squinted tightly. *Please, please fix this mess. And—and if You do, I'll try my hardest to never play matchmaker again!*

Then Amanda thought of Angie and Wayne and how happy they were. If Amanda hadn't played matchmaker, they'd have probably never met.

All right, Lord, Amanda amended, *I won't play matchmaker again unless it's absolutely necessary. Amen.*

Her fingers unsteady, Amanda opened her eyes and read the note a last time. Finally she slipped the message back into the envelope, turned on the water, and placed her finger under the cool flow. Amanda touched her finger to the seal, reclosed the envelope, and inserted it back into her purse's side pocket. She turned off the water.

Her fingers bumped a package of peppermint gum, and Amanda retrieved it from her bag. She unwrapped a piece, popped it into her mouth, and vigorously chewed while the burst of mint filled her senses.

"I will not let Haley down," she said into the mirror, then nodded. Amanda put the gum back in her purse, washed her hands with liquid soap that smelled of coconuts, and dried them on the plush towel.

I've got to get out of here, she thought, her mind already churning with ways to convince Haley that Mason wasn't the right man for her after all. The primary plan involved luring her away from Mason with another man. The man would have to be *absolutely suited* for her in order for Amanda to keep her promise to God. Who that man was, she presently could not imagine.

Roger certainly is not the one! Amanda had nearly died when she saw him with Nate. She'd already been in a dither over seeing Nate. Seeing Roger, too, had nearly sent her into a faint. She never remembered him being at any other church function and suspected he'd come with the hope of seeing Haley.

I can't even imagine her marrying him! Amanda thought. *He's as stylish as a bag of potatoes and about as witty. I've got to get her directed toward someone else,* she stewed, then once again remembered her prayerful pledge.

"But it will be with the perfect match this time," Amanda whispered and glanced toward the ceiling. "I promise."

Snapping her gum, Amanda opened the bathroom door, stepped out, and prepared to tiptoe toward the front door. No way was she going back into that party. She'd return to Haley's, sit with her, and try to determine the easiest way to hint about forgetting Mason.

"Oh, Miss Amanda! There you are!" Betty's shrill voice ricocheted off the spacious entryway.

Amanda hunched her shoulders, darted a glance toward the party room, and stopped herself from hissing, *Sssshhhh!*

"Hello, Betty," she said instead and peered toward the party, then back at Betty. She'd chatted with dear Betty only once in the food line but hadn't crossed her path since.

Who could I talk to with Mason in my hair all night? she thought. Amanda hadn't been able to say a word to Franklyn without Mason barging into the conversation.

The one conversation she'd shared with the housekeeper had involved Betty's apology for crashing the Young Adult Christmas party. But Amanda had assured her no one minded. Betty said she'd come for Janet's sake.

"Do you remember I mentioned a little secret I'd share with you later?" Betty whispered and rubbed her palms along the front of her cotton dress as if it were her cleaning smock.

While Amanda nodded, she noticed a smear of hot pink lipstick near Betty's nose. Unfortunately, the shade was wrong for Betty's orange dress, her thin lips, *and* her pudgy nose.

"Well, here's the secret," Betty whispered. "Someone has sent Janet a baby grand piano for Christmas!"

"What?" Amanda gaped.

"Yes!" Betty pumped her head up and down. "Believe me! It's the truth, Amanda! It's sitting in my living room as we speak. And get this!" She grabbed Amanda's arm, looked from side to side, then lowered her voice even more. "It's from her *secret admirer!*"

Amanda attacked her gum like a starving woman devouring her first meal in weeks. "Her secret admirer?" she repeated. Her eyes wide, she began a mental search for a man who'd *do* such a thing.

He'd have to be rich, that's for sure, Amanda thought. "Baby grands cost thousands."

"Tell me about it!" Betty crossed her arms and stuck out her bottom lip like the prime authority on all Janet's business.

"Does she have an admirer in Queenstown?"

"She *says* she doesn't, but Janet is so infernally modest." Betty shook her head. "If it's not someone in Queenstown, I've decided it has to be someone she's just met. Maybe he's even here tonight," she hissed and pointed toward the party room.

In Amanda's mind, Nate Knighton had to be the primary candidate. He'd been talking to Janet when she arrived, and he sat by her during the performances. He spent most of Janet's party with her, and he'd told Amanda he thought Janet was pretty the first time he met her.

Amanda chomped on the gum with a vengeance. Her heart thumped as ferociously as her jaws worked. She imagined Nate and Janet standing at an altar while a solemn minister recited the "I do's," "I will's" and the "duly, doethly's."

"This is just *awful*," Amanda breathed and clutched her thin purse with the grip of a woman losing her life...or a friend who'd been there for life.

"Why is it so awful?" Betty squinted.

"Oh, I mean, uh, I...uh...did I say awful?" She said and blinked so rapidly she hoped she convinced Betty of something—anything but "awful." "I guess I should have said mysterious, shouldn't I?"

"That's what I think." Betty shifted her weight. "It's mysterious and *so romantic!*" She looked toward the ceiling and sighed in melodramatic theatrics that could have won an Oscar.

"Would you look at that chandelier?" Betty gasped. "Isn't it the most beautiful thing you've ever seen?"

Amanda glanced toward the ceiling and noted the brass-and-crystal fixture that she'd help Angie pick out. The piece truly was a masterpiece.

"There you are, Amanda!" Mason's whiny voice interrupted the chandelier moment, and Amanda nearly jumped.

Oh no! she thought. *Not the leech again!*

Mason hurried across the foyer and stopped within inches of Amanda. He placed his arm around her waist and looked at Betty as if she were an interloper.

"Amanda and I were just going out on the deck," he hinted. "Angie says it's gorgeous out there, especially in the moonlight."

"Oh," Betty said, her pink lips remaining in the "O" shape. And Amanda couldn't imagine what her lifelong friend must be thinking.

She stepped out of the minister's reach and said, "Mason, I don't think I can stay any long—"

"Of course you can," he insisted and propelled her across the entryway to a hall door she knew led to a massive deck over-looking a landscaped yard.

Amanda, feeling like a cruise ship being bullied by a tugboat, tried to resist but grappled with keeping her balance on the stilts posing as shoes. Mason flung open the door and urged Amanda forward. Before the door snapped shut, she shot a panicked glance over her shoulder. Betty gaped after Amanda, her bugged eyes magnified threefold by her thick glasses.

Seventeen

❧ ❧

Amanda stumbled onto the deserted deck with Mason pulling her hand. "Please, Mason," she panted as the balmy air swathed her. "I really need to go. Haley's waiting on me. She's sick, remember?"

"Who can think of Haley at a time like this?" Mason declared. "I've got something that needs to be said. I've decided to tell you how I feel."

"How you feel?" The smell of earth and ferns reminded Amanda of the relaxing evenings she'd spent chatting with Angie near the heated pool. This visit was anything but relaxing.

"Yes, I've got to say it or I'll burst. Besides, with the likes of that Franklyn barging in…" He nudged her toward a shadowed alcove near the pool, but Amanda refused to budge another inch.

I'm bigger than he is, she thought. *Why am I letting him drag me around?*

Mason grabbed both her hands and said, "Amanda, surely you know what I'm thinking?"

She silently shook her head from side to side. "Mason, I—"

"You've *got* to know that I've been crazy about you ever since our date at O'Brien's."

"Our date?" She tried to extract her fingers from his sweating paws.

He tightened his grip. "Of course! You asked me out!"

"No!" Amanda jerked her hands from his and stumbled backward. "No!" she repeated. "I asked you to meet Haley."

"Ah, come on, babe." His eyes heavy, Mason closed in. "You know you asked for you."

"No, I didn't!" Amanda yelped and promptly swallowed her mint gum. "I invited you for Haley," she said and hacked against the wad slithering down her throat. "I thought you liked *Haley!*"

"Haley? Who's she?" He waved away the very thought of her.

"She's my best friend!" Amanda stomped her foot. "And I refuse to allow you to two-time her!"

"Two-time her?" Mason laughed and reached for her waist. Amanda scurried back another few feet.

"I barely even know what she looks like. It's *you* I'm all about."

"But—but—but—" Amanda stumbled into a wrought-iron chair and plopped on the cold metal. The legs squeaked on the wooden deck as her body crashed against the chair's back. Her purse plopped at her feet.

"I'm so about you…I'm here to ask you to marry me." He bent on one knee and earnestly gazed into her eyes.

"Mason!" Amanda gasped. "We barely know each other."

"I know enough to know you're the woman I want to spend the rest of my life with!"

"But I'm nearly twice your size," Amanda babbled. "Haley is so much more suited for—"

"That prawn?" he scoffed. "No! I like my women bigger than dreams like *you!*" Mason stood, placed his hands on either side of the chair, and inched toward her face.

"Mason, no!" Amanda said and shoved against his chest. He was amazingly strong, and her resistance did little to stop his progress toward the kiss.

"I've *got* to kiss you, Amanda, or I'll explode," he mumbled, his gazed fixed on the object of his words.

"*No!*" Amanda gritted her teeth and shoved with all her might.

Mason's face contorted. He yowled, jerked backward, and grabbed at his shoulder.

Amanda, shocked that her effort had reaped such results, scrambled to her feet—only to notice Nate Knighton towering behind Mason. Furthermore, Nate's fingers were biting into Mason's shoulder with enough pressure to make even Amanda wince.

"What do you think you're doing?" Mason hollered and jerked away from Nate.

"I'm protecting the lady," Nate growled.

"Nate!" Amanda panted. "How long have you been out here?"

"If you're wondering if I heard everything, the answer is yes," Nate replied and glowered at Mason. "It's time for you to leave."

"I'm not leaving!" Mason retorted, his face darkening.

"Amanda?" His features accented by the deck's lighting, Nate silently encouraged her to make Mason's departure imminent.

"Mason, I…" Amanda shook her head. "There's been a terrible, terrible misunderstanding." She rubbed her temple. "Please, I don't want to hurt you in any way, but understand me when I tell you I had no idea you were even remotely interested in me. I thought you were all for Haley."

Amanda lowered her hand and helplessly gazed down at the minister. "If I'd known, I would have—".

"I thought you knew when you finished the portrait," he defended. "I wanted to take it home because it was your art, remember?"

"We thought you took it because it was of Haley," Amanda explained.

"No, it was because *you painted it!*" His voice rose, and the shadows intensified his stricken expression. "And how could you not know how I feel after the flowers?" he accused.

"I thought you meant them for Haley." Amanda's voice had never sounded so tiny; neither had she ever felt so small, so naïve. Nate had been right, and she'd scoffed his every warning.

"And Haley thought…" His eyes widened.

"Yes."

"And the same about the portrait?" Mason prompted.

"Yes."

"How could you do this to me?" he demanded.

"I didn't do anything to you," Amanda squawked. "I was just trying to find someone for Haley."

Nate's deep laughed echoed across the backyard.

Mason stiffened and glowered at Nate. While the seconds stretched, he began to visibly tremble.

As if he were bent upon doing what he shouldn't, Nate laughed again. This time he had the decency to cover his face. "Oh man," he said, "I'm sorry. It's just that—" He broke into another chortle.

Mason turned and stomped toward the door. He banged through it with the force of a man scorned.

Only the distant sounds of Highland's traffic and the crickets remained. Amanda eyed Nate, who solemnly observed her, before bursting into a fit of uncontrolled laughing.

"This is not funny, Nate Knighton!" Amanda exclaimed and placed her hands on her hips.

"No, it's hilarious!" Nate wheezed as he covered his eyes. "You should have seen your face when you came out here."

"So you really were out here during the whole thing?"

"I told you I was." Nate bit his bottom lip.

"Why didn't you say anything then?"

"What could I say?" He lifted both hands.

"You eavesdropped on us!" Amanda accused.

"Well…"

"How dare you! That's the rudest thing anybody could ever do!"

Nate laughed again. "You're a fine one to say that."

Amanda's face warmed as her traitorous mind flashed through instance after instance of her eavesdropping. The final image involved Haley's letter she'd just read. While that wasn't technically classified as eavesdropping, she still partook of information Haley meant for someone else.

But it was for her good! Amanda argued and observed Nate.

For some unknown reason, she was reminded of his comments from the villa's balcony—something about his being a man and not being one of her girlfriends. If he did have a mystery woman, then Amanda was sure that lady appreciated the way his brown eyes might make a lady remember she was all woman…or the way his trim physique fit so well in a suit…or his prominent brows that made him resemble a classic Greek statue.

"You know, Amanda," Nate said. "You really shouldn't try to play God. It'll backfire on you every time."

"Play God?" she repeated and tried to forget what the mystery woman might or might not appreciate about Nate. What she thought was really none of Amanda's concern. "Whatever do you mean by that?" she asked and relived the last few months of vigorous matchmaking like a dying soul whose life is flashing before her.

But I repented! she defended. *In the bathroom!*

Then she thought of poor, poor Haley, who believed Mason Eldridge was in love with her. Amanda wanted to groan with the weight of responsibility. Her eyes stung in sympathy for the sweetest lady who ever lived. She was so innocent and so susceptible to manipulators like Mason. The longer Amanda thought about the whole wretched situation, the more her eyes stung and the greater her soul churned with the need to release the frustration.

Nate sighed and debated how to explain his comment without getting into the Roger–Haley issue all over again. The last time they'd talked about that romance, they'd argued. He rubbed the side of his nose and stared toward the pool, frosted in the moon's radiance. The enchanted water seemed much more inviting than the heat of this conversation.

"I guess what I'm saying," Nate finally drawled, "is that maybe you should let some relationships flow along and not, well, not try to, you know..." he shrugged, "uh...alter things."

Amanda stared at him in wide-eyed appraisal, and Nate had no choice but to calmly stare back, despite the fact that his legs felt like gelatin. He'd thought Amanda was more beautiful than ever when she sat at the piano, but he hadn't imagined the magic of a bright moon on a clear, Tasmanian night. Amanda's hair glimmered as if it were alive with fairy dust. Her deep-red dress heightened the effect. And Nate couldn't say that he blamed Mason for thinking he'd explode if he didn't kiss her.

But even if Mason thought that, the cad didn't have to act on it! Nate fumed.

He glanced away and grimaced. Nate had never been a fight-monger, not even as a child. But when other boys bullied him or hurt some weak, defenseless kid, he was ready with all his might. Tonight he'd been tempted to grab Mason by the hair and sling him into the pool's deep end.

A cry erupted from Amanda, and Nate dashed a concerned glance back to her. Her shoulders hunched, she stepped toward the wrought-iron chair and dropped into it. Sniffling, Amanda picked up her purse and scratched through it until she pulled out a package of tissue. She propped her elbow on the patio table, covered her eyes, and hiccoughed over another sob.

Nate's heart dropped. He was having enough trouble exercising willpower without having Amanda crying on him. He hardly remembered seeing her weep and didn't quite know how to handle the shocking experience.

What if she decides to cry on my shoulder? he stressed.

Despite all his worries, Nate was propelled to her side. And before he even registered what he was doing, he hovered over her, patted her back, and muttered several original platitudes such as, "There, there, Amanda."

"I don't know what I'm going to dooooo!" she wailed and covered her face with her hands. "I've made such a royal mess of everything! Poor Haley! Poor, poor Haley! There she is in—in—in bed, sicker than sick, thinking that—that—that Mason has sent her flowers!"

She threw the used tissue on the table and fumbled with the plastic wrapper in quest of another. Finally Nate relieved the wrapper of its misery, neatly extracted a tissue, and tucked it into her hand. She dabbed at her eyes and hiccoughed.

"Then you laughed at me!" she huffed.

Nate groaned and sat in the chair next to her. "I'm sorry," he said and stroked her fairy-dust hair. "It's just that, well, I...uh...I saw it all along. Then...oh well," he sighed. "I shouldn't have laughed anyway, especially not after Mason tried to force himself on you. *That* made me mad, actually." Nate resisted the urge to plunge his fingers deeper into her hair and relish the texture. Upon that resistance abounded the urge to bury his nose in her soft locks and drink of the heavenly scent she'd called jasmine. He lowered his hand instead.

Amanda lifted her face, rubbed at her eyes, and glanced toward him. "Thanks," she said, her voice unsteady. "I guess he's stronger than he looks."

"Yeah." Nate nodded and wished he could caress her cheeks.

"I really don't think he'd have done anything but kiss me," she said.

"Which is too much if you didn't want him to." Nate leaned away from her, told himself not to touch, and folded his arms. If he had to, he'd sit on his hands.

"I know." Amanda sniffed and smiled weakly. "What have you been doing with yourself these days?" she asked and blotted her cheeks.

"Working. The Christmas rush is on, y'know."

"Yes." She glanced down, fidgeted with her tissue, and looked toward the pool. A stray tear wandered from the corner of her eye, and she dabbed at it with unsteady fingers.

"I'm sorry to get so emotional," she quivered out. "But it's just been a b-bad—a really bad—bad night." She sucked in an unsteady breath.

"Yes, I know," he assured.

Out of nowhere, Nate wondered what she'd say if he told her he loved her. *Would that make you feel any better, Amanda?* He blinked.

Is Roger right? he questioned as a prickly rush swept him. Incredulity followed. He leaned back, gazed toward the stars, and used every ounce of willpower to maintain a calm persona.

Oh God, he silently pleaded, *show me. Show me what's going on. Am I really in love with her, or is this just some sort of infatuation that's going to pass?*

The first thought that entered Nate's head involved the quality of woman he wanted to spend his life with. She'd have to be full of life, smart, witty, with an independent streak. She needed to be someone whom Nate could respect. Someone who could look him eye to eye and hold him tit for tat in any verbal interaction. And while she might possess external beauty, Nate was more interested in her heart and her character.

Of course, if she was a redhead who looked incredible in a red Christmas dress...or black party dress...or blue jean cutoffs, that would be fine as well.

With an amazing swoop of insight, Nate realized he'd just described Amanda, almost down to her red-tipped toenails. He closed his eyes as his veins vibrated with the weight of the truth. There was a reason he'd been so frustrated in O'Brien's when she was emphatic about never marrying.

I'm in love with her, he thought. Looking back, Nate realized he'd fallen so gradually he hadn't even registered the process. Shoving her presents in his closet was the act of a tormented lover gone wacky.

Now what? He opened his eyes and looked at her again.

She was studying him like an astronomer who's mesmerized by a newly discovered planet. "Are you okay?" she questioned. "You really haven't been acting like yourself lately—for quite a while actually?"

"Who me?" Nate questioned and noticed her eyes were puffy and tear-smeared. Even so, she was still more exquisite than all the stars.

"No, I'm talking to the mouse sitting on your shoulder," she quipped.

"Humph." Nate looked down, rested his elbows on his knees, and gazed at the deck's fresh lumber. "So I haven't been acting like myself?"

"Absolutely not," she said.

Nate sensed her examining the top of his head. In a fit of panic, he feared she might be able to see his thoughts. Even though logic insisted his feelings were irrational, he jerked his head up, straightened, and silently appraised her.

She leaned forward, and a line formed between her brows. Without a blink, Amanda said, "Be honest with me, Nate. Are you seeing a *woman?*" Her mouth twisted over the word "woman." "You're acting like a—a husband who's gotten distracted with some female his wife won't be happy about."

Nate laughed.

Amanda narrowed her reddened eyes. "Please don't do that. I don't like it," she snapped and crossed her legs with a vengeance.

Oh yeah, he thought, *and I'd want my wife to be feisty.*

"Are you really never going to get married, Amanda?" Nate asked and was tempted tell her the truth. *Yes, I'm seeing a woman. I'm seeing her in my dreams…in my daydreams. I'm seeing her photo in my office—the one I shoved in my desk drawer, then pulled back out. I'm looking at her now.*

She gazed past him, tucked her bobbed hair behind her ear, and barely shrugged.

"You told me in O'Brien's you were going to stay with your dad until…well, as long as he needs you. Are those still your plans?" Nate panted for the slightest hint that Amanda might have thought of him in some vein other than invisible friend or brother. If she gave him only the tiniest encouragement, Nate might very well act like Mason, fall to his knees, and beg her to marry him.

"Well…" she hedged and fumbled with the tissue in her hands. "I guess if I *did* meet someone—"

"And have you?"

"Uh…"

"Want to tell me about him?" Nate gripped the iron chair's cool hand rests.

"Uh…"

"Someone I know?" He inched forward.

She stood. "I think this conversation has gone far enough."

"Why?" Nate stood as well. His chair scraped against the deck. "You asked me about my mystery woman. Why shouldn't I be allowed to ask you the same sort of questions?" His brows rose.

Amanda's lips quivered. "There is someone, isn't there?" she pressed.

Nate searched her eyes for any hint of an attraction, any encouragement whatsoever…anything, that would let him know if he told her the truth she'd be receptive. But all he saw was Amanda flirting with Franklyn West.

In O'Brien's she'd been emphatic about never marrying. Now she wasn't quite as committed to that whole plan. She hadn't indicated that Nate had done anything to change her mind. But she had spent the last month and all of this evening making eyes at Angie's stepson.

Nate's wild hopes plummeted.

"Well, are you going to answer me?" Amanda asked.

His first inclination was to remain evasive, then Nate decided to just be honest. "Yes," he said.

"Yes, what? Yes, you'll answer me, or yes there's a…a…a *woman?*" she said as if "woman" tasted atrocious.

"Yes to both," Nate replied and barely smiled despite himself.

Amanda's mouth fell open.

And you're the woman! he added and wondered if the idea of another woman might jolt Amanda to jealousy. If she *were* jealous, then perhaps her feelings ran deeper than even she realized.

"What did you think, Amanda, that I'd act like you and want to stay single forever? Like I already told you, I'm a man." He pressed his fingertips against his chest. "I'm not your sister or your girlfriend. I have desires for a wife like any other man."

"So you're going to marry her?" she gasped.

"Who knows?" Nate shrugged and searched her demeanor for any scrap of jealousy. All he encountered was shock mixed with vestiges of Franklyn West. "I guess that all depends on her," he said and nudged the toe of his shoe against the chair's leg.

A quiet voice suggested Nate was blurring the lines of honesty a bit. He considered clarifying the fact that there really wasn't *another* woman—only the one he was talking with. But Nate realized he'd talked himself into a trap. Telling Amanda that she was the woman meant he'd risk the same rejection Mason had endured. While there were many comical facets to that whole ordeal, Nate couldn't say he'd laugh if he were dealt the same fate. He couldn't tell Amanda who this "other woman" was—not yet, anyway. Maybe not ever.

"*There* you two are!" Angie's voice floated from the house. "I was afraid you'd left without my knowing it, Amanda. Franklyn is asking for you."

Nate's chest tightened.

Amanda jabbed the tissue at her eyes again, sniffed hard, and strode toward her surrogate mother. "Sorry to desert you," Amanda said, her voice strained. "We were just talking," she continued as if they'd been chatting about nothing.

Eighteen

Sunday, after morning services, Amanda sat in Haley's sunroom and nibbled the Big Mac she'd picked up on the way to Haley's. But she couldn't even enjoy the special sauce this time. She'd purchased a burger for each of them along with a large fry they were sharing. Haley was half finished with her burger and slurping her soda.

"I can't believe how much better I feel today than yesterday," Haley claimed. "It's like the antibiotics have finally taken over. I might even get dressed in some regular clothes before the day's over." She looked down at the satin pajamas and house robe Amanda bought yesterday. "Imagine that!"

Amanda hoped her smile appeared more genuine and interested than it felt. She'd worried all weekend about telling Haley the sordid Mason saga. Amanda hadn't wanted to upset Haley when she was so ill. Now that her friend was better, she knew the inevitable must happen. It wasn't honest or fair to leave Haley believing Mason was her man when he was anything but.

He hadn't been in church this morning. Several were whispering about his taking an unexpected leave of absence—a month—from his ministerial position. He had supposedly gone to Launceston where his parents lived. Amanda didn't need anyone to piece together the clues for her. She knew his leaving town was directly related to her rejection.

Sighing, she observed Haley. While her hair was a bit frizzed and her eyes still somewhat hollow, her cheeks were beginning to show some signs of color, even without makeup. Amanda placed her barely eaten burger in its box, closed the lid, and placed it on the table.

"Did you get to talk to Mason today?" Haley put the remainder of her burger in her box as well. "You *did* give him my note Friday night, didn't you?" she asked, her brow wrinkled.

Haley's question nearly made Amanda choke on nothing. Her friend had felt so bad yesterday, Amanda had been relieved of the necessity of such a question. She stared toward Mt. Wellington and prayed the Lord would give her some scrap of wisdom He'd never imparted before. This morning during the service's prayer time, Amanda had reminded the Lord of her pledge to not play matchmaker again unless it was absolutely necessary. Amanda wished she'd stated that prayer last winter.

"I, uh…" Amanda cleared her throat, plopped her burger box on the wicker table, and reached for her bottle of mineral water. She downed a swallow of the chilled liquid and waited for it to hit her stomach. "Haley," she said and gripped the water bottle, "Mason wasn't at church today. He—he's taken a one-month leave of absence."

"At Christmastime?" she asked, her eyes widening. "What about the Christmas cantata?"

"Haley…" Amanda shook her head back and forth and gurgled out something that sounded like a drowning frog.

"But he didn't even call me to tell me he was leaving," Haley whimpered. She laid her burger box on the table and pulled one of the plaid pillows to her midsection.

Amanda gulped another swallow of water, set the bottle near her burger box, and moved to Haley's side. She held her hands, peered into her disillusioned eyes, and then didn't have the fortitude to do anything but look down. The emotions that brought tears Friday night and last night assaulted Amanda anew.

"There's been a dreadful mistake," she breathed as warm rivulets trickled along her nose.

Haley's fingers flexed against Amanda's.

"Mason wasn't—the flowers, they weren't—there's been a terrible—terrible—" her voice caught, "mis–misunderstanding." A tear splashed onto their entwined fingers. Amanda sniffled and swiped at her cheeks.

"You mean he wasn't…with me?" Haley whispered.

Amanda looked up and shook her head. "Oh Haley, things are so botched up. He thought *I* was the one!"

"You?" Haley gasped, the trace of color in her cheeks draining to nothing.

Amanda sniffed through a nod.

"But the flowers…"

"He sent them to the travel agency. They didn't have my name on them, so I thought they were for you. But they were really for…" Amanda covered her face with her hands and coughed through another surge of torment.

"Poor Haley," she cried, "poor, poor Haley. I feel as if I've betrayed the sweetest soul in the world. You feed injured wallabies and volunteer at the children's home! I don't know how this ever happened to somebody so wonderful, but it's *absolutely dreadful!*"

Haley wrapped her arms around Amanda and buried her head against her neck. Her silent shaking indicated the measure of her own turmoil.

Amanda gently nudged at Haley's arms so she could embrace her. "It's okay, Haley. *Please* don't cry like this," she encouraged. "You're going to be okay, I promise," Amanda assured and admonished herself to control her emotions. She had to be strong for Haley.

A fit of bark-coughing attacked Haley, and she jerked away to finish the fit. "I don't need to let myself get this upset," she wheezed. "I'm still too congested to be crying so much. It's just that—I really h–h–had begun to care for him!" Haley covered her face and hunched forward.

Amanda reached for the tissue box on the edge of the coffee table, pulled out a wad, and shoved them into Haley's hands. Then she extracted her own wad and mopped at her face. Now that the telling was complete and the emotions were spent, Amanda experienced an odd release, a peculiar freedom. And she knew she must remain steady.

"No w–w–wonder he hasn't called me! He hasn't even *thought* of me!" Haley lifted her face and shook her head. "But what about the portrait? He wanted to show it to his mother and sister. He *did!*" She nodded like a tot and pressed her index finger against her chest. "I heard him say it."

"He said he wanted it because…" Amanda looked toward the potted fern hanging in the corner, but the plant offered about as much inspiration as her water bottle might.

"Because *you* painted it," Haley slowly stated. "Yes, that was it. Wasn't it?"

Amanda fumbled with the hem of her knee-length skirt, turned to her friend, and simply nodded.

Haley slumped against the love seat, and the wicker fibers creaked with her movement. "Oh no!" she shrieked and sat up straight. "Please tell me you didn't give him my note!"

"I didn't!" Amanda affirmed. "I never had the chance."

"Thank God!" Haley flopped backward again and stared out the window.

Amanda reached for her water bottle, unscrewed the lid, and gulped a generous portion while Haley continued her blank staring. Unless Haley pressed for more details, Amanda decided not tell her about Mason's proposal or the resulting upheaval.

She toyed with the bottle's plastic cap and relived that revolting episode all over again. When she got to the part where Nate stepped into the picture, Amanda told herself to think about something else. She continued thinking about Nate anyway and especially dwelled upon his mystery woman.

She must be Janet French, Amanda thought and hoped the lady appreciated the quality of man she was getting. Nate had *never* bought Amanda a baby grand piano. If he had, she might have practiced more. If this woman was Janet, Amanda hoped she knew she was costing her one of her best friends. She pressed the bottle cap between her index finger and thumb.

Nate had been right. He really was a man. Every time Amanda thought of him now she pondered how much this mystery woman must appreciate his masculinity. She was certain his wife-to-be would find his quick mind fascinating, his sense of humor refreshing—even though he did sometimes laugh at the wrong times.

After a season of stewing over pianos and other women, Amanda decided to put the whole ordeal out of her mind. She shifted in the love seat and observed Haley.

Still trapped in her silent staring, Haley mumbled, "Poor Roger."

Roger? Amanda thought. *Who can think of Roger at a time like this?* Then she began a mental inventory of the single men whom even God would agree would be an absolutely perfect match for Haley. The last thing Haley needed was to revert back to Roger Miller. He absolutely was not good enough for Haley—not even a little bit!

Nineteen

By mid January, Haley had fully recuperated from the upper respiratory infection, which lingered for three weeks. Even though she still pondered Mason on occasion, she had to some degree also overcome the mortification of that entire episode. Today's shopping trip was part of her recovery from the whole scenario. Nothing lifted the spirits like finding a good bargain.

She'd walked to the shopping center down the street from the travel agency, eaten a quick lunch at Frank's Fish 'n' Chips, and now she had a full hour to search for deals. When Haley shopped with Amanda, she didn't get to focus solely on the mark-down racks. While Amanda was all for seasonal sales, she never liked to investigate the back-of-the-store bargains. Amanda believed the whole process was a waste of time. She preferred to just buy what she needed rather than sift through the "tired leftovers." But Haley had found many "gold nuggets" others had overlooked.

As she stepped into the women's clothing store aptly named "Delightful," Haley considered herself a prospector looking for fashionable treasures. The store's cool interior offered a reprieve from the summer heat. Today had spanned into the mid 80s, which was warm enough to make more than a few Tassies sweat.

Enjoying the smells of new carpet and the latest clothing, Haley dabbed at the perspiration along her hairline as she passed a mirror. She gleaned a glimpse of herself in the cream-colored pantsuit Amanda surprised her with last week. The color brought out the highlights in her hair and the peachy undertones in her skin. Inwardly, Haley smiled.

Even though she believed Amanda wrong in her take on the bargain rack, Amanda was so right about so much—including Haley's need for a new wardrobe and makeover. Haley had never felt more confident, and she enjoyed the passing glances of men who noticed. Of course, as petite as Haley was, she knew she'd never be able to touch Amanda's stunning effect with her willowy height and fiery hair. Nevertheless, Haley felt better about herself than ever, despite Mason's rejection.

While she had spent a week crying herself to sleep, Haley had finally come to the conclusion that she and Mason just were not meant to be. This realization brought a sense of peace upon Haley's wounded heart that she attributed to God Himself. Still, she longed to say she belonged to someone and to be part of a family that also belonged to her.

At last Haley spotted the sign that she knew so well: *Clearance. 75% Off.*

When the frigid salesclerk asked if Haley needed assistance, she called, "Just looking," and zoomed toward that sign like a pilot landing a plane. She attacked the racks of clothing with a hard eye and a certainty that she would not leave empty handed.

Forty-five minutes later Haley walked toward the store's exit, weighted with a bag full of goodies she suspected even Amanda would swoon over. *Amanda's just wrong about the bargain scene. That's all there is to it,* she smugly thought.

Of course, she thought, *Amanda was also wrong about Mason.* And while Haley seldom mentioned Roger around Amanda, she'd begun to wonder if Amanda also misjudged the Roger business. Haley had deeply cared for him, and there was no doubt his love ran just as deep. While Amanda insisted Haley would feel trapped on a dairy farm, Haley had thought she might enjoy the experience, especially since Roger's extended family lived within sight of each other. Haley had hungered for the comfort of being in a family for so long; that element alone had nearly been enough to make her accept Roger.

But that chance is gone, she thought and tried to prevent herself from sinking back into the grips of despair that Mason's rejection had thrown her.

When she touched the door's metal handle, a rumble of thunder boomed over the parking lot. Haley jumped and gazed toward the dark clouds rolling across the sky.

"Oh no," she breathed and counted the minutes it would take her to walk back to the travel agency. She glanced down at her bare toes in strappy, gold sandals. Even though the shoes were flats, she'd still be forced to trudge through rain without an umbrella.

Unless I can get there before the rain starts, she thought and imagined herself racing a fourth of a mile while holding her purse and the bulging bag of clothing. *Oh well,* Haley mused, *sometimes you've just have to do what you have to do.* She scanned the parking lot and didn't spot even one raindrop on any windshields.

With all the gusto of the Australian spirit, Haley shoved open the door and hurried onto the sidewalk. The second the door shut, a flash zipped across the sky while a crackling roar jolted

Haley into a lurch and yelp. She stumbled backward, clutched her purse and shopping bag, and hovered near the glass storefront. Haley hated storms as a child—especially if her foster mother hadn't checked on her crying.

A gust of wind bearing the smell of rain predicted the inevitable. As if someone in the clouds flipped a water switch, the heavens pelted the cars and parking lot with fat drops that splashed with a vengeance. A flash in the distance preceded grumbles that floundered among the clouds.

"Oh no," Haley groaned again and checked her fashion watch—a demurely glitzy number with tiny, black crystals that she'd liked the second she saw it. Today Amanda had taken a two-hour lunch with one of the travel-agency managers visiting from the mainland, and she'd told Haley to enjoy a long lunch as well. However she was supposed to be back at the office by one thirty. She glanced at her watch and noted she had exactly 12 minutes left.

But this rain is just too hard! Haley thought and decided to stay dry and safe until the rain stopped. Amanda would understand. She was one of the most understanding people Haley had ever known.

The door opened to the shoe shop next to Delightful, and a man bustled out while wrestling a black umbrella. "Terribly wet today, isn't it?" he commented and glanced toward her with a friendly nod.

Prepared to offer an amiable response, Haley opened her mouth, then stopped. Her eyes rounded as she observed the thin face and kind eyes she knew so well.

"Roger!" she gasped.

"Haley?" Roger leaned forward and scrutinized her.

"Yes, it's me," she replied.

"You—you've changed!" he exclaimed and lowered the unopened umbrella.

Haley touched her hair and blinked. "Yes, I've, um, made a few changes. Amanda said I should." She stopped herself from asking the question that popped into her mind, *Do you like the new me?*

"You look great!" The appreciation cloaking Roger's rugged features validated his claim.

"Thanks." Haley looked down and talked herself out of a severe blush. The best she could tell, her face heated to only a moderate tinge of the cheeks.

She eyed Roger's work boots and the worn jeans that touched the tops, then glanced upward. As usual, he was dressed in farm gear—blue jeans and a denim work shirt. A gust of wet wind whipped at her hair and tasseled his.

Haley flinched against the cool spray that dashed her face, and a spontaneous chill shook her. The temperature must have dropped 15 degrees.

"This is a nasty storm, isn't it?" Roger said with a gleeful smile. He wiped at his face and looked toward the clouds as if he were receiving the best of gifts. "Looks like it's spitting at us now."

A nervous giggle tottered out of Haley, but another gust of wind dampened her humor. She pressed her body against the window and noted a stream two inches deep flowing along the curb.

The whoosh and pop of his opening umbrella accompanied Roger's stepping toward her. "Would you like to use my umbrella?" he asked and twirled it.

"*Please,*" Haley replied and moved from the glass toward the man she once thought would be her husband.

Instead of handing her the umbrella, Roger walked to her side and held it at an angle against the storm. The rest of the world was blocked out, and Haley felt as if they were in a world of their own, all cozy and isolated.

"There," he said with a comforting smile. "This way, you'll stay dry."

Haley nodded and detected a whiff of freshly laundered clothes. Roger never had gone for anything fancy in men's fragrances, and that fit his uncomplicated personality. He'd always been like the sun—forever present, forever steady, forever warm. She didn't expect the flutter in her chest. After all, she'd convinced herself she was over Roger Miller...or needed to be.

His eager gaze scanned her features, and Haley was left with no doubt that he hadn't even begun to get over her. As her heart pummeled her ribs, Haley wondered if this chance meeting might be an answer to her prayer for divine guidance this very morning.

Another flash and boom sent Haley into such a leap she dropped her shopping bag. When she stooped to pick it up, she found Roger right beside her, still holding the umbrella against the rain.

"Storms always *did* terrify you," he said, the umbrella capturing his voice's rhythm.

"And you always thought they were the greatest things ever," Haley responded and shook her head. She gathered the bag full of clothing and stood.

"There's nothing more beautiful than lightning against a dark sky." He paused, looked down, then smiled into her eyes. "Well, almost nothing," he added with a sly wink.

Haley caught her breath and couldn't stop the hot blush this time.

"So where are you headed?" Roger questioned, a satisfied tenor to his voice.

"I walked down here from work. I was going to walk back, but…" She pointed toward the rain.

"Want me to give you a ride?" he asked and jerked his head toward the parking lot. "I'm in the farm truck, but I can move some clutter and make a spot for you."

"Would you mind too terribly?" Haley asked and glanced at her watch again. "I'm supposed to be back in five minutes."

Roger touched the face of her watch. "I say, Haley," he teased, "this is a flashy little guy. Have you gone and bought your cat a rhinestone collar too?"

Haley lifted her wrist between them. Even in the dim light, the tiny black crystals shimmered with life. "Do you like it?" she asked.

"I think it's just right and goes great with…" he looked her head to toe, "with everything…with the new you," Roger babbled.

"Amanda got one a lot like it with clear crystals. If you think *this* one's flashy, you should see hers. It will put your eyes out." Haley's snicker didn't sound any less nervous than Roger's voice. Her spine felt like jelly, and her knees had gone liquid.

A slight frown rippled his forehead. "Well good, then," he said and glanced toward the parking lot. "I'll pull my truck up, and you wait here. Do you mind if I take my umbrella?"

"No, of course not." Haley shook her head. "I insist."

After a nod, Roger bounded into the rain, sprinted across the parking lot. With his every footfall, water splashed up and covered his jeans while rain rushed off his umbrella. The sounds of tires slapping the lot's watery pavement meshed with the hiss of cars rolling along the thoroughfare. The smell of fresh rain, the lazy rumble in the distance, the smile and question in Roger's eyes all insisted Haley would never view storms the same.

Twenty

Amanda sat at her desk and stared across her office at a mural from South Africa. The artist had captured the arrogant stance of a charging elephant, trunk lifted, tusks strong, and eyes gleaming with challenge. Behind her stood an army of like-minded elephants.

When Amanda awoke this morning, she could have identified with the hulking mammals. She'd been ready to take on her day. Then she'd gone to lunch with the branch manager from Sydney, fully expecting to have a success report from the lively, young executive. He, on the other hand, had planned the whole luncheon as a nice way to resign.

Amanda slid her forefinger and thumb down the shaft of the silver-plated pen she'd found at the "Noah" level of her desk clutter. She flipped the pen and repeated the gesture. The irritation over having to find a replacement for Ken-the-working-machine had driven her to deal with the mound of receipts, stacked up notes, and miscellaneous nothings she normally avoided. Now her trash can was overflowing, her desk was clean, and she'd found the pen Nate Knighton had given her for her twenty-fourth birthday.

But Amanda still hadn't found a solution to her hiring needs. Ken was a one-in-a-million manager. No one currently on staff could even touch him. Even though Amanda had offered him a big pay raise and a bonus, he'd declined. As things turned out, Ken was marrying a Canadian lady and moving to Canada after the wedding next month.

Amanda sighed and observed the pen. Nate had gotten her name engraved on the barrel. She touched the cursive script and wondered what Nate was doing these days. He hadn't even been to church, which made Amanda really question what was going on. Nate never missed services. He often said the corporate worship experience kept him going through the week.

He's probably having sing-alongs with Janet and her piano, she thought.

Betty had been bringing Janet to work with her these days. Unfortunately, Janet looked good even in her cleaning smock. Amanda tried to talk herself out of the growing irritation she felt every time Janet entered the room. According to Betty, her sister had adopted Janet from a Korean orphanage. At four years old she had little hope for a family due to the fact that most adoptive parents prefer younger children.

Once Amanda learned these facts, she lambasted herself for struggling over her attitude toward the Asian beauty. She could think of no crime Janet had committed—aside from being a perfect size three and gorgeous...and Nate thinking exactly that.

This morning the sweet-spirited young woman had even brought Amanda some cookies she'd baked yesterday. The invitation in her eyes said, "Let's be friends."

Amanda wanted to howl, *But we can't be friends! Not if you're Nate's mystery woman!*

She dropped the pen, laid her arm across the desk calendar, and rested her forehead on her arm. Sighing, Amanda stared at the calendar squares. The fact that Nate actually admitted to a mystery woman had astonished Amanda nearly as much as hearing herself ask him. The last few weeks had been a journey from shock to hurt to strangely feeling betrayed.

It's almost like I'm a little sister who can't accept her big brother leaving home, she thought.

This morning, Amanda with her "charging-elephant mentality" had decided it was time to move on, to accept that Nate was not going to be a part of her life anymore. Then she found the pen. Her eyes stung.

"Oh Father," she prayed, "please help me. I'm having a bad day." She held her breath and rapidly blinked. Amanda refused to fall into another fit of tears. After crying over the Mason–Haley fiasco, she'd done the weepy thing all she wanted to for a while.

"I know Janet doesn't deserve my dislike, and I'm not even sure I understand it," she prayed. "I've n–never felt this way before. Please, please help me."

An eager rap on her office door prompted Amanda to sit up straight. The knock sounded like Betty's. The housekeeper and Janet had been here all day, and Amanda fully expected Betty to simply report they were leaving. Amanda plucked a tissue out of the box on her desk's corner, dabbed at her eyes, blinked again, and cleared her throat.

"Come in," she called.

Sure enough, Betty opened the door and stepped into the room. But instead of beginning a brief goodbye, she closed the door and scurried forward.

"Before I leave, there's something I've *got* to tell you, Miss Amanda," she whispered and glanced toward Haley's ajar office door as she passed it. "Do you mind if I shut this?"

"No." Amanda checked her watch and noticed it was one thirty-five. "But Haley's not back from lunch yet," she said and thought, *That's odd. Haley's never late.*

"Well, just in case she gets back." Betty snapped the door shut and waddled forth like a goose on a mission. She didn't stop until she'd rounded Amanda's desk and hovered over her.

Amanda leaned back in her chair and looked straight into Betty's magnified eyes. "Have you heard the latest about Mason Eldridge?" she hissed.

"M—Mason?" Amanda stammered.

"Yes! He's just come back home. Arrived two nights ago. And guess what?" Betty leaned back and crossed her arms.

"What?" Amanda shifted forward.

"He's *married!*" Betty hissed.

"Married!" Amanda exclaimed and stood. "How—wh–what? He's *married?*"

"Yes!" Betty nodded and began crumpling and releasing the front of her smock.

"Are you sure?" Amanda asked.

"Perfectly." The housekeeper pressed her pink lips together.

"When did you find out? How do you know for sure?" Amanda placed her flattened hand on the desk, leaned into it, and wondered how poor Haley would respond to this bit of news.

"I found out yesterday," Betty explained. "I've started cleaning the church, you know."

"Yes, you mentioned that a couple of weeks ago."

"Well, I was there yesterday and he came in with *her,*" Betty said. "And I've got to tell you she's the most brassy creature I've *ever met* in my life! And not half as pretty as Haley."

"Haley?" Amanda questioned.

"Well, yes." Betty shoved at her glasses. "Didn't Haley and he have a thing for a while?"

Amanda looked at the tortoise-shell trash can and panicked over how best to answer. Betty was always the source of all sorts of news. Ironically, her information was usually too correct to be mere gossip.

"Where did you hear *that?*" Amanda asked.

"Sarah told me."

"Sarah." Amanda repeated in a flat voice. Their cook was like an all-seeing eye who never said much but never missed much either. She'd cooked cod for them the night Amanda invited Mason and Haley over for dinner. That same night, Amanda and Nate had exchanged a heated discussion on the balcony. While Amanda couldn't imagine that Sarah had heard the whole conversation, she could see how the cook might have picked up some clues, added them to Haley's body language, and arrived at an assumption.

"We were thinking they must have broken up and that's why Mason took the leave of absence. I figured that's what he wanted to talk to you about at the Christmas party." Betty silently blinked, and Amanda put up her guard. The housekeeper was obviously doing more than sharing information. She was also trying to glean the bits missing in her story.

"I see," Amanda said and was relieved Betty had no information regarding Mason's proposal. Hopefully that whole shameful ordeal was limited to her, Mason, and Nate.

"Well," Amanda finally said, "I can honestly tell you that Haley and Mason were never an official couple. If Mason has gone off and gotten married, then maybe he already knew this lady."

"Maybe so," Betty said, her features wilting in a veil of disappointment. "Oh well, I just thought you might be interested."

"Thanks," Amanda said and noticed Betty's smock was buttoned crooked. She suppressed a laugh and figured that if Betty ever got it all together, she'd forget where she put it. On an impulse, Amanda fingered the buttons on her white blouse and was satisfied that she was buttoned evenly.

"The church secretary told me Mason's wife is rich," Betty added. "She also said it's a good thing because Mason's got tastes higher than his income."

"Oh really?" Amanda questioned and wondered if that had been part of his attraction for her. While the Priebes weren't the wealthiest family in Australia, Amanda could have chosen the rich, idle lifestyle over a career if she'd so desired. But that never had and never would suit her personality. She was far too goal-oriented to dither her time away at a pool side.

"Credit card bills to here," Betty added and sliced her index finger across the middle of her sagging neck.

"Wow!" Amanda whispered and plopped back into her chair. "That explains a lot."

"What do you mean?" Betty asked.

"Uh…" Amanda picked up her silver pen and examined it.

Haley's door whipped opened. "Amanda, you're not going to believe who I just—"

Amanda had never been so glad to see Haley, and never had Haley looked so flushed.

"Oh!" Haley said and glanced from Amanda to Betty. "I'm sorry. Did I interrupt you?"

"No!" Amanda stood. "We were just chatting," she continued and hoped Haley read between the lines. In case she didn't, Amanda mouthed, "Don't go" while Betty's attention was fixed upon Haley.

"Actually, I need to be leaving," Betty explained as if they'd been chatting about the weather. "Janet's waiting on me."

"G'day, then," Amanda said and nearly slumped over the desk when Betty ambled along without blurting anything else about Mason and his new wife. Haley's discovering the truth was inevitable, but Amanda preferred for her to hear the facts tactfully and gently.

"Be back Monday!" Betty waved and disappeared into the hall.

The second the door snapped shut, Haley hurried forward. "You're never going to believe who I saw at the shopping center," she blurted.

"Who?" Still holding the pen, Amanda slipped her hands into her blazer pockets and steeled herself against Haley's having already seen Mason with his new wife.

"Roger!" Haley said.

"Roger Miller?" Amanda wondered if the man was omnipresent. He seemed to pop up at all sorts of places lately—including the church Christmas party.

The secretary nodded. "I was coming out of that new clothing store in the shopping center," she pointed north, "and Roger was coming out of the shoe store next door. He had his umbrella. It was raining. He gave me a lift back to the office."

Amanda held Haley's gaze and didn't respond. She didn't know how to respond. She glanced away. That's when she noticed the long streak of grease on the leg of Haley's new suit.

"Haley," she gasped, "your suit!" She pointed to the dark line.

Leaning over, Haley eyed the stain. "How did that happen?" She touched it and rubbed her index finger and thumb together.

"Was Roger's truck as junky as always?" Amanda questioned.

"Well…" Haley didn't finish.

Amanda sighed and nearly gave up on trying to steer Haley from Roger. If she wanted to spend her whole life swathed in tractor grease and chicken feathers, then perhaps Amanda should let her. But a stubborn voice in the back of her mind hinted that Amanda should make light of this encounter with Roger and continue to search for a replacement.

"Roger said he was at the church Christmas party," Haley continued and gave no more attention to the grease. She tilted her head and awaited Amanda's response.

"Yes, he was." Amanda nodded.

"Why didn't you tell me?" Haley pressed, a wrinkle forming between her brows.

"To be perfectly honest," Amanda said and lifted her hand, "it never crossed my mind. That was at the same time we had the problem with M—" She stopped and squeezed the pen.

Haley looked down.

"I was so upset over all that trouble, I honestly didn't think to mention Roger." She stepped forward and gripped Haley's hand to underscore her honesty.

"I understand," Haley said and smiled.

Amanda sensed this would be the perfect opportunity to share Betty's news. Still, she cringed and nearly backed away from telling all. Finally Amanda reminded herself that if she didn't tell Haley someone else would. Or even worse, Haley would *see* Mason with his new wife.

She cleared her throat. "Since we're on the subject," Amanda began, "I've got some really…disturbing news about Mason."

"Oh?"

"Yes. He seems to have gotten himself a—" Amanda tucked her hair behind her ear and focused on the collage of pictures lining the wall. Squaring her shoulders, she swung her attention back to Haley and blurted, "He's married."

"Married?" Haley gasped as her fingers flexed against Amanda's. "So quickly?"

"Yes. Betty just told me."

Haley held Amanda's gaze and shook her head back and forth. Then she released Amanda's hand, moved to the sofa, and sat down. Haley stared straight ahead and hugged herself. The patter of rain on the picture window accompanied her gentle rocking.

"He's really a fast mover, isn't he?" she finally mumbled.

"*Very* fast," Amanda agreed. *Especially if his credit card bills are due.* She stepped to Haley's side and patted her back. "Are you okay, sister?" she asked.

Haley jerked her focus to Amanda. "You've never called me 'sister' like that before," she said.

"I guess I haven't. Really, I didn't even realize I did then. It just came out," Amanda said and was relieved to see the spark in Haley's eyes. For two weeks after Christmas, there was a dull veil where life once reigned in a soul gentle yet passionate.

Rising, Haley wrapped her arms around Amanda for a tight hug. Amanda rested her head on Haley's and hugged back.

"I don't think Mason and I were ever meant to be," Haley mumbled.

"I'm so glad you feel that way." Amanda inched away and laid her hands on Haley's shoulders.

"I do. I really do." Haley nodded and smiled, although her eyes were misty.

"Will you just promise me one thing, Haley?" Amanda said and decided the time had come to get really honest with her friend.

"I'll try." Haley blotted the corner of her eye.

"Promise me you won't decide on Roger just because you think he's all you can get."

Haley's silent question hung between them.

"If you love him and really don't mind breathing bird feathers and the fumes of cattle," she wrinkled her nose, "then fine. But if you just care for him because you believe he cares for you," Amanda shrugged, "that's not love."

Her eyes churning, Haley hugged herself again and stared toward the opened window. Only the computer fan's soft hum filled the contemplative silence.

"So how do I know if what I feel is really love?" Haley asked and searched Amanda's face. "How will you know when *you* fall in love?"

Amanda pondered Franklyn and the growing attraction she felt for him. She'd lain awake for a week wondering if this was the beginning of love, but she had no answer. Franklyn was certainly a striking man. He would be a doctor in the near future, so his profession was solid. He also made Amanda laugh. And Angie had hinted several times that she thought her stepson would make a fine husband.

But is any of that love? Amanda questioned.

As Haley patiently waited, Amanda scrambled for an answer. Finally she shrugged and said, "I guess I'll just know."

"A lot of help *you* are!" Haley teased.

Twenty-One

Saturday night Amanda sat at the piano playing one of her father's favorite hymns, "The Love of God." Her Siamese, Cuddles, sat beside her on the bench and occasionally offered an off-tune howl. After a particularly long yowl, Harold Priebe, lounging in his recliner, laughed.

"I believe the cat thinks she's singing," he said.

"At least my music inspires someone," Amanda replied as she came to the hymn's final chords.

"You shortchange yourself, m'dear," Harold crooned. He closed his eyes, rested his head on the back of the recliner, and said, "Play it again." His lips tilted into a mild smile.

"Again?" Amanda asked. "That will be three times."

"Yes, again." Harold rested his hands on his round belly and settled in for the next rendition. "What time did you say that Franklyn was supposed to be here?" he asked.

"He didn't say an exact time—just after dinner," Amanda replied. Franklyn had called mid-afternoon and asked if he could come over this evening. Amanda had readily agreed. Upon arriving home, she told her father of the visit. His lack of response had left her a bit undone.

"If we aren't careful," Harold said and slid her a glance, "Franklyn will replace Nate. This is three times in two weeks that he's been by. And I don't even remember Nate showing up for Christmas—except at the family get-together."

Amanda laid her hands on the smooth piano keys and recalled that impersonal shopping card he'd given her for Christmas. He hadn't even bothered to buy her a present this year while she had at least presented him a non-red tie and matching shirt. "Nate has *dis*placed himself." She lifted her fingers from the keys and huffed. "You might as well know, Daddy," Amanda crossed her arms and picked at the sleeve of her T-shirt, "Nate told me there's a *woman*."

"Another woman?" Harold sat up. He swiveled to face his daughter, and his Bermuda shorts twisted near his knees.

"Well," Amanda hedged, "I wouldn't exactly put it *that* way. But yes, he says there is someone. I think Nate has quit us, Daddy." Amanda placed her fingers on the piano and pressed what she thought were the right keys to begin "The Love of God" only to discover she'd played a minor chord.

"Hmmm," Harold mused and stared across the room. "I need a cup of coffee to think on this."

"I'll get it." Amanda stood.

"Okay, if you insist, I'll let you."

"You're so spoiled," Amanda crooned and fondly touched her father's arm on the way by.

"Yes, and I love it," Harold replied. "Maybe it's best that Nate has quit us. I'd be terribly lonely without you here."

Amanda slowed her pace and didn't give in to the urge to ask her father if he meant what she thought he meant. Surely her dad didn't think there was anything but friendship between her and Nate. Amanda shook her head and walked toward the dining room. Perhaps her father's clarity of thinking was starting to decline.

But he really isn't that old, she argued.

Amanda paused near the sideboard where Sarah always kept an urn of decaf coffee for Harold's after-dinner indulgence. Near the urn sat a bowl of dark chocolates wrapped in golden foil. Amanda helped herself to one of the delicacies Franklyn had brought the last time he visited. He *said* they were for Amanda's father, but she believed they were as much for her as not. Soon, one silken chocolate led to another. After she consumed the third chocolate, Amanda busied herself pouring her father's coffee and wondered what Franklyn might bring her dad tonight.

Before she could deliver the fragrant brew to her father, the doorbell rang.

"I guess that's Franklyn," Harold grumbled. He scooted to the edge of the recliner and accepted his daughter's offering. "You might as well know, I don't like him nearly as much as Nate." Harold looked up through his bushy brows. "I guess if this whole man business is inevitable, I'd rather have Nate hauling you off than Franklyn."

"Oh," Amanda answered. She started to tell her father that there really was nothing between her and Nate when the doorbell chimed again. Deciding to save the conversation for later, she said, "Well, I guess I'll go get that." She pointed toward the front of the house and avoided looking at her father again.

"Yes, all doorbells were meant to be answered," Harold said, a smile coloring his voice. "Old ancient proverb, you know."

Amanda chuckled as her father hoisted himself from the chair. "Such wisdom, such wisdom," she chanted.

"Well, I try." Harold planted a kiss on her forehead. "G'night, dear. Give my regards to Franklyn. Maybe this time he'll be man enough to say the chocolates are for *you*."

Amanda followed her father to the stairs and stood at the base while he ascended to his room. His shoulders were as broad as they'd been in her childhood. Yet his graying hair and thickening midsection betrayed his senior status. So did the completely odd statements he was making about Nate.

Who knows what he's thinking, Amanda thought and imagined Nate's expression if he heard Harold's assumptions. In light of his mystery woman, he'd probably fall on the floor laughing.

When the doorbell rang for the fifth time, Amanda decided to think about how best to end her father's assumptions later. Franklyn was waiting.

Only after she opened the door and smiled into Franklyn's enchanting blue eyes did she realize Cuddles was at her feet. Her hiss and growl mingled with Amanda's cheerful, "Hello!"

Franklyn's attention shifted from Amanda to the feline. "Well, hello down there," he called with British glee. "You are so cute with all your hissing. Quite an attack cat, aren't you?" Franklyn mocked before stooping toward the feline.

"Don't!" Amanda yelled, but she wasn't swift enough. Cuddles lurched at Franklyn with all the focus of a tiger on a mission.

"Run!" Amanda commanded while groping for the feline. Ears flat, Cuddles slipped past her owner and hurled straight at Franklyn.

He jumped sideways and bellowed, "Olé!" before outwitting the cat and slithering into the villa.

Laughing, Amanda shut the door. Cuddles responded with a wail that was even less melodious than her singing.

"No, no, Cuddles," Amanda called through the closed door. "Bad, bad kitty! You stay outside and *think* about what you've done now!"

"Quite a beast you've got there, no?" Franklyn quipped and rubbed his hands against his fashionably faded jeans.

"I found her as a stray. She feels threatened by any of my male friends," Amanda said and slipped her hands in her walking shorts pockets.

"Really? I'd have never guessed."

She cut him a droll stare.

"Where has she been the other times I've visited?"

"Upstairs in my room," Amanda explained. "I forgot to lock her in there tonight."

Cuddles' mellow howling sounded like a sad, sorry soul who'd lost her mate.

"Poor thing," Franklyn said and moved to the window beside the door. "Why not go ahead and put her upstairs where she belongs? If I'm forced to listen to her very long, I say, I believe I would slit my wrists."

Amanda chuckled. "Okay, okay," she agreed.

"Besides, I've left something in the back of my car—or, Angie's car, rather. Can't believe I'd be so absentminded." He placed his fingertips together and tapped them against each other. "Of course, I have much on my mind these days." He stared into the distance, and a troubled mask cloaked his features. After several blinks, he shook his head.

"What was I saying? Oh yes." He lifted his finger. "I stopped by the market on my way here. Thought perhaps Sarah—that is your cook's name?"

She nodded and soaked in the lilt of his beautiful accent.

"Yes, I thought she might be glad to place some fresh flowers on the dining table. You and your father and she could all enjoy them."

"Of course we will," Amanda answered and wondered what her father would think of *this* excuse for another gift.

As she retrieved Cuddles from the doorway and maneuvered past Franklyn, Amanda was certain the man must be courting her. She nuzzled Cuddles' neck and enjoyed the smell of soft cat fur and the way it tickled her nose. By the time she'd climbed the stairs and reached her bedroom door, a giggle escaped Amanda. She'd never been in love before, and wondered if this bubbly, expectant feeling was the beginning of the real thing. If so, then she might be able to answer Haley's question soon.

With Cuddles secure in her bedroom, Amanda trotted back downstairs in time to hear Franklyn's timid knock. She opened the door and motioned for him to come in.

"There was no need to knock," she exclaimed. "You could have just stepped back in."

"Oh no, never." He shook his head as severely as if she'd asked him to rob a bank. "That would be the epitome of impoliteness." Without further comment, he thrust forward a large bouquet of mixed wildflowers. "Here you are. These reminded me of you, but I'm at a loss as to why."

"You're *so* poetic." Amanda fluttered her lashes then accepted the offering.

"Yes, I am, even if I do say so myself," Franklyn responded.

Amanda lifted the multicolored arrangement to her nose. "Mmmmm…fresh!" she enthused.

"Maybe that's why they call them 'fresh flowers.'" He drew invisible quotation marks in the air.

"You think?" Amanda replied in an exact replica of his voice.

"Now she's mocking me!" Franklyn cried before they both laughed.

"Come on back to the living room," Amanda invited and led the way. "Sarah's still in the kitchen," she said over her shoulder. "She's already made decaf coffee, but she can make anything else you like. What will it be?"

"Nothing for me," Franklyn said. "I'm not here for a long visit anyway. Just for a wee chat, that's it."

"Well, okay," Amanda said and tucked her hair behind her ear in an attempt to mask some of her disappointment. She'd hoped Franklyn had planned to stay a couple of hours, as he'd done on his previous visits. But a "wee chat" was better than nothing for a woman who might be on the brink of love.

Sarah received the flowers with all the appropriate oohs and aahs and promised Amanda she'd have them in a vase in no time. At last Amanda faced Franklyn in the living room. He'd chosen her father's recliner. She perched on the edge of the couch.

Franklyn rested his elbows on his knees, tapped his fingertips together, and stared at the floor. All his smiles and jesting were no more. Even his blond curls, once appearing carefree, now took on a serious swirl—that is, if curls *could* be serious.

"I'm about to go back home," he said. "My aunt is terribly ill."

"I'm sorry." Amanda leaned forward. "Angie's mentioned her sickness a few times, but I had no idea it was serious." She didn't add that her governess had hinted that she thought her husband's sister was a hypochondriac.

"Well, it seems to come and go, you know. The doctors can't seem to find out what's wrong, if you want the truth." He stopped tapping his fingertips and looked up at Amanda. "I think my stepmother believes she's a hypochondriac."

"Really?" Amanda said and didn't blink.

"Absolutely." He nodded. "But I just can't believe that." He scratched at his neck and stared out the window behind Amanda. "So I'll be gone for a while, but I do have plans to come back as soon as I can. I've enjoyed being with my father."

"And he's enjoyed you," Amanda affirmed.

"There was one other item I needed to discuss with you, Amanda dear," he said and searched her eyes.

Amanda was too distracted over his calling her "dear" to read his expression.

"You see…" Franklyn stood and paced the room. "You've been such a good friend," he said and stopped near the faux fireplace. Franklyn worked his mouth, picked up a brass fish, set it down, and picked the thing back up.

Amanda's pulse began to thud as she imagined any number of things Franklyn might be working toward. In a panicked dither, she wondered if he was about to act like Mason and propose.

Please, not so soon! she thought and stood. While she was very much attracted to Franklyn, she was by no means ready to deal with a proposal. One per season was plenty for any woman. The least Franklyn could do was have the decency to wait until fall.

The doorbell's unexpected ring sliced through Amanda's anxiety, and her stiffened spine relaxed. "Who could that be?" she questioned.

"Ah, more guests." Franklyn raised his hands and looked heavenward. "Maybe this is Your way of saving me from myself," he said toward the ceiling.

When the doorbell rang a second time, Amanda realized she was staring at Franklyn.

"Aren't you going to get that?" he asked.

"Uh, sure," Amanda said and strode toward the hallway. Thinking the night couldn't get any odder, she opened the door to discover Nate Knighton standing in the twilight.

"Hello, 'Manda," he said with a hesitant grin.

Twenty-Two

While Nate had expected Amanda to be somewhat surprised by his visit, he hadn't anticipated her shock. She stood in the doorway staring at him like he was a talking kangaroo.

Once he realized she wasn't even close to inviting him in, Nate decided to take the initiative. "Mind if I come in?" he questioned.

"N–no." Amanda shook her head, opened the door wider, and stepped aside. "Not in the least."

"I saw Angie's car in the driveway," he said. "I guess she's here?" Nate asked as Franklyn stepped into the entryway.

"Hello," Franklyn said.

"Oh, it's you!" Nate replied. As his eyes adjusted from the shadows to the chandelier brightness, his designs for the evening spiraled to a crashing death. Simultaneously, Nate wished the floor would open and swallow him alive. He felt like a youth arriving to pick up his date, only to find she was leaving with someone else.

"So good to see you." Franklyn stepped forward, vigorously shook Nate's hand, and smiled a warm welcome. By the time Franklyn stopped the hand-pumping, Nate realized the young doctor possessed no clue that he was viewed as a rival.

In the middle of Franklyn's friendliness, Nate noted he was just as tall and blond and broad-shouldered as ever. *Like I thought he would change,* he scorned.

Nate's mission had seemed unavoidable upon Betty Cates' departure this afternoon. After several hours of walking and thinking along the beach, Nate had decided the time had come for him to at least hint of his feelings to Amanda—especially if he saw any kind of admiration in her eyes.

But now, again, all he saw in Amanda were shades of Franklyn West.

So much for that *plan,* he thought.

"Looks like you already have company then." Nate shot a glance just past Amanda and prepared to facilitate a swift and humiliating exit.

"No." Franklyn raised his hands, palms outward. "I was just leaving, actually."

"You were?" Amanda questioned, her brows arching.

"Absolutely." Franklyn nodded. "I mainly wanted to tell you I'm going back to London. Now that that's done..." He rubbed his hands together. "I'll be off."

Franklyn gripped Nate's shoulder as if they were the best of friends. "Amanda says there's a pot full of decaf that needs to be drank. I'm no good at that. I'm sure you'll do a good job of it, though."

Nate's smile felt much less stiff than he would have imagined. He could have really liked Franklyn if he weren't the good-looking, charming, Amanda-focused sort. *No wonder Amanda is so taken with him,* Nate thought and had never felt so inadequate in his whole life.

By the time the door shut on Franklyn's departure, Nate was trying to remember what had possessed him to believe he should hint of his love to Amanda. Then he recalled Betty's babbling about how she was so glad he'd decided to clean out his closet and how she'd told Amanda all about the things falling out on her and how she'd assumed he must be turning into a slob and how she now took it all back.

At that point, Amanda's comment at Janet's party made perfect sense. With an accusatory edge to her voice, she'd told Nate she still had all his gifts. At the time, he'd grappled for her meaning. When Betty told him she'd informed Amanda about the closet contents, he then fully understood Amanda's innuendo. So Nate had wanted to explain the closet problem…and so much more.

An uncomfortable silence settled upon them, and Nate tried to smile.

"*Would* you like some decaf?" Amanda finally asked.

"Sure." Nate shrugged and decided to make the most of his visit. "Why not?" As he followed Amanda through the hallway that led to the living and dining rooms, Nate wondered if he'd been using all the wrong strategies in dealing with Amanda. He'd thought staying away from her might help him control his wild heart. When in reality, Nate was experiencing the opposite affect. The less he saw of Amanda, the more desperate his love.

He thought of the old clichés "Absence makes the heart grow fonder" and "Familiarity breeds contempt." When he stepped into the living room, Amanda turned for the dining room. She looked great, even if she was dressed in faded shorts and a casual T-shirt. Several weeks had lapsed since he'd seen her, and Nate couldn't look at her enough. He wondered if he should go back to the old pattern of seeing Amanda nearly every day. Even if familiarity did not breed contempt in this case, maybe it would at least help cool his fervent feelings.

Nate felt anything *but* cool. He tugged at the collar of his polo shirt and wondered why he'd asked for coffee. The last thing he needed was something to make him warmer.

He'd barely settled on the sofa's edge when Amanda arrived with the decaf. "Two sugars, no creamer," she said with a smile. "Just the way you like it—unless you've changed."

"Still the way I like it." Nate accepted the mug, took an obligatory sip of the hot, sweet liquid, and set it on the coffee table. "Did I hear Franklyn say he's going back to London?" he asked and tried not to sound as thrilled as he was.

"Yes." Amanda settled in the wing-backed chair near the sofa. "His aunt is sick—Wayne's sister. She's the one who raised him, so she's like his mom."

"Aah." Nate nodded.

"Angie thinks she's a hypochondriac and that she's trying to manipulate Franklyn to come back home." Amanda picked at the seam on the chair's arm. "But Franklyn believes she's really ill." She shrugged and glanced at Nate. The green eyes that had always been clear and candid now observed him through a veil of uncertainty...almost distrust.

Nate had never felt such a wall between them, and he struggled to breathe as well as to form something coherent to say. The whole idea that he should explain about the closet...about his love seemed beyond ridiculous at this point. Even if Amanda did know about the closet, she probably deduced he was just cleaning house or something. He must have imagined the accusation in her voice when she told him she still had all his Christmas presents. Nate grabbed the mug of coffee and downed a large swallow. The liquid scalded his throat and trickled into his stomach with a burn that made him wince.

"Yow, that's hot!" Nate complained.

"That's what you get for drinking it like a crazy person," Amanda sparred with a bit of the old spunk that used to characterize their relationship.

Nate lifted his brows and smiled. "Thanks for the sympathy," he retorted.

"Anytime," she said with a smile that nearly made him dizzy.

"Nate, m' boy!" Harold Priebe's voice boomed across the living room.

"Mr. Priebe." Nate nodded and stood. "Good to see you."

"Likewise! Likewise!" Harold rushed into the living room, his cup and saucer rattling with his every step. He plunked them onto the coffee table next to Nate's mug, reached across the table, and pulled Nate into a fatherly hug. After thoroughly slapping his back a few times, the older gentleman released him.

"I thought you were another fellow when you rang the doorbell. What's his name?"

"Franklyn," Amanda drawled.

"Oh yes, Franklyn. How could I have ever forgotten?" he said with a forced British accent and an extreme grimace.

"He was here," Amanda informed.

"What happened to him then?" Harold glanced around the room.

"He left already." Amanda pointed toward Nate. "When this guy showed up, Franklyn left."

"Ah! I see!" Harold nodded. "I guess I went upstairs with one man after my daughter, and I've come back down to another one!"

Nate nearly swallowed his tongue.

"Like I told Amanda, if I have to choose one of you for a son-in-law, my first choice is *you*. I don't know why she persists on wasting her time with—"

"Daddy!" Amanda laughed and stood. "*Please!*" She playfully slapped at his arm. "The last thing Nate and I need is to have you proposing for us. I'm sure Nate would come closer to marrying a sister than he would me—and I'd feel like I was married to my brother." She laughed again and looped her arm through her father's. "You're just too ridiculous for words."

Nate had no choice but to laugh with Amanda, but his heart wilted and wept.

"Well, maybe so," Harold acquiesced, "but you can't blame an old man for trying." He hit Nate's upper arm with the side of his fist. "The way things are going, the two of you have me worried. Franklyn's on the verge of camping here, and Amanda says you've got some other interest these days."

"*Daddy!*" This time Amanda was not smiling.

Nate slipped his hands into his slacks pockets and didn't know whether to laugh outright or run. Harold Priebe certainly could get to the point when he wanted to.

"You know I've never been one to beat around the bush, Amanda," Harold said, and Nate felt the older gentleman examining him again. "I just want you to know that if this other…attachment doesn't work out, you're always welcome here, m'boy."

Looking up, Nate struggled for a way out of the awkward moment—until he glimpsed Amanda's face. The poor woman looked like someone was choking her. He couldn't stop the laugh.

"See!" Amanda exclaimed. "He thinks it's as ridiculous as I do. Now, stop all this." She wagged her index finger from side to side.

"Well, you can't blame an old man for trying." Harold repeated. He picked up his coffee cup and turned for the dining room, all the while mumbling something about hardheaded redheads.

Amanda rolled her eyes, flopped into her chair, pulled the throw pillow onto her midsection, and said, "I'm sorry, Nate." She glanced over her shoulder toward her retreating father. "I'm beginning to think he's worried I'm going to marry Franklyn and move to London or something."

Well, are you? Nate thought, but wasn't sure he wanted an answer any more than Harold did.

"I can see why he might think that," Nate said and purposefully kept his voice light, "especially if Franklyn's been here quite a bit lately."

"He hasn't proposed by any means," Amanda replied and sat straighter in the chair. "We haven't known each other long enough."

"How long will he be in London. Do you know?"

Her focus on the coffee table, Amanda said, "I have no idea. He just told me he was going."

"Is he even planning on coming back, then?" Nate resumed his seat.

"Yes." She nodded. "He definitely said he'd be back. I just don't know when."

The closed curtains prohibited the fading evening light from penetrating the room. The soft lamplight bathed the room in a golden aura that did wonderful things to Amanda's hair. Nate wondered what she might do if he moved closer and kissed her pouty lips. On a whim, he toyed with the possibility that winning Amanda just might require such a drastic measure.

But what would I do if she slapped me silly? he thought, and a chuckle leaked out before he could stop it.

"What's so funny now?" Amanda asked and smoothed at her hair. "Do I have problems? Half the time Betty Cates has lipstick smeared by her nose." Amanda began rubbing at her nose.

"No, no." Nate shook his head. "Nothing like that."

"I promise," Amanda held up her hand, "yesterday, her cleaning smock was buttoned crooked. And at Janet's party, she still had a curler in her hair."

"I know. I see her all the time," Nate said and tried not to recall how captivating Amanda looked that night in her little black dress. He eyed the steam swirling off the coffee and was tempted toward another sip. His irritated throat protested the very idea. Nate decided to down another swallow anyway. This time it wasn't as hot.

After his third gulp, Nate heard himself say, "Do you think Franklyn would mind if I took his lady out to lunch Monday?"

"Who me?" Amanda asked while Nate wondered where that proposition had come from. It certainly hadn't been on his to-do list when he walked in.

"Who else? We haven't done lunch together in ages. I miss it." *That's an understatement,* he thought. "Don't you?"

"Maybe," Amanda admitted and crossed her legs. "I have to admit that nobody else harasses me quite like you." Her impish smile both charmed and invited.

If this was anybody but Amanda, Nate would assume she was flirting with him. But he knew better. Amanda had made her thoughts clear. She could never view him as a husband prospect. Nevertheless, Nate was so desperate at this point, he was willing to even take Franklyn's leftovers.

"So do I pick you up or do you want to meet somewhere?" he asked and didn't even bother to convince himself this wasn't a date. Whatever Amanda might or might not think, it was a date to Nate.

"Wait a minute!" She scooted to the edge of her seat and sat stiffly straight. "What about your…your…uh, your *friend?*"

Nate propped his elbows on his knees, gazed at the carpet, and laughed.

"What's so funny *now?* I promise, you've got the weirdest sense of humor on the planet."

"Thanks," Nate said and chuckled. "At least I've got something. Just let me worry about my friend, okay? She already knows we've been friends a long, long time." He didn't look up.

"I guess there won't be a problem then—especially if she understands there never could be anything, you know, romantic between us," Amanda said.

"Yeah," Nate replied and didn't even try to read her expression. He was too frustrated and couldn't remember a time when he'd ever been more so.

"Well, then, why don't we just meet at the new café by my office? It's called Arlene's. Have you seen it?"

"Yes. I've seen it." Nate didn't bother to tell Amanda he'd eaten there three days last week in hopes of bumping into her. Never had he felt like such a wretched beggar.

Twenty-Three

Three weeks later, Haley stared at the e-mail that had just popped into her inbox. She blinked and leaned forward to make certain her contacts weren't playing tricks on her. Sure enough, the name "Roger Miller" claimed the message line. Haley's pulse leaped. She hadn't heard from or seen Roger since the day he gave her a lift from the shopping center, despite the fact that she'd looked for him on nearly every corner. While she had been tempted to revisit the church the two of them attended together, Haley had refrained. She didn't want to give Roger the idea she was chasing him.

She also hadn't wanted to attend Amanda's church, given Mason's presence with his new wife. Amanda felt the same. So the two friends had avoided seeing Mason at all and had chosen another congregation with which to worship. The church was small and sweet and welcomed them with open arms. Nate Knighton had even attended with them last week. Amanda said she'd confidentially explained a few things to Angie West and that

Angie understood why they wouldn't be attending her Bible study class for a while.

Never taking her gaze from Roger's name, Haley moved her cordless mouse. The cursor jumped to the command and landed on his e-mail. Haley clicked the message and devoured the text.

> Hi, Haley! It was good to see you the other day. Do you shop during lunch often? I'll be picking up a pair of boots I ordered today. RJM

Haley stared at the e-mail a full 30 seconds and tried to determine some meaning. About the time she decided she'd gotten excited over nothing, she gasped.

"I get it," Haley whispered and checked her watch. Her lunch break wasn't for another two hours, but Roger was hinting that he'd like to see her again if she so chose. He was going to be at the shoe store where they bumped into each other. Haley drummed her fingers along the tidy desktop and debated how best to answer Roger.

The last few weeks had been a time of intense soul-searching. She'd taken Amanda's advice and tried to determine if what she felt for Roger was the beginning of true love or just a heavy dose of gratefulness because he had noticed her. Even though she often turned heads these days, Haley found herself looking back at the men—not because she was responding to *them* but because she was searching for Roger. Still, she wasn't certain if he was "the one."

After that chance meeting several weeks ago, Haley had been tempted to e-mail Roger. But she'd talked herself out of even thinking about writing him. The last thing she wanted was Roger thinking she was chasing him. When days spanned into weeks, Haley finally decided she wouldn't hear from Roger ever again.

She'd even come close to resigning herself to this fate as of last night. Then the message popped into her box.

I could just arrive at the shoe shop at noon, she thought and never considered not meeting him.

Then she imagined Roger sitting in front of his computer at the farm. He lived in a modest, one-bedroom house five acres away from his parents' homestead. The computer was in his tiny living room that also held a couch, a TV, and nothing else. Haley pictured him staring at the screen, awaiting her response. She placed her fingers on the keyboard and typed the first words that came to mind.

> Hello, Roger. Good to hear from you. I often shop
> for bargains during lunch. Nice to know you
> ordered new boots. Haley.

She snickered as she pressed the "send" button. If he could communicate in code, then so could she.

A wave of caution swelled from the aftermath of glee. Haley decided this was one meeting Amanda didn't need to know about. Amanda would not be happy—not in the least. Not adept at being sneaky, Haley squirmed with the realization that she'd have to think of a way to keep Amanda from wanting to go to lunch with her today.

Amanda had already mentioned that Nate Knighton was involved in a business meeting and wouldn't be joining her for lunch. That statement had been accompanied by a silent understanding that the two friends would enjoy their noon meal together. Haley's mind churned for a means to discourage Amanda from a girlfriend lunch session.

Finally the key word hurtled through her thoughts: *Bargains!* If Haley was determined to look for bargains, Amanda would find somewhere else to lunch. Amanda would rather eat Betty Cates' mop than be dragged from sales rack to sales rack.

"Perfect!" Haley whispered and balled her fists upon the base of the computer keyboard. This way she'd be free to meet Roger, and she wouldn't have to lie. She *would* go into the store and search the 75 percent-off rack for any new additions.

"If I find something, I'll buy it," Haley whispered at the screen and giggled. Being sneaky had never been so easy...or so thrilling.

☙ ❧

Amanda meandered to the travel agency's exit and idly wondered what she might do for lunch. She and Nate had shared lunch numerous times in the last few weeks, but today Nate had a major business luncheon he was set to attend.

She had asked Haley if she was free for lunch, but Haley was determined to shop for bargains today. That was the *last* thing Amanda wanted to do. While Haley seemed to have a good eye for spotting the racks with the best buys, Amanda could look a week and never find half the steals Haley could stumble upon in an hour.

So Amanda had decided to just lunch on her own today. She stopped by the coat rack and slipped on her light jacket. With March just around the corner, the promise of fall was nipping the air. Amanda was delighted. She was ready for cooler temperatures.

As she neared the glass doorway, Amanda wasn't as delighted to be dining alone. The last few weeks with Nate had been nearly like the good ol' days. They had shared many energized hours bantering away about who knew what. To an onlooker, they would have appeared as good of friends as always. But Amanda detected a new wall in their relationship...and a definite strain in Nate's features. She attributed it to his mystery woman and wondered if Nate would ever confide in her.

Oddly, Amanda hadn't seen him with the woman once. No one else had mentioned seeing them either. Furthermore, while Highland was a successful suburb of Hobart, it was far from the size of Brisbane—where Knighton's Department Stores head-quarters were located. Since Nate manned the satellite office in Highland, he was considered one of Tasmania's leading busi-nessmen and quite the man around town. The newspaper society pages loved it when they caught any local person of Nate's suc-cess in the throes of something new. A new home. A new busi-ness venture. A new girlfriend. She'd halfway expected to see Nate's photo in the *Highland Progress* with some wilting Asian on his arm. And if the snapshot weren't Janet French, she looked just like her in Amanda's mind.

Amanda's greater dread involved his arriving at lunch one day with his love interest in tow. And every time she considered the possibility, Amanda coached herself on how to behave in a civilized manner before she found an isolated place to cry. She was gradually accepting the fact that good old Nate would not be her good old Nate forever. But thoughts of having to meet the person who was taking him away still gave Amanda fits.

She sighed and pushed open the door. The afternoon sun belied the chilly wind blowing in from the ocean; the breeze tossed her hair in all directions at once. Amanda adjusted the "Open" sign to the "Gone to Lunch" setting, shoved the door closed, and inserted her key in the lock. The streets were charged with the hustle of commerce, the whiz of traffic, a stream of pedestrians targeting the intersection crossover.

Amanda recognized one pedestrian she'd seen often in the last few weeks. Mr. Samuel Adair and his wife lived across the street in the new, luxury apartment building. Amanda and Nate had met them at Arlene's one day when they'd all been waiting to be seated. But Amanda saw him around town now on his own as much as she did with his wife. As usual, Mr. Adair was confidently striding toward the intersection with his guide dog leading the way. The blind retiree's assured independence never ceased to amaze her.

She stepped toward him, touched his arm. "Hello, Mr. Adair," she said. "Good to see you out today."

"Amanda! Great to see you too," he replied. "Is Nate with us?" He lifted his chin, and Amanda imagined invisible sensor antennas feeling the space around them. Mr. Adair had a way of sensing as much or more than most sighted people.

"No, I'm on my own today. Have you already had lunch?" she hopefully questioned.

"Yes." Mr. Adair nodded and fidgeted under his overcoat sleeve. When he pressed the button on his watch, a mechanical voice stated, "Twelve-fifteen."

"I'd offer to go with you, but I've got an appointment in 15 minutes. An old client," he added. "I can't seem to hide from them, even in Tasmania. They still come by and ask for legal advice. Sometimes they just won't let you quit."

"Well, when you're good, you're good. That's all there is to it," Amanda said.

"I wouldn't go *that* far," Mr. Adair said with a modest grin.

Amanda joined his humor and was stricken once again with how much Mr. Adair reminded her of Nate—or what he might look like in 30 years. The former lawyer was tall, aristocratic, self-sufficient, and sure of who he was.

His guide dog, Goldie, restlessly shifted. "I won't keep you," Mr. Adair said. "I'm sure you're hungry, and Goldie is ready to go. The traffic makes her a little nervous these days." He reached down and laid his hand on his dog's head. "Good girl," he mumbled. "We're almost home."

"Okay. G'day, then. It's been nice to see you."

"And you." Mr. Adair moved along the sidewalk.

Amanda brushed the hair out of her eyes and turned back to the task of locking the door. The faint whiff of home cooking invited her to enjoy Arlene's café once again. She and Nate were now regulars there. Amanda only hoped his "business lunch" didn't also involve the mystery woman and Arlene's.

"Amanda!" a vaguely familiar male voice cut through the traffic's hum and Amanda's thoughts.

She pulled her key out of the lock and looked toward a man scurrying past a mother with a baby stroller.

Mason Eldridge! she thought and was tempted to run. Her next thought was for Haley, and Amanda was immediately thankful her friend had already left. They had purposefully avoided the very sight of Mason by avoiding his church. Amanda had hoped to never see him again. She'd finally stopped reliving that awful proposal episode and was thankful Haley hadn't mentioned him in two weeks. The last thing either of them needed was Mason barging into their lives.

"Hello!" Amanda said and noticed a tall brunette hustling behind him. When they stopped three feet away, Amanda realized they were holding hands.

"I'm so glad I caught you," Mason huffed. "I wanted to introduce you to my new wife, Sonja."

Amanda's smile had never felt more fake. "Hello." She smoothed her hair. "It's so good to meet you," she said and prayed that God understood the feigned pleasantries of a panicked soul.

"And you as well." Sonja extended her hand and Amanda politely shook it. But that was not enough for the over-made bride. She enveloped Amanda's hand in both of hers and squeezed. Amanda glanced down to see enough diamonds to start a jewelry store. Immediately, she wondered if that had been the purpose of the whole handshake.

Once her hand was her own again, Amanda decided Sonja needed the opposite kind of makeover that Haley received. She was wearing enough makeup for *two* women, and her dark hair was teased into a frenzied do that made 1950 pageant hair seem small. At closer vantage, Amanda deduced that the dark hair color probably wasn't Sonja's own. It belonged to some bottle labeled "Boom Boom Brunette" or something equally obnoxious. Furthermore, the feather of lines around her eyes testified to at least ten years longer on earth than Mason had endured. And while she wasn't as tall as Amanda, she *was* significantly taller than Mason, especially after you calculated the foot of hair reaching to the sky. He'd told Amanda he liked his women bigger than dreams. Amanda would never doubt his claim.

"Mason has told me so much about you!" Sonja oozed, her blue eyes too bright to be of natural hue and too cold to be sincere. Amanda deduced Sonja was also wearing colored contacts and wondered if there was anything about the woman that wasn't enhanced or teased or plastered.

It's a good thing she's got money, Amanda thought and eyed Sonja's sculptured fingernails, which were long and red and square. They were every bit as bold as her musky perfume. *Her grooming bills alone probably cost a fortune. She's like an oversized poodle!* Amanda nearly acted like Nate and laughed, but somehow she managed to keep the humor harnessed.

"We were just dropping by for a chat." Mason smiled up at his bride.

"Oh!" Amanda jiggled her keys and wondered what possessed Mason to pay such a visit. "Well, I was…just going to lunch." Her brain whirled with a barrage of options. In a swift decision, she decided that inviting the pair to lunch would be the safest option. That way she could politely leave at the end of the meal and remain in control of her own destiny. If they entered the travel agency, they'd be free to leave when they so chose…or *didn't* choose.

"Why don't you join me?" Amanda offered and pointed toward Arlene's café.

"We already ate, actually," Mason explained.

"Maybe you could enjoy some coffee while I eat?" Amanda offered as her stomach grumbled in response to the aroma from Arlene's.

A horn's angry blast accompanied the screeching of tires and Amanda twisted toward the noise. Mr. Adair stood in the middle of the intersection, his head high, his face cloaked in confusion. Goldie pulled him toward the traffic, but the man refused to budge.

"My word, he's blind," Mason said.

Twenty-Four

"It's Samuel Adair!" Amanda said and scanned both corners. While pedestrians ambled too and fro, no one seemed interested enough to stop their activities in preference for saving a life. As another car swerved around her new friend, Amanda lurched forward and smacked into a business woman who'd just bypassed Mason and Sonja.

"Excuse me," Amanda mumbled into the woman's glare. Meanwhile, her keys and purse clanked to the sidewalk. Half of her wanted to retrieve the lost possessions while the other half insisted she ignore them in preference for Mr. Adair.

"Get my keys and purse!" she hollered at Mason. Glad she was wearing loafers and slacks, Amanda dashed toward the intersection. A glance over her shoulder assured her Mason had responded to her plea.

By the time Amanda reached the curb, the pedestrian light had changed to green. She raced into the walkway and slowed as she neared Samuel.

"Looks like you're having a time of it," she called.

"Amanda," he said, his shoulders sagging. "I was praying you'd come."

"Let's get you across the road, shall we?"

"Please," he said.

Amanda took Mr. Adair's arm and guided him to the other side of the street.

Once they made the curb, he patted Amanda's hand and said, "I'm afraid Goldie's getting too old for this." They strolled toward the Brown Street Apartments, and the traffic droned forward. "She's been with me 15 years. I keep hoping she's just going through a phase." His clouded eyes jerked in their sockets, and the wind-blown trees cast dappled shadows upon his lined face. "But—"

"You could have gotten killed back there," Amanda interjected and, for the first time, noticed the aging dog was graying around her mouth and eyes.

"So I suspected." Samuel smiled and sighed.

Goldie woofed and increased her pace.

"I think we're good from here," Mr. Adair said. "She's back to her old self."

"You're sure?"

"Yes." He smiled toward her voice. "Heel, Goldie," he commanded and paused. "You've been a lifesaver, Amanda."

"Just helping a friend, that's all," Amanda said and patted his arm. "We all have to stick together, ya know."

"There's something I've wanted to ask you," Mr. Adair began with a respectful air. "Do you mind?"

"No, not in the least."

"Are you by chance American?"

"No." She laughed. "I've just spent a lot of time there."

He nodded. "I can hear it in your voice. A lovely voice. And you aren't married?"

"No." She chuckled through the admission.

"Engaged?"

"No." Amanda's smile broadened.

"I've decided you're about 30. Am I correct?"

"Twenty-five." She crossed her arms and scrutinized the perceptive man.

"If you weren't so young, I'd marry you myself."

Amanda laughed and chalked this up to yet another proposal—or near proposal—for this season.

"Except I'm not so sure my wife would be happy with me," he replied and stroked the corner of his mouth. "She doesn't like me bringing home wives."

"I can't imagine why," Amanda parried.

"Beats me." His winning smile reminded her of Nate all over again. *And that other woman will be the one who'll enjoy him,* Amanda thought.

"Well, you've been a lifesaver. *Literally.*" He reached for her arm, gave her a pat, and said, "We need a million 25-year-olds just like you."

Basking in his compliment, Amanda said, "Good luck with Goldie." She eyed the dog. No one could ever deny her loyalty to her master.

He sighed and bent to touch Goldie's ears. "Thanks. Sometimes it's just hard to let go." The dog whined and licked his hand.

"Why can't you keep her as a pet and just get another guide dog?" Amanda asked.

"Apartment rules." He shook his head. "As you know, we just moved in a month ago. They'll only allow one dog—and that's only because I'm blind. No one else is even allowed that."

"So what will happen to her?" Amanda's concern kicked in.

"I'll have to find her a home." He coughed, pressed at his eyes, and lowered his head. "I've kept you long enough," he finally said. "You're young. You don't need to be tangled up in my problems." With a tight smile, Mr. Adair nudged the dog's harness and began to stride forward.

"But what about one of your former clients?" Amanda suggested and hurried to catch up with him.

"I'm trying." Mr. Adair laid his hand on her shoulder. "Believe me, I'm trying. But it's hard to find a place for a grown dog, especially an older one. I was hoping for someone close so I could go see her. But we're new in the area, so…"

Amanda pressed her lips together. "Let me see what I can do, okay?"

"You'd do that?" Mr. Adair asked.

"Of course."

"But you just met me."

"So." Amanda shrugged. "A friend is a friend."

Mr. Adair lifted his chin like a sailor assessing the ocean. A distant horn blasted. The smell of exhaust accompanied the surge of traffic. Oak leaves danced to the tune of the coastal breeze.

Finally Mr. Adair said, "Like I said, we need a million more just like you." He smiled. "Let me know what you come up with, okay?"

"Absolutely," Amanda agreed.

"Well, my client will be here soon," he said and nodded toward her. "G'day, then."

"G'day." Amanda watched until he entered the building, and the whole time she brainstormed for someone who would be willing to take Goldie. The very thought of the animal being separated from her owner when she'd served him her whole life made Amanda want to weep.

She turned back toward the street corner and wished for a piece of the gum she'd placed in her purse this morning. As a child, she'd been convinced that chewing gum would help her think. Amanda wasn't so certain the assumption was false. She reached for her purse, only to realize she wasn't carrying it. That's when she remembered she'd left her bag and keys with Mason Eldridge and the Queen of Plaster of Paris.

She stopped at the pedestrian crossing and scanned the sidewalk across the street. While the lunch rush was dwindling, there was no sign of Mason and his new wife.

Twenty-Five

Amanda paused outside the travel agency and looked up one side of the street and down the other. No sign of Mason and Sonja. On a whim, she tried the agency door. It opened with ease.

Frowning, she stepped inside. Apparently, Mason had used the keys to let himself and his bride into her business. *It's almost like breaking and entering*, she thought.

"And this is Amanda's office," Mason's muffled voice floated down the hallway.

Her scowl deepening, Amanda strode toward Mason's voice. All the while, she was deducing what Mason was up to. *Sounds like he's giving Sonja the grand tour*, she fumed and couldn't remember a time when Mason had ever been in the agency himself.

Telling herself to keep a cool head, Amanda stepped into her office to find Mason and Sonja examining it like two clients at a museum. For the first time she noticed they were dressed much alike. Each wore a stylish, navy suit—like a designer's answer for his and hers. While Sonja sported a fuchsia silk scarf around her neck, Mason wore a fuchsia tie. The suits screamed of big money, and Amanda figured Mason didn't have to use his credit card to buy them. A fleeting intuition suggested that Sonja had purchased herself a male doll whom she planned to spend the rest of her life dressing up.

Meanwhile, the rich lady and her doll were invading Amanda's privacy and neither seemed aware of the violation. Amanda crossed her arms and squeezed while clearing her throat.

"There you are! I was just showing Sonja around," he explained as if he owned the place. "Here are your purse and keys."

"You have a wonderfully quaint little place," Sonja crooned as if Wood-Priebe International was anything but a nationally acclaimed corporation.

"Thanks." Amanda gritted her teeth and accepted the purse and keys. Her nose prickled against Sonja's perfume and she sneezed. "Excuse me," she squeaked and dropped the keys in the top of her purse.

"No prob, dear." Sonja laid her hand on Amanda's arm. "This terrible wind would give anybody a chill. That's the reason Mason and I decided to come inside. I was afraid the wind would make me sick. I have problems with my sinuses, you know." She touched the side of her nose, and Amanda wondered if it was fake too.

Amanda pulled a stick of gum from her purse's side pocket, unwrapped it, and placed it in her mouth. She focused on the explosion of peppermint and not upon the potential explosion bubbling within. The longer she stood here with these two invaders, the warmer her temperature grew. Instead of giving into the fury, she chomped her gum and prayed for guidance.

An immediate idea pierced her irritation. "Would you like to see my saltwater aquarium?" she asked and hoped the invitation would lead to a swift exit from her office.

"You have a saltwater aquarium?" Sonja enthused and moved into the hallway. Mason followed.

"Yes." Amanda set her purse on the love seat, shut her office door, and strolled forward. "It's in the lobby off the entryway," she said, her words stiff. "You'll have to excuse our mess in there, though. We're getting ready for the corporate party in a month, and we've got boxes of decorations stacking up. We're going to start sorting through them in an hour or so," she casually claimed and hoped the newlyweds would take the hint and leave soon. The last thing Amanda wanted was for Haley to arrive from lunch and have to face Mason's new wife.

"Nate Knighton told me all about you, but he never mentioned the aquarium or this big fall party. Sounds like fun!" Sonja said.

"You know Nate?" Amanda slipped off her fur-trimmed jacket.

"Excuse me a minute," Mason said as they grew even with the restrooms. "I'm going to step into the men's room."

"Of *course* I know Nate!" Sonja ignored Mason and gestured as if Amanda were daft to even ask such a question. "I met him at church and have known him for weeks."

I wonder why he hasn't mentioned you? Amanda thought and pushed up the sleeves of her short-waisted sweater.

When Sonja and Amanda rounded the corner toward the corporate entertainment room, she grabbed Amanda's arm and stopped. "And isn't he the most scrumptious piece of manhood you've ever seen?" she whispered.

Amanda's eyes widened, and she wondered how any new bride could say such and still be dedicated to her husband. Furthermore, thinking of Nate Knighton in terms of a "scrumptious piece of manhood" was as foreign to Amanda as imagining him wearing a skirt and pantyhose.

"W–w–well," she stammered and didn't exactly know how to respond to such blatant yearning in the eyes of a new bride. *At least she's not being fake now*, Amanda thought. *She really thinks Nate is something!*

So do a lot of other women! The thought stomped across Amanda's mind, and she recalled all the envious female glances she received lately every time she and Nate shared lunch. Interestingly enough, Amanda hadn't noticed those gawking women before the last few weeks. And she had to admit that Nate *had* gotten better looking with age. The last three months had been especially good to him.

"If I weren't already married…" Sonja mused and gazed across the room. Amanda expected drool to drip from the corners of her mouth. Furthermore, she wondered if a mere marriage ceremony would stop Sonja from pursuing Nate or any other man for that matter.

For the first time, Amanda felt truly sorry for Mason. Even as quirky as he was, she detested the thought of anyone being miserable for life. Once Mason woke up and realized he'd been bought, she couldn't imagine him being anything *but* miserable.

The door to the men's room squeaked open, then closed, and Mason bounded around the corner. He removed a large diamond ring from his left hand and ran his index finger inside the ring.

"I can't stand water under my wedding band," he explained and slipped the ring back on. The oversized stone twinkled with the life of ten diamonds, and Amanda sensed the whole act was staged for her benefit.

She held Mason's gaze for a few seconds and read a wealth of gloating therein. Her momentary pity for the man vanished.

Mason seemed perfectly thrilled to have been bought and just as delighted to flaunt his new wealth at Amanda.

She hung her jacket on the coat tree, stepped toward the aquarium, and wondered if Mason really believed she cared.

॰ ॰

Haley clutched the shopping bag that contained her bargain of the day—a peach-colored cotton blouse she would put up until next summer. She'd been so distracted over the prospect of seeing Roger, she'd forgone lunch and trudged straight to Delightful. After spending 30 minutes in the store, browsing near the window as a cover for watching for Roger, Haley had decided to mosey toward the shoe store.

However, a detailed perusal through the store's windowed front revealed no sign of Roger. Haley had examined the store just as intensely before she entered Delightful. The results were the same. No Roger.

Her stomach churned in an odd combination of hunger and nausea, and Haley knew her jittery nerves were to blame. She tugged her knee-length sweater jacket closer, but enjoyed the cool wind, despite its biting at her nose and fingers. Haley had worked up a sweat in Delightful, but all the anticipation was for nothing. Roger simply was not here.

She checked her watch and noted what she already suspected. Haley needed to be back at work in ten minutes. *I must have misunderstood that e-mail,* she thought. Her shoulders sagged as she recalled her response. Haley was so thankful she hadn't revealed her faulty interpretation of Roger's e-mail...or her expectation over what she thought was his invitation.

She strolled away from the shoe store and headed across the parking lot toward the busy street's corner. Haley would go back to her office and eat some of the fruit and snacks she and Amanda kept in the kitchen. Then she'd get back to the usual. Amanda had her organizing the corporate party next month. This week the final RSVPs from Wood-Priebe upper management were trickling in. Next week Haley would be able to give a head count to the caterer. She'd already hired a jazz band to provide live entertainment. This afternoon or tomorrow, Haley would begin assessing what decorations they had and what they'd need for the jazz theme.

Amanda went with a different theme every year. By popular demand, her choices usually reflected an American flair. Last year, the whole group had raved over the western theme and had swooned over the life-sized poster of John Wayne. How Amanda sniffed out some of her decor was as much of an enigma to Haley as Haley's bargain abilities were to Amanda.

By the time Haley reached the street corner, she was purposefully allowing the party preparations to engross her. Anything was better than pondering the awful letdown over not seeing Roger. A blaring horn's irritating interruption heightened her exasperation. The sun's glare added to the mix with annoying persistence.

The pedestrian light turned green, and Haley trudged forward. The horn grew louder until she finally realized she was walking in front of the very vehicle causing the disturbance.

How rude! Haley thought and glowered toward the vehicle, only to recognize a very familiar farm truck. And Roger Miller was behind the wheel waving madly.

"Roger!" Haley exclaimed. She turned to the truck and gaped at him.

He gestured for her to join him, and Haley didn't need him to ask twice. As she hurried to the passenger side, she noticed every driver was focused on the drama. By the time Haley reached the truck, Roger had leaned over and opened the door.

"Hurry!" he encouraged as the vehicle beside them purred forward.

A horn's blare behind Roger testified to a line of drivers who were ready to move along. Haley climbed onto the seat and noticed the clutter free cab smelled like window cleaner. She snapped the door shut and clicked on her seat belt.

"Sorry about all the horn blowing," Roger said and pressed the accelerator. "My window's stuck over here. The thing hasn't budged in months."

Haley laughed. "Lifestyles of the rich and famous?" she said.

"Really," Roger agreed as the truck picked up speed. "Sorry I was so late too," he said and glanced at her again.

Haley curled her toes.

"We had an emergency at the farm. One of our fences went down, and we had more cattle outside the fence than in it. Not good." He leveled a swift grin at her that reminded Haley of their first date. Roger had taken her to his farm. They'd sat in a field with his parents, watched the stars, and enjoyed his telescope.

This rapid turn of events had her so disconcerted she couldn't think of a thing to do but stare at her purse and the shopping bag claiming her lap. A new rush of nervous nausea erased all traces of hunger.

"What do you say to lunch?" Roger asked.

Haley's eyes rounded. She swallowed against the swell in the back of her throat, said, "Sure," and couldn't fathom a way to sound more enthused. She dashed him a hesitant grin, only to discover a flutter of confusion rippling across his features.

"I guess I'm just a little…" She couldn't exactly tell him she was so excited about seeing him again that she'd worked herself into a nauseated flurry. "My appetite's not the best right now, I guess."

"Mine either," Roger rubbed his palm along his jeans and wowed her with another grin. Haley was reminded why she always thought his smile was his most endearing feature. "But anyway," he shrugged, "maybe there's a waiter somewhere who wouldn't mind letting us look at a steak for a while."

"Okay," Haley said and underscored her acceptance with another shy smile.

Twenty-Six

❧ ❧

Amanda had done everything but the tango trying to get Sonja and Mason to leave. But they'd lingered over two hours chatting about anything and everything and nothing at all. With her stomach growling, Amanda had the full recounting of all Sonja's father's international investments, a complete list of the public greats their family had met or known, and all the reasons Sonja was just better than Amanda or any other woman in Mason's past.

They'd never moved beyond the aquarium, and Mason stayed in clear view of the outside door. Every time the door was opened—by the postman, a salesman, and the newspaper boy— Mason turned toward the sound as if he were specifically awaiting the arrival of someone.

While Amanda suspected Mason was interested in encountering her secretary, she hated to foist even that low of a motive upon Mason. His spiteful need to show Amanda he had married a woman wealthier than she was understandable. Despicable, but understandable. After all, Amanda had hurt his pride when she rejected him. But Haley had done nothing but make the mistake of believing Mason was attracted to her.

She's already been the victim of a misunderstanding, Amanda reasoned and found no logical explanation for Mason wanting to further hurt her. Therefore, Amanda gave Mason the benefit of the doubt.

Then he looked at his new gold watch and said, "I was hoping to introduce Sonja to Haley. Is she not here today?"

All doubts on Mason's behalf disappeared. Amanda crossed her arms and gazed past him to the gurgling tank. The lion fish was particularly feisty today. As her ire increased another notch, Amanda wondered if she might have a bit of the lion fish in her. Her empty stomach rumbled.

"She's here," Amanda explained and glanced at her watch again. It was now two-fifteen. "She left for lunch right before you arrived. We usually only take an hour for lunch. Haley's *never* been this late!" Even though she'd realized in the back of her mind that Haley was late, she'd been too focused on how to calmly deal with Sonja's boasting to register alarm over her secretary's absence. "I hope nothing bad has happened!" she exclaimed and hurried toward the expansive window. She shoved aside the brocade drapes and examined the street as far as she could see.

Although she detected no sign of Haley, she did notice Samuel Adair across the street. He sat on a bench near the apartment building with Goldie at his knees. His chin lifted, Samuel seemed to be sightlessly watching the city with his highly tuned senses while lovingly stroking his dog's ears. Her heart bulging with fresh concern, Amanda made a quick, mental commitment not to forget Goldie's need for a home.

But first, I've got to find Haley, she thought. Amanda dropped the drapes and turned toward Mason and Sonja.

"I'm really worried about Haley now," she said. "I hate to be rude, but I'm going to see if I can find her. She mentioned going shopping. I'm just hoping she hasn't been involved in some kind of an accident."

"Well…" Mason hedged and silently questioned his wife.

Fearing the pair might entrench themselves until she returned, Amanda decided to be more direct. She was on the verge of telling them they'd just have to leave when Sonja spoke up.

"I guess we'll plan to meet her later." She fussed with her "Boom Boom Brunette" hair while the diamonds delivered another well-aimed message.

Not if I can help it, Amanda thought and determined to never mention this visit to Haley. The less Haley heard of Mason from now on, the better.

"Mason has told me so much about all his friends, and we're just trying to meet them all before we move to Launceston permanently." Sonja's smile was as brittle as her thick mascara.

I'm sure you are, Amanda sarcastically thought and couldn't ever remember meeting anyone as brassy as Sonja Eldridge. Given Mason's gloating arrogance, Amanda decided the two deserved one another. Furthermore, Sonja's claims of their moving to Launceston only strengthened Amanda's resolve not to mention their visit to Haley. Once they left the area, Haley would never have to see them, and there was no reason for her to even know that they'd been here.

Finally Amanda stood in the wind again and watched Mr. and Mrs. Eldridge stride toward a new Jaguar parked across the street. Amanda couldn't conjure even a scrap of the earlier sympathy for Mason. And she was stricken with a deep realization that Nate Knighton had been right—all the way right—about the Reverend Mason Eldridge. He was *not* a highly respectable man of God. He was a wolf in sheep's clothing and nothing more.

☙ ❧

By the time Haley picked at her steak and salad and laughed at all of Roger's humor and fulfilled his request for the latest tidbits from her life, she realized it was after two o'clock. And that happened only when the waiter cleared their table and inquired about dessert.

She glanced toward the refrigerated tower near the register. Slices of pies and cakes and nut-topped brownies each beckoned her indulgence. The little bit of food she had consumed took the edge off her hunger and nervous nausea, and the prospect of dessert was definitely appealing. But the voice of wisdom suggested she check her watch. The shock of reality blotted out all caloric temptations.

"Is it really two twenty?" she breathed.

"I hope not. I was supposed to meet my banker at two fifteen," Roger said and glanced at his watch. His eyes bugged. "I've got to go!" he said and jumped to his feet.

The young waiter backed away from the table.

"Me too." Haley grabbed her teacup and downed a final sweet swallow while standing.

"I can't believe I let time get away from me like that. What was I thinking?" Roger glanced toward the waiter. "Sorry." He reached into his hip pocket, pulled out his billfold, removed some bills, and shoved 50 dollars at the steak-house employee. "Here. That should cover everything and your tip."

"Thanks!" the waiter exclaimed.

"Don't need a receipt!" Roger said and hustled toward the exit before Haley could even say goodbye.

She was so focused upon shrugging into her sweater jacket, retrieving her purse, and deciding how to face Amanda an hour late that Haley barely noticed his oversight.

Six feet into his journey, Roger stopped and hurried back to Haley. "So sorry!" he said and smiled his apology. "I just left you with it all, didn't I? You were walking," he stated and helped to adjust her sweater. "Let me give you a lift back to the travel agency before I go to the bank."

"No!" Haley shook her head and frowned.

Roger flinched and stepped back.

Without another thought, Haley reached for his hand and gripped it. "It's not because—it's just that—"

How could she explain her desire to keep this meeting from her boss, who also happened to be her dearest friend? While Haley loved and respected her friend, she was beginning to realize that Amanda's heart sometimes got in the way of her better judgment—at least in Haley's case. Amanda so desperately wanted Haley to be happy she'd talked her into declining Roger's proposal and falling for another man who never had a thought for her. While Haley understood Amanda's challenging her to test her love for Roger, she also recognized the determination in Amanda's eyes. Amanda was resolved to find another man for her secretary.

Haley *did* want to make certain she truly loved Roger, but she wanted to come to those conclusions in privacy and on her own. Therefore, she knew beyond doubt that this meeting and any future meetings must be kept from Amanda. But she possessed no idea how to communicate all that to Roger without sounding like she was hinting about another proposal or begging him to contact her again.

Roger's fingers tightened around hers. Haley silently begged him to understand while he searched her face. His brown eyes, as considerate as ever, also held threads of caution…and pain.

Haley's heart pounded. The nausea returned. And she suspected that what she felt for Roger Miller was far beyond the mere infatuation she'd experienced with Mason Eldridge.

"I just wanted this to be our secret," she finally breathed and lowered her gaze. She took in his angular shoulders, cloaked in the typical denim work shirt—except this work shirt was new. So were his jeans. And Haley knew he'd dressed in his finest, just for her.

"Roger!" A familiar male voice erupted upon their moment, and Haley stiffened as Nate Knighton appeared at their side.

As usual, he was dressed in a business suit, a white shirt, and one of the red ties she'd heard Amanda tease him about. He was also running with a small herd of similarly clad business professionals.

"So good to see you!" Nate exclaimed and gripped his cousin's shoulder. He cast a cursory glance toward Haley, and his eyes bugged. "Haley! I didn't realize that was you! How did I miss you?"

Haley grappled for something to say as her desire to keep the date with Roger "our secret" mingled with her chagrin over seeing Nate. He was the first person who'd tell Amanda and the last person who needed to know.

Why did I ever think I'd be able to get away with this? she fretted and wondered if this was some kind of divine justice for trying to be so sneaky. *Your sins will find you out.* The cliché she'd heard so many times now took on a haunting, new meaning as she recalled all the stories of married people being caught in secretive relationships. Although she wasn't married and there was nothing sinful about her relationship with Roger—unless being sly and late back from lunch could be counted sinful.

A knowing veil settled upon Nate's features and filled his dark eyes with a mischievous glint. "I didn't know you two were—"

"Nobody knows," Haley rushed and once again silently implored Roger to understand.

He rubbed the back of her hand with his thumb, and never had such a small gesture communicated so much insight. Haley's legs wobbled.

"Can we keep it that way, Nate?" Roger asked.

The very thought of dessert, no matter how sweet and delectable, now left Haley spinning in a fresh wave of nausea. The tingles spreading from Roger's thumb heightened the effect.

Nate's brows flexed as a new understanding mingled with the mischief. "Of course we can," he agreed with a sage nod.

"Good." Roger nodded too and shared a meaningful glance with Haley. "I hate for us to run like this," he continued and tugged Haley's hand, "but I've got an important meeting ten minutes ago, and I've still got to take Haley back to work."

"I can give her a ride," Nate offered.

"Would you?" Roger said, then turned to Haley. "Do you mind?"

"Not in the least." She shook her head. "But I can take a taxi."

"Absolutely not." Nate nodded toward Roger. "I'm glad to help. Just a minute," he said and waved toward the klatch of men and women hovering near the register. "Go on without me. I'll meet you at the office in 30 minutes."

They returned his goodbyes and disappeared into the lobby.

"There. It's all arranged," he said with an assuring smile.

"Great!" Roger said. He offered Haley another pulse-stopping grin and threw in a sassy wink.

She wiggled her fingers at him. As he hurried from the restaurant, Haley hoped he understood her weak smile had nothing to do with a lack of enthusiasm and everything to do with feeling light-headed.

"So you're getting sneaky these days?" Nate teased as he politely nudged Haley's elbow and the two walked toward the lobby.

"Maybe…I don't know…" she hedged. "It's just that—"

"Amanda's too nosy for her own good. That's what it is," Nate groused.

"I never said that," Haley defended.

"You're right. I did. And I mean it," Nate parried. "We all love her to pieces, don't we? But sometimes she means *too much* good."

Haley laughed. "I really don't know what to say."

"So say nothing." Nate paused by the baroque wooden door and opened it. He extended his hand for Haley to exit while delivering a smile every bit as cocky as Roger's was charming. "And I'll say nothing as well," he added.

"Thanks," Haley breathed and had never appreciated Nate Knighton more than now.

Twenty-Seven

The morning of the corporate party, Amanda knew beyond doubt that Haley Schmitz was hiding something—or someone. The clues were too clear and too frequent. Haley's being late from lunch last month had begun the whole scenario. After Amanda had combed the shopping center with no sign of Haley, she'd arrived back at the office to find her secretary placidly typing away at her computer.

She stopped long enough to show Amanda her new peach blouse and vaguely mentioned that time had gotten away from her, she'd seen Nate, and he gave her a ride back to work. Relieved that her friend was safe, Amanda hadn't bothered to further pry into Haley's lame explanation for being so late. Since Haley had an impeccable work record, Amanda decided to give her some grace.

But in the last month, Haley had strained that grace. She now arrived late from lunch about once a week. She'd even been late for work three mornings and complained of being up too late.

And five minutes ago, she'd just hung up from a phone call a little too quickly when Amanda entered the room and asked for a file. That was the fourth guilty hang-up in two weeks.

Amanda sat at her desk and tapped the front of the file with the silver-plated pen that bore her name. She'd been impressed with herself for keeping up with Nate's gift without losing it again. On top of that, she'd maintained a clutter-free desk for a whole month. This had to be some kind of record.

But now being impressed with herself was the furthest thing from Amanda's mind. Instead, she was worried senseless that Haley was in the mix again with Roger Miller. She possessed no definite evidence—only a strong intuition that Haley was trying to hide a Roger revival.

The phone's distant buzz announced another incoming call. Amanda eyed the blinking orange light and was tempted to silently pick up the receiver so she could determine if this call was from Roger as well. With her index finger hovering over the button and her other hand on the receiver, Amanda talked herself out of this eavesdropping session. At some point, she was going to have to learn to let Haley make her own mistakes, even though she wanted to help her as much as she was helping Samuel Adair.

Nate had offered to take Goldie. Samuel couldn't be happier. He was even coming to the Wood-Priebe International party tonight as Amanda's special guest. Even though this annual event was very much for the corporation, Amanda used it as a way to thank special people in her life and to get to know others a little better.

She dropped the pen and decided to leave the contents of the folder until later. She'd narrowed the applicants for the management position in the Brisbane branch down to three. It might take all three to replace Ken-the-working-machine. She'd planned to take a few minutes poring over the resumes once more because she'd invited all three to tonight's party. But the time had come to get to work on the party itself. Betty Cates would be here soon. She and Amanda would be putting the final touches to the décor. Thankfully, Janet French was getting her hair and nails done for the party tonight, so she wouldn't be here to help.

Amanda grimaced and wondered at her own lack of logic. The last thing she should be thankful for was Janet's making herself more beautiful for tonight. Amanda imagined Nate's focusing on Janet all evening and was tempted to gnaw the silver pen in half. Even though the man was regularly back in her life, the wall between them seemed to grow thicker by the day. Amanda was beginning to expect him to announce his engagement any time. Or worse, just elope without a word to her.

She stood, pushed aside the folder, and likewise shoved everything else out of her mind. Tonight's party must take precedence over all else.

The intercom's buzz interrupted Amanda's journey. She pressed the button and said, "Yes, Haley?" in as natural a tone as she could conjure. During the last week, Amanda found herself straining to keep all threads of suspicion from her voice and couldn't decide if she was convincing or not.

"Angie's on line one," Haley said. "I've just been chatting with her. She's wondering if there's anything last minute she can do for tonight."

"Wonderful," Amanda replied. "I've got a shopping list she can take care of."

"That's what I told her," Haley said and hesitated. "Or at least I told her that's what I thought you'd say."

"Thanks!" Amanda released the intercom, pressed the button for line one, and picked up the receiver. "Hello Ang," she said.

"Amanda," Angie replied, "I was just talking to Haley about how I could help, and she said you've got a shopping list."

"I do, and I'd kiss your feet if you'd be willing to take care of it." Amanda's mind whirled with the mental recollection of those who'd be arriving by seven. Since no one new had been added to the list, that meant the count was still at 85—the same as last night. "I'm beginning to feel the crunch."

"You know I'm thrilled to do whatever you need, dear," Angie crooned.

"I'm afraid it's not a very glamorous list—things like toilet tissue and a new vacuum cleaner bag."

"No problem at all. Would you e-mail it to me? I'll hit the shops and bring it early tonight."

"Great!" Amanda said. She picked up the list sitting under the brass piano posing as a paper weight.

"One other thing, Amanda," Angie continued. "I also wanted to call and ask a favor. Franklyn's back in town. But I guess he told you already."

"No, as a matter of fact he didn't!" Amanda exclaimed and stood. "I haven't heard a peep out of him since he left."

She'd been so busy the last few weeks, she'd hardly given Franklyn West a thought. In retrospect, Amanda realized he hadn't even so much as e-mailed her. All at once these facts seemed rather odd for a man who'd been on the brink of proposing weeks before and doubly odd for a woman who'd debated if she was falling in love.

"Well, I was wondering if you'd mind if he came to the party tonight with Wayne and me."

"Not at all," Amanda enthused and sat on the edge of her desk. *Eighty-six,* she thought and was thankful she'd told the caterer to prepare for 100. Yesterday morning only 78 had been scheduled to come.

"Bring him," Amanda encouraged. "I can always use somebody like him. He's full of life and funny. He'll be perfect."

"Great," Angie said and hesitated. "Did you say you haven't heard anything from him?"

"Not a word," Amanda admitted and realized she felt nothing in regard to his lack of communication. Nothing at all. She'd been too focused on planning the party and wondering when Nate would elope and what Haley was hiding and trying to help Mr. Adair find a home for Goldie that she'd hardly given Franklyn a thought.

"That's odd," Angie said. "I'd really hoped..."

"I don't think we're meant to be, Angie," Amanda said and understood that all she'd felt for Franklyn was the natural reaction of a young female to an attractive bachelor and nothing more.

"Well, I guess we'll just have to wait and see," Angie replied with a resolve that wasn't foreign to Amanda. She'd felt everything Angie was implying when she was certain Mason was the one for Haley. Amanda covered her face with her hand and nearly groaned. Mason was the *last* person she wanted to think about today.

"Amanda? Are you still there?" Angie prompted.

"Yes." Amanda stood and tapped her fingertip along the side of the receiver. All the while, she debated the least abrupt way to tell Angie her stepson never would be the one.

"You've gotten really quiet," Angie observed, and Amanda lowered her gaze as if Angie were present. "Are you sure you're okay about Franklyn not keeping in touch?"

"Absolutely!" Amanda responded and hoped she didn't sound as if she were faking enthusiasm in order to cover disappointment. "Really," she added with less emphasis, "I'm perfectly fine. I guess I'm just distracted over the party tonight." She gazed toward the elephant mural, then the Leaning Tower of Pisa replica. Presently, she could identify more with the Leaning Tower of Pisa.

"Good, then," Angie said, but her voice held the weight of a concerned mother. "I'll see you about six fifteen."

"Six fifteen is great!" Amanda chimed, then cheerfully added, "G'day," before hanging up the phone.

Amanda strode around the desk and headed toward Haley's open door. She gripped the side of the doorjamb, leaned into Haley's office, and said, "Will you scan this shopping list and e-mail it to Ang? I'm going to the lobby to finish decorating. If you need me, you know where I'll be."

Haley looked up from a pile of paperwork. The dark circles under her eyes had gotten worse as the day progressed. Haley looked like she hadn't slept in a week. "Sure," she said through a yawn.

"Are you going to be able to make the party tonight? You look like you could just drop and it's barely one thirty," Amanda said and eyed the flickering candle on the edge of her secretary's desk. The ocean breeze scent seemed the antithesis of everything Roger Miller offered.

"I'll make it," Haley claimed with a tired smile. She stood, stretched, picked up the candle tin, and blew out the flame. A tendril of smoke spiraled from the wick. "But not without some coffee. I'll make a fresh pot and bring you a cup, okay?"

"Okay," Amanda replied.

Out of nowhere, a brainstorm nearly knocked Amanda flat. *Franklyn West and Haley would really look great together! His fair hair, blue eyes, and height would perfectly complement her darker hair and eyes and petite frame. Furthermore, Franklyn was the ultimate extrovert while Haley was more the introvert. They'd be like two halves of a whole.* No sooner had the idea entered her mind than she relived that prayer she'd breathed in Angie's bathroom...

something about repenting of matchmaking. She also recalled the amendment she'd made to that prayer, *I won't play matchmaker again unless it's absolutely necessary.*

Given the probability of Haley's seeing Roger again, Amanda determined this was an absolutely necessary situation. Despite her earlier thoughts toward allowing Haley to breathe chicken feathers and the fumes of cattle for life if that's what she wanted, Amanda still couldn't shake the desire to see her friend settled better. She envisioned Haley, bone thin and sunburned, feeding chickens in a tattered dress and holey shoes.

Yes, this is absolutely necessary, Amanda thought. *When Haley is 40 and married to a successful physician, she'll thank me.*

"You're staring at me," Haley said. "Is there something wrong?"

"No! Nothing. Not in the least. Nothing at all. I was just thinking. I was thinking, that's all." Amanda pointed toward the hallway. "Well, I guess I'll go on and finish the decorating. Betty should be here any minute." She backed away from the door, waved at Haley, then scurried toward the hall. All the while Amanda knew this time she'd acted anything *but* casual and unaware of Haley's "other life."

Twenty-Eight

Nate stood on the edge of the party and watched Amanda work the crowd. The hum of voices and the smell of crab puffs blended with the band's inviting sounds to create a pleasing atmosphere that could only have been better if Nate and Amanda were throwing the party as one. The musicians merged one light jazz number with another and provided the perfect ambiance for a relaxing and rewarding evening.

One married couple on the edge of the crowd expertly twirled and stepped in time to the upbeat music while a few others looked on with admiration. Nate imagined the couple being him and Amanda, and his fingers tightened against the glass of club soda. He inserted his index finger between his shirt and neck, tugged, then smoothed his hand along the silk tie. He lifted the tie and looked at the purple number Amanda had given him for Christmas along with the gray shirt. He'd bought the charcoal-colored suit to match and wondered if Amanda would notice. Nate touched the silk scarf in his breast pocket. It perfectly matched the tie. Amanda had barely looked at him all evening, let alone registered he was red-free.

She'd spent extra time with several people and none with Nate. One of those people was Mr. Adair. At Amanda's bidding, Nate had walked over and escorted him and his wife to the party. Amanda fondly referred to the Adairs as her new neighbors and fussed over Goldie as much as she fussed over her cat, Cuddles. Fortunately, Goldie was much better mannered than Cuddles. As far as Nate was concerned that sour-tempered feline needed a few years in cat prison.

He sipped his club soda and savored the carbonated tingle as it slid down his throat. He wondered why he'd even bothered to come. With Franklyn back in town, Amanda had other things to ponder. She and Haley and Franklyn were in a semicircle, discussing who knew what. When Janet French joined the group, Franklyn seemed to forget Amanda existed.

Nate narrowed his eyes. How Franklyn could flirt with Amanda one second and ignore her the next went beyond Nate's comprehension. While Janet did look lovely, Amanda stole the hour in her chocolate-brown crushed-velvet number. The short jacket emphasized her waist while the skirt hugged her hips and flared to just above her ankles. The spike heeled boots set off the whole outfit and gave her that "bigger than dreams" appearance that Mason said he liked so much.

Thoughts of Mason made Nate grimace. He looked into his short glass, swirled the liquid, and downed the final drops of soda. The last thing he wanted to do was think of that buffoon and his tasteless wife tonight. Every time Nate had attended Mason's church in the last few weeks, Sonja had spent so much time focused on him that he was left with no doubts about her thoughts. And those thoughts made him highly uncomfortable.

A movement out of the corner of his eyes tugged his attention toward Samuel Adair who was moving to the edge of the crowd with Goldie in the lead. Nate stepped forward and touched Mr. Adair's arm.

"Want to come stand by me?" Nate questioned.

"Of course. I thought I remembered your heading off this way," Samuel replied. He lifted his chin toward Nate and smiled. "And here I've found you. Quite a party Amanda is throwing."

"Yes, quite," Nate agreed and gazed toward the cutouts of oversized jazz instruments, covered in glitter and attached to the wall. "She does this every year," he added and noted that the life-sized cardboard replica of Kenny G was now commanding the same corner John Wayne had ruled from last year.

Nate reached down to scratch Goldie's ears, then remembered Samuel's earlier warning. No one was allowed to touch Goldie except Samuel when she was on duty. That meant no playing, petting, or eating.

"Amanda Priebe is quite the lady," Mr. Adair said. "Quite the lady."

"Mmmmm," Nate said and eyed Amanda again. She gracefully threw back her head and laughed at something Franklyn said. Now that Janet had left the group, Franklyn's focus was on Amanda again.

"Does she know?" Samuel asked.

Nate cut his glance to Samuel. His cloudy eyes gave no clue to the meaning of his statement. But Nate's instincts suggested Samuel had picked up on some vibes Nate thought he'd hidden.

"Does who know what?" Nate cautiously asked and hoped if he acted ignorant the older gentleman would be thrown off.

Adair's smile reminded Nate of some mountain-dwelling sage who saw all and knew all. What the man lacked with physical sight, he certainly made up for every other way.

"Aaah, I guess not," Samuel mused. "But I can't say that I blame you for the way you feel. She's a fine woman—a fine woman indeed. Like I told her, if I were her age, I'd marry her myself. Of course, my wife would have to approve."

Normally Nate would have smiled. Instead he nearly choked. If he was so obvious that Mr. Adair had picked up the clues, did Amanda and everyone else know as well?

"Don't worry," Mr. Adair continued and laid his hand on Nate's arm. "You've probably got everyone fooled—except me. My wife says I'm annoyingly perceptive. Imagine that! She actually used the word 'annoying.'"

"Humph." Nate jiggled his ice and decided not to commit to any of Samuel's observations.

"Whatever that is you're drinking, I'll have some," Samuel said. "And a few of those crab things my wife tried to get me to eat earlier."

"Amanda's got a whole spread. We're all supposed to just help ourselves. Want me to fix you a plate?"

"Yes. That would be fantastic."

"There are some tables straight ahead. I'll lead you over there so you can wait on me." Nate took Samuel's arm and noticed the man was dressed in a suit every bit as fine as his own. Amanda said he'd been a lawyer and a successful one at that.

"What do I need you for when I've got Goldie?" Mr. Adair said and stepped away from Nate. "You go get the plates. Goldie will sit me. I'll be waiting. While I eat, we'll take her harness off and let you two get better acquainted."

"Sure," Nate replied.

"Goldie sit Samuel," Adair said. The faithful canine moved toward the corner, and Nate watched as Samuel confidently found a table and chair.

Over the last month, Amanda had fretted so about poor Goldie that Nate had finally been moved to agree to take her until he could find a good home for her. Amanda had repeatedly said she'd take the dog but she was afraid how Cuddles might react.

Cuddles would probably kill *Goldie!* Nate thought and wondered if they had maximum security in cat prison.

But this morning brought a new turn of events. Roger Miller had agreed to adopt Goldie. Nate was much happier about this arrangement than about his keeping the dog. First, he didn't know how Gary would react to a rival. Furthermore, with his work schedule, he was hard-pressed some days to give Gary all the attention he needed. On top of that, Goldie would have more freedom on Roger's farm than in Nate's beach house. Roger said she'd have the run of the farm and plenty of family members to spoil her. He also said Mr. Adair was free to visit her anytime.

As of tonight, Amanda still didn't know of Roger's offer, and Nate wasn't so sure he was ready to tell her. For Haley's sake, he wanted to keep as much focus as possible off Roger.

Within minutes, Nate had filled a plate with veggies and dip as well as stuffed morsels and several cheeses. He was heading straight for Mr. Adair when a movement near the entryway stopped him.

Mason and Sonja Eldridge invaded the party as if they were royalty and everyone else had been awaiting their arrival. Sonja was dressed in a mink stole and some velvet number that didn't look half as good on her as Amanda's outfit. She strode toward the crowd as if she were perched on a catwalk with the world as her audience. Mason, dressed in a butterscotch-colored suit, followed close behind like a good little boy.

The crowd parted as Sonja and Mason merged into the group. Several heads turned, and Sonja arrogantly lifted her chin. Someone forgot to tell the big-haired, attention seeker that she wasn't the most beautiful woman in the world. And Nate was nearly ready to be the one.

He searched out Amanda. Her wide eyes and ashen face attested that yes, she had spotted the two, and no, she did not invite them. They mingled through the crowd and waved toward Amanda. She halfheartedly returned their gesture and reached for Haley's arm. Haley stared at Sonja like she was seeing a clip from a horror movie. Amanda's gaze swooped the crowd until it landed on Nate.

"Help!" she mouthed.

Nate nodded and pointed toward Mr. Adair. Amanda returned his nod. He hurried to the gentleman, who was being joined by his wife—a tall, gray-haired woman every bit as distinguished as her husband. Nate placed the plate in front of Mr. Adair and looked toward his wife.

"If you don't mind getting his drink and telling him how I've arranged the food, I've got another issue that needs to be dealt with immediately." He glanced toward the Haley situation. Franklyn had meandered toward the food table, and Amanda and Haley stood alone. Sonja and Mason had reached their target and were making short work of introducing themselves to a stiff-lipped Haley.

"Of course," Mrs. Adair encouraged.

"Go on. Enjoy your night," Samuel agreed. "We'll talk about Goldie later."

"Yes," Nate absently stated and hurried toward the small disturbance. The closer he grew, the more distinctly Sonya's clear voice floated over the music and the crowd's hum.

"So you're Haley?" Sonja crowed while several people turned toward her voice. "Mason has told me so much about you," she said, yet her eyes communicated cold disdain mixed with cruel humor.

No telling what Mason has told his wife, Nate thought and saw the same conclusion hit Amanda.

With Haley's face flushing, Amanda glared a warning at both Sonja and Mason and stood beside her friend like a tower of defense.

While the nonverbals flew, Sonja laid her hand on her chest and stretched to her full height. Unfortunate for her, Amanda was still four inches taller. Mason protectively placed his arm around Sonja. His face stiffened.

Nate nearly laughed. Mason protecting Sonja was like Amanda protecting Cuddles in her attack mode. Nate stopped beside Haley and gently put his hand upon her shoulder. All his humor vanished.

Some people were nothing but pain-inflicting vultures. And Sonja could be the founding mother of the whole lot of them. The more harmless the victim, the more vultures enjoyed the sport. Nate imagined a hole in Haley's heart and blood dripping from a gleeful Sonja's beak.

"Come on, Sonja," Mason muttered just loud enough for several to hear. "Let's don't waste our time here."

Despite his comments, Sonja remained focused on Haley, who appeared to be shrinking by the second.

Amanda's eyes darkened. She looked toward Nate, at Sonja and Mason, then back to Nate with a "do something" demand in her eyes.

Nate patted Haley's shoulder and said, "If you don't mind, I need to chat with Haley for a few minutes. Come on, Haley," Nate said and tugged on her arm. "We need to talk."

She didn't falter as Nate swept her to the edge of the crowd and toward the exit. "I have never been so humiliated in my whole life," Haley whispered as they hurried forward. "That woman looked at me like I was a piece of trash. She is despicable!"

"So is he," Nate growled.

Glancing over his shoulder, Nate noticed that Amanda had pulled out her secret weapon. Betty Cates had latched onto Sonja and Mason and backed them against the wall. Both of them looked like they were being forced to eat live worms. If not for Haley's pathetic sniffle, Nate would have snickered.

"I need some privacy," Haley wobbled out.

"What about your office?"

"Yes. That's great."

Nate placed his hand on Haley's back and offered as much respectable support as was acceptable. By the time they stepped from the lobby, Haley was leaning against him. Nate assisted her all the way to her office and settled her into one of two tightly stuffed chairs. The second she sat down, Haley broke into a sob, and Nate hustled to get the box of tissue from the corner of her desk.

"I can't believe…" He mumbled and gently placed the box on Haley's lap.

She grabbed a wad of tissue and mopped at her face while Nate patted her back and got angrier by the second. *Haley Schmitz wouldn't hurt a soul,* he thought. *Mason and his wife should be excommunicated from all social gatherings for life! The nerve of them!*

The closer Haley got to controlling herself, the nearer Nate grew to losing control. By the time she wadded her sixth tissue, Nate had paced the office as many times and was ready to coldly usher Mason and Sonja to the nearest exit.

"I'm sorry to get so—so emotional," Haley said. "I don't care about him in the least. I really don't! But I'm already exhausted from all these secret meetings with Roger. And besides all that, it always hits a nerve when anyone treats me like that." She tossed the ball of damp tissue onto the oak coffee table between the chairs. "I struggle with feelings of w—worth anyway. The last thing I need is someone to act like—like that."

Nate settled in the chair opposite Haley. "Listen, Haley," he began, "you didn't deserve one bit of that. You're an intelligent, attractive woman, and you have a lot to offer the world. You've got poor Roger so distracted, I don't think he even remembers how to button his shirt."

Haley giggled, and her teary smile unraveled some of Nate's tension. "That's m'girl." He slid out of the chair, knelt beside her, and took her hand. "You just don't pay any attention to that idiot and his wife."

"Okay." Haley sniffed and blotted away the final tears.

"Listen, I'm not on the church board and I try to keep a low profile around church, but the pastor and church board do respect me. I've decided it's time to drop a few hints. Mason should have never been hired in the first place. He's a fake!"

"But Amanda says they're supposed to move soon."

"It can't be soon enough," Nate growled. "After tonight, I'm going to make certain they're gone within the next couple of weeks. We've all had enough."

Haley took a quivering breath. "Thanks."

Nate squeezed her hand and said, "So what about Roger anyway? Are things going well?"

She nodded with an eagerness that spoke volumes, tugged at her bottom lip with her teeth, and lowered her gaze.

"Do you think Amanda suspects at all?" Nate asked.

"I hope not." Haley's wide-eyed appraisal underscored her desire. "She acted a little odd in the office today. It made me wonder, but then she never even hinted that she suspected. What do you think?"

"I haven't said a word to her about him, or you either for that matter. She hasn't brought either of you up either." Nate released Haley's hand.

"That's a good sign."

"Maybe. Maybe not. Since we've argued over all of this, she might not ever tell me. It's hard to say."

Haley laughed. "I don't know how long she could keep a secret from you, Nate. She really thinks a lot of you."

"Really?" Like a neglected child eager for any scrap of approval, Nate panted for some news of Amanda's miraculously awakening to her love for him.

"Oh, you know that, you silly man." Haley slapped at his arm. "Stop acting so dense. You're like the big brother she never had."

"You're right," Nate replied and stared at the carpet. "Of course I knew that," he added, his momentary expectations mocking him.

The door opened, and Amanda bustled into the room, her skirt swishing with every step. "There you are!" she said, and Nate stood. "Is everything okay?" She hurried toward Haley. As Amanda knelt at her side, Nate backed away.

Her perfume reminded him of a Paris sunset…just the two of them and their love. While Amanda spoke to Haley, Nate turned and strode toward the window behind Haley's desk. He pulled the curtain cord and took in the city lights. Never had Nate been so intimate with loneliness and desperation. Never had the city left him so cold, so hopeless.

When someone placed her hand on his arm, Nate fully expected Haley. But when he turned, he was looking Amanda eye to eye. He glanced toward the chair where Haley had been sitting, then noticed her slipping out of the office. The door clicked shut, and the two of them were alone.

Twenty-Nine

"Thanks for what you did for her," Amanda said, every nuance of her expression supporting her words.

Nate inserted his hand into his pocket and looked into the night. "She's a special lady," he said. "She deserved better treatment than that."

"I asked them to leave," Amanda admitted.

Raising his brows, Nate observed Amanda again. "That took some guts."

"Yes, it did." Amanda crossed her arms, lifted her chin. "I also told Mason I wanted the portrait back. He's supposed to give it to you at church."

"I'm thoroughly impressed," Nate said and was reminded all over again why he relished her confidence, her independence. "And they actually left?" he asked.

"The very idea made Sonja so mad she stomped out. Mason had to follow, of course. That's what his job is," she drolly added with the lift of one thin eyebrow.

Nate chuckled and nearly burst into applause. "Good job."

"I told Haley they're gone. She's in the restroom trying to repair herself. Poor thing." Amanda shook her head.

"You know I'm not on the church board, but I've decided it's time to tell them and the pastor a few things about Mason. He and Sonja keep saying they're moving to Launceston. I believe it's time."

"Good." Amanda placed a hand on her hip. "If they're gone, I'll come back. I'm missing Angie's Bible teaching."

"She's good."

"*Very,*" Amanda affirmed and looked toward the city.

Longing to hold Amanda, Nate drank in her profile and appeased himself with imagining her in his arms...his lips on hers. All the while, he kept his face impassive. He didn't figure anyone but Mr. Adair would be able to discern his true thoughts.

Amanda looked at him. "I just had to thank you." Her eyes had never been so full of respect and appreciation. It was nearly enough to make Nate think...

"I love Haley as much as my own sister," Amanda continued. "It makes me furious to see someone purposefully hurt her."

In Nate's mind, their kiss deepened. He whispered sweet nothings in her ear. Then Amanda promised she'd love him forever. Nate broke eye contact and stroked the front of his tie.

"You're wearing my purple tonight!" Amanda picked up the end of his tie and dropped it.

"You noticed." Nate smiled. "There's not a scrap of red on me."

"What is the world coming to?" Amanda teased and touched the matching scarf in his breast pocket. "This is such a shock it might cause a major national disaster. Maybe an earthquake!"

"Humph." The sassier she grew, the greater Nate's temptation to kiss her. He casually shifted away and gripped the windowsill.

Amanda sighed, looked out the window, and gazed back at him as if she were being forced to eat her own serving of earthworms. "You were right, you know," she finally admitted.

"Of course I was," Nate replied. "And if you'll tell me what I was right about, I'll agree again."

"Oh you." Amanda wrinkled her nose. "About Mason. I seem to have made a mess of all that. You tried to tell me, but…" She shrugged. "Sorry I didn't listen."

Nate clutched at his chest and staggered backward. "*Now* there's going to be an earthquake!" he mocked.

Amanda rolled her eyes, pursed her lips, and Nate relived that kiss she'd thrown him in O'Brien's. Her bronze lips looked as inviting now as they had then—maybe even more so. His legs began to betray him, and Nate nearly dashed aside all caution in preference for taking the chance of a lifetime.

But what if she rejects me? The dreaded fear that accompanied that worry stopped him. While Nate's torment increased by the hour, he'd rather live a lifetime as Amanda's friend and never touch than take the chance of losing her altogether.

Cool it! he commanded and decided the best means to that edict was simply getting some distance.

"Your guests are probably wondering what happened to you," Nate said and pointed toward the doorway.

Amanda glanced across the room, then looked back at Nate. She hesitated as curiosity and hesitancy swirled through her eyes. "Um…" Amanda hedged and tucked her hair behind her ear. She looked down and finally said, "You're right. I should be out there. I've got a hiring decision to make. Tonight will be a huge help toward that."

"Ah yes," Nate said as he accompanied her to the doorway, "you mentioned those three earlier. Want me to chat them up for you and give you my opinion?"

"Would you?" Amanda asked and laid her hand on his arm. "That would be such a huge help. I'm not nearly as good a judge of character as you are."

Nate covered her hand with his, casually removed it from his arm, and, as much as he hated to, released it. Having Amanda compliment him *and* touch him all at the same time was nearly too much for his willpower.

"It's the least I can do," Nate mumbled and opened the door for her.

When he flipped off the light switch and shut Haley's door, Nate decided the time had come for a vacation. A steady diet of Amanda was nearly driving him to the brink of doing something he might regret forever. Gordon had e-mailed him yesterday, saying it was time for a corporate meeting in Brisbane again. The two were facing some management issues and needed several conference days. The potential trip would do Nate good and give him some much-needed distance from Amanda.

As he watched her sway up the hallway, Nate realized no tactic had helped him cope with his growing love. Stuffing all signs of Amanda into a closet hadn't worked. Keeping his distance hadn't worked. And the very idea that he could go back to their old patterns and find some relief for his torment now struck him as sickeningly hilarious.

No matter what I do, I'm falling deeper in love, he thought and decided the time had come to consult an expert. Gordon had been married 15 years, and he and Amanda's sister were happier than any married couple Nate had ever known. The man just might be able to offer some advice.

Amanda stopped near the end of the hallway and looked over her shoulder. "Are you coming?" she asked and walked back to his side.

"I guess," Nate drawled and acted a thousand times more carefree than he felt.

Amanda looped her arm through his and pulled. "Come on, Grandpa," she urged with a saucy cadence. "We'll never make it back to the party at this rate."

"Well, you know I'm ten years older than you," he teased. "I'm not as young as I used to be. Not the man I used to be," he added in a piteous voice.

"Yeah, right," Amanda grumbled, "tell that to Sonja Eldridge, the whole Singles Department at church, and nearly every other woman in Tasmania."

"What's *that* supposed to mean?" Nate asked and prayed for some sign of feminine appreciation in her eyes.

"Don't play ignorant with me, Nate Knighton." Amanda barely pinched his cheek and offered no sign that she was among the group of Tasmanian women who appreciated his masculinity. "This is *me* you're talking to. Just because I'm like your little sister, doesn't mean I don't have eyes. I see more than you *think* I see."

As they moved toward the lobby, Nate's hopes plummeted, and he knew that trip to Brisbane was his sole ticket to sanity. Gordon would know what to do. Even if it meant relocating, Nate was ready to put an end to this agony.

Franklyn West appeared near the lobby's entry. "There you are, Amanda!" he said. "I've been looking for you." He gazed past her. "And where's Haley? Is she okay?"

"Haley's going to be fine," Amanda said and looked at Nate. "Franklyn saw everything and heard me ask Sonja and Mason to leave."

"She was *good*," Franklyn bragged. "I don't know how many people would have had the courage to handle that whole situation as well as she did."

"I'm sure she was remarkable, as usual," Nate mumbled. He stepped toward the party and kept on walking. *He* didn't have the courage to watch Franklyn and Amanda charm one another. He spotted Mr. Adair and decided to focus on Goldie the rest of the evening.

"Nate?" Amanda called. He turned to see her trotting after him.

He also spotted Haley near the entry with Franklyn smiling down at her. Now that her makeup was repaired, she didn't look as if she'd cried in years. And none of it was wasted on Franklyn. Hiding a frown, Nate knew Roger would not be happy.

"She looks great, doesn't she?" Amanda said.

Nate swung his attention back to Amanda. "Yep. At least Franklyn seems to think so."

"They look good together, don't you think?"

Nate shrugged. "As pretty as Haley is these days, she'd look good with just about anybody."

"I agree," Amanda replied, then hesitated. "I hate to be a pest, Nate, but please don't forget what you said about talking with the three management candidates. Daddy and Angie are doing the same." She nodded toward her father, interacting with a tall blonde female and Angie, talking to an overweight young man with a keen eye.

"At this point, I'm so confused over which one to hire, I'd like to hire all three."

Nate chuckled. "What if I think the same thing?"

"Don't *do* that!" Amanda admonished.

"Okay, point out the other one, and I'll see what I can do."

By ten o'clock Amanda declared the annual event a huge success. As usual she'd ended the evening by discreetly handing out annual bonuses to all 12 managers who helped maintain

Wood-Priebe International at the multimillion dollar level. On top of that, her father, Nate, and Angie had all agreed upon the best replacement for Ken-the-working-machine. And success had compounded on top of success when Franklyn and Haley spent the rest of the evening in each other's company.

This might be one match I don't even have to work for, Amanda thought as she observed Franklyn walking Haley toward the exit.

Haley waved goodbye and called, "Franklyn's giving me a lift home."

"Good!" Amanda replied and recalled Haley's mentioning her car was in the shop. She turned toward Nate, who was approaching with the Adairs. His frown was all for Haley and Franklyn, and Amanda wondered why. Then Amanda remembered Nate glowering at Franklyn and Haley several times during the last half of the party.

Amanda's mind so churned with possible motivations, she was hard-pressed to focus on what Nate was saying. Finally she forced herself to absorb his words.

"I'm going to walk Mr. and Mrs. Adair home," he explained as the couple paused near the agency's exit. "Are you about to leave?"

"Well…" Grappling for the reason for Nate's question, Amanda looked toward the room, once full of a lively party. Only the band now remained, and they were packing up their equipment.

"I'll certainly be here until the band leaves. But I'm *not* going to stay here until midnight trying to clean up," she said in case Nate was on the verge of delivering a brotherly lecture about how she should get plenty of rest. "I'm going home and leaving this mess until tomorrow. Betty and Haley and I are coming back to clean house in the morning."

Amanda wiggled her toes and looked down at the new suede

boots that so perfectly matched her outfit. Much to Haley's exasperation, Amanda *hadn't* found them on sale.

"My feet are killing me," she admitted with a tired smile.

"Sit down then," Nate said and motioned toward the row of tables and chairs near the window. "I want to talk with you for a few minutes. Do you mind staying?"

"Not at all," Amanda agreed. "I think I'll go to my office and take these boots off." She lifted one foot and angled it to give Nate a clear view of the heel. "I've got a pair of flats in my office I'd rather wear home."

Nate winced. "I don't know why you women insist on such torture."

"It's *fashion*. It's *the rules*." She wiggled her eyebrows, nodded, and took in the Adairs in her antics.

"We're fine walking ourselves home," Mrs. Adair interjected.

"Yes we are!" Samuel bragged. "If Goldie loses her edge, I've got a beautiful backup." He slid his arm around his wife's shoulders and mumbled something into her ear.

Her expression sharpened.

"Are you sure?" Nate asked.

"It's just across the street," Mrs. Adair quickly added as the two hustled out the doorway. "Samuel roams the street by himself all the time. We're fine. Really. G'day," she called, and the door closed before Nate had time to object.

Amanda wondered exactly what Mr. Adair had said to his wife. She'd gone from casually waiting to urgently exiting.

"Think they'll be all right?" Nate asked and stepped toward the doorway.

"Sure." Amanda waved toward the street. "It's not like they're in their nineties. This is a good neighborhood, and the street is well lit. Besides, I'm wondering if they weren't up to something anyway. Whatever Mr. Adair said to her, it changed everything and she was ready to fly. Did you notice?"

"Yes, I noticed," Nate mumbled with a knowing undertone to his voice.

Amanda studied him but gained no insight into his thoughts.

Her aching feet insisted she shouldn't care. Amanda walked past Nate and trudged toward her office. "I'm going to change shoes so I can think better," she said. "You know my brain's in my big toe."

Nate followed close behind. "I guess it could be worse," he drawled.

Amanda narrowed her eyes and debated whether or not to even take the bait. But in the end, she couldn't resist. "Why do you say that?"

"It could be in your *little* toe."

"Like yours, for instance?" she shot back.

His laugh was as rewarding as Amanda expected.

Thirty

Nate followed Amanda into her office and waited while she slipped out of the boots.

"Oooohhhhh," she moaned and closed her eyes as her feet flattened against the tile. "That feels *so much* better." Amanda eyed the couch. She kicked the boots out of the way, walked to the sofa, and dropped into the corner.

"I don't think I'm going to make it home right now." She stretched her feet along the cushions, rested her head on the back of the couch. "I might just take a nap right here. It's been a long day," she added through a yawn.

Noticing the dark circles under her eyes, Nate's love was moved to action. He gave in to an impulse he didn't bother to question. Sitting on the other end of the couch, he took her feet in his lap.

She lifted her head and looked at him. "What are you doing?" she asked.

"I'm going to give you a foot massage," Nate replied with as much emotion as someone reciting a grocery list.

"Oh!" Amanda said and blinked.

Never taking his gaze from hers, Nate pressed his thumb in the middle of her foot and began to knead. "Does that help?"

Amanda closed her eyes and sighed. "Extremely," she breathed.

Nate concentrated on her toes next and kept his mind focused on the task at hand. "I actually didn't come in here for this," he mused when he switched to her other foot.

"Who cares," Amanda said. "I would *pay* you to do this every day."

You don't have to pay me, Amanda, Nate thought. *Just say you'll marry me, and I'll give you free foot massages for life.*

"Where did you learn how to do this?" She lifted her head and suspiciously scrutinized him.

"Beats me." Nate smiled. "This is my first time."

Her gaze softened. She flopped her head back against the couch and said, "You're a natural."

"Actually, I was thinking my turn would be next."

"No way!" Amanda pulled her feet out of his grasp. "I'm not rubbing your stinky feet."

"Get back here," Nate drawled and coaxed her feet into his grasp. "I was just joking. But just for the record, my feet do not stink. They smell like roses."

"Humph," Amanda replied.

"Now she's started 'humphing' me," Nate complained. "First, she criticizes my rosy toes, then she 'humph's' me. What's next?" He felt Amanda looking at him and leveled a smile at her he hoped made her remember him when he was in Brisbane.

"You're terribly chipper, aren't you?" she said. "What was in all the club soda you were drinking anyway?"

"Clubs I guess," Nate quipped.

Amanda giggled and wiggled her toes. "That's feeling so much better."

"If you don't stop wearing those spikes, you're going to have a whopper of a podiatrist bill when you're 60," Nate predicted and offered the final rub.

"Yes, Father," she mocked.

"I'm not your father," Nate growled and released her feet. *Neither am I your brother,* he thought.

"No, you aren't," Amanda said and gazed at him with a lazy droop to her eyes that Nate nearly interpreted as an invitation.

Then he just as quickly talked himself out of the impression. *Gordon…I've got to talk to Gordon,* he admonished himself and stood.

"Actually, I just wanted to let you know that I'm going to be gone for a while—a week or so," he said.

"Gone?" Amanda swung her feet to the floor and looked up at him. "B-but where?" She stood, clenched her fists, and licked her lips.

"Actually, I'm—"

"No! Don't tell me." She covered her ears, closed her eyes, and swallowed hard.

Laughing, Nate stepped closer, pulled her hands away from her ears, and whispered, "I'm going to visit Gordon and Beverly."

Amanda's eyes popped open, and she said, "Oh."

"What did you think I was going to do? Disappear from the planet?"

"No, I thought you were going to get—" She swiveled toward the closet, and her skirt swirled with the movement. "Never mind," Amanda said and opened the closet. She stooped, retrieved a pair of loafers, and slipped her feet into them.

"Going to get what?" Nate pressed.

"Nothing," Amanda said and picked up her boots.

"Going to get a new car…a new house…a different position…what?" Nate waited for her answer as he further brainstormed.

"Just *never mind!*" she insisted.

Finally a word popped into his mind, and it was the only word that made sense with her reaction. He laughed out loud. "Did you think I was going to say I was getting *married?*" he blurted.

Her head lowered, Amanda stepped to her desk, pulled out the bottom drawer, and extracted her purse. "I never said that!" she snapped.

"No, you didn't," Nate agreed and couldn't deny the warmth that spread through him.

"But you told me about—about some mystery woman at Angie's Christmas party," she blurted. "What was I supposed to think?"

Nate crossed his arms and gleefully challenged her. "You're jealous!" he exclaimed like he'd just won a million bucks.

Her mouth fell open. "I am not! That's the most ridiculous thing I've ever heard in my life." She strode toward the door with her boots in one hand and her purse in the other. Amanda opened the door and turned to face him. "No, it's *not* the most ridiculous thing…it's the most arrogant thing! Why in the world would I be jealous?"

Nate laughed out loud and didn't even try to find logic in his reaction. If she really *wasn't* jealous and she really *did* think he was ridiculous and arrogant, then he should be crying.

She stomped. "I already told you, Nate Knighton, I don't like it when you laugh when you're not supposed to."

"And who's the judge on when I'm not supposed to?" he parried and lifted his chin.

Her face reddened, she glared at him a full five seconds, then stormed from the room.

Nate turned off the light, closed the door, and followed at a distance. He planned to stay until the band departed. Then he'd help Amanda lock up. He didn't like the idea of leaving a beautiful woman alone with several men and the necessity of walking to the shadowed parking lot—especially not when she was the woman he loved.

Fortunately the wait wasn't a long one. The band was just hauling their final cases out the door when he and Amanda exited the hallway. "G'night and thanks!" Amanda called.

"Call us if you need us again," the bushy-haired saxophonist said.

"I will," Amanda replied and switched off the light in the oversized lobby.

As they exited the agency and stepped into the cool night, Amanda didn't look at him. She didn't talk to him. She didn't even acknowledge his presence. Still, Nate followed her toward the parking lot. After the band's van exited, the only two vehicles left were a red Mercedes and a sporty, white BMW.

"Sorry I made you mad," he mumbled as she stopped near the BMW.

Finally Amanda looked at him. The parking lot lights cast an inviting glow upon her hair, and Nate came within a breath of telling her exactly how beautiful she was. Only the fear of her rejection stopped him.

I'm a coward, he lambasted himself, but possessed no means to overcome the problem. If Amanda was a new friend and this whole progression of love had happened in a normal vein, if she'd give him any hint that she might even think of him as a potential love, Nate would know how to handle the situation. But none of that was how his love for Amanda had progressed. Instead it had sneaked up on him after years of friendship. Now he was still seeing nothing but the same friendship he'd depended upon in Amanda.

"Do you want the truth?" Amanda asked.

"No," Nate stated with a smile. "Why would I ever want the truth?"

She adjusted her purse strap on her shoulder and narrowed one eye in a sarcastic squint. "The truth is, I think I *am* a little jealous."

"Oh?" Nate said and held his breath in hopes of more.

"Yes. It's like I'm an eighth grader and my big brother is going off to college," she explained. "In a lot of ways, I guess I feel like you're abandoning me. I mean, you've always been there, Nate. Now, *she's* in the picture."

His face went cold and stiff. "Yeah," he mumbled and searched for anything else to say. Nothing came.

"Well, she's in *your* picture," Amanda amended. "But I still haven't met her. I guess we need to arrange for that when you get back." She hung her head with a resigned weariness.

The hum of traffic attested to the highway just meters away. The cool wind stirred the oaks lining the parking lot, and Nate begged God to give him something to say. Nothing verbal came—only the need to communicate with Amanda in a way he never had. Nate wrapped his arms around her and gently hugged. He was reminded once again of the Paris sunset, of the months he'd loved her, of the years his love had taken root.

When she didn't pull away, he dared to smell her hair and relished the softness against his lips. "I guess our relationship has been changing for a while," he mumbled. "It's been stressful for me too." Nate closed his eyes and savored her warmth. "Sometimes, though, the death of one relationship has to happen so another can be born."

He held his breath and waited for her to respond to the well-placed hint. After several seconds, she offered no reply. Nate inched away and looked into her face. All he saw in the shadows was confusion laced with anxiety and exhaustion. Nate sighed and stepped away.

"I'll call you when I get back from Brisbane, okay?" he said and walked toward his Mercedes.

"Sure," Amanda agreed, and he felt her watching him as his shoes grated against the concrete.

Nate paused and verified that she was indeed staring at him instead of trying to get into her vehicle. "Are you going to get into your car?"

"Yes. Of course. Right," Amanda replied and fumbled with her keys. When they clanked to the pavement Nate moved back to her side.

"Here, let me help," he said. Nate retrieved the keys and pressed the remote. The lock chirped. He popped open the door and extended the keys.

"Thanks," Amanda said and accepted the keys. "I'm just so tired, I'm almost a zombie."

"And here I've held you up," Nate admitted. "Sorry 'bout that."

"No, it's perfectly fine," Amanda said through a yawn. She settled into the driver's seat, clicked on her seat belt, and gazed up at him.

Nate searched her face for any hint of encouragement. All he detected were the memories of a 12-year-old who followed him around like a groupie every time their families got together. Many years had lapsed since her Nate fan club era. During those years, he had tolerated Amanda's constant chattering with patient amusement. Nevertheless, Nate couldn't deny that the hero worship in her eyes had bolstered his ego. Now he would fall to his knees for even a scrap of what she'd exhibited then.

"G'night, Amanda," Nate said and gave into a chaste version of the urge that would no longer be denied. He leaned into the car and brushed his lips against her forehead.

Thirty-One

Amanda ran through the streets of Highland chasing a red convertible Mercedes. Every time she got within reach of the car, it would disappear, then reappear, zooming in the opposite direction. Again Amanda lurched after the vehicle, running and falling and crying for Nate to stop. But to no avail. He just continued the insane driving.

The rejection would have been bad enough, but the ghostly, feminine image sitting in the passenger seat threw Amanda to new heights of anguish. And Nate's haunting words from last week echoed through the streets: *Sometimes the death of one relationship has to happen so another can be born.*

Covering her ears, Amanda tried to break free of the heart-rending words. No relief came. None. Only the sickening reality that she was losing Nate...that their relationship was dying...or rather, *that woman* was killing it.

When the Mercedes swerved in her direction, Amanda strained to identify the mystery woman. Her image loomed familiar yet elusive as the vehicle zoomed past Amanda again. She pulled at her hair, writhed from side to side, and screamed, "No! No! No!"

A disgruntled yowling jolted her senses. Amanda opened her eyes and stared through the morning twilight at the brass-trimmed fan on her bedroom's ceiling. Her night shirt was damp with perspiration. Her fingers were tangled in her hair. And Cuddles was howling like someone had died.

Amanda sat up. The covers, knotted around her leg, had somehow trapped the cat. Cuddles' writhing body bulged the sheets as she struggled against the linen prison.

Amanda, grimacing against the taste in her mouth, unwrapped her legs and fumbled with the cover until Cuddles was free. The feline bolted from the bed, raced to the door, and stopped. Back arched, tale fluffed, she hissed at the bed and lowered her ears.

With a dry chuckle, Amanda swung her socked feet to the rug. "You're so brave," she mocked as the haunting dream crashed through her mind anew. Amanda hugged herself.

Nate had been gone a whole week. He hadn't called or e-mailed or even sent a postcard. Nate's neglect, unlike Franklyn's lack of communication, plagued Amanda every second of every day. And his telling her that their friendship must die so he could continue the relationship with *that woman* was awakening Amanda to the depth of her dependence upon him. She was gradually realizing that she was in no way ready to allow their friendship to die.

She hugged tighter and relived Nate's hug, his lips on her forehead. Even though Amanda hadn't expected the contact, she accepted the brotherly tokens of affection for what they were—Nate's way of expressing his apologies for dumping her.

Standing, Amanda stumbled into the white marble bathroom, flipped on the light, and gazed into the mirror. Her hair looked like one of Betty Cates' used-up brooms. Her skin was pallid. And during the last week, the dark circles under her eyes had worsened. Fortunately, Haley was punctual, fresh, and cheerful all week because Amanda had been tardy, tired, and as grouchy as Cuddles.

Amanda had barely been able to concentrate. Presently, there was a list of phone calls she needed to return Monday and a pile on her desk that looked like clutter but was actually high-priority business. Amanda hadn't wanted to deal with the stack last week and didn't want to think about it now.

"This was a bad week," she mumbled at her reflection and wondered if Nate's "friend" was in Brisbane. She thought about e-mailing her sister the question but decided against it. Amanda just knew Bev would leak the question to Gordon, who would then "casually" mention it to Nate.

Nevertheless, the fixation over who he was with was nearly driving her insane. *If he was with some woman, wouldn't Bev have let me know?* Amanda worried, then wondered why her sister would even feel the need to let Amanda know. *It's not like we're an item or anything.*

I'm obsessing over him, she thought and grabbed her toothbrush and toothpaste. Amanda smeared a dollop of paste on her toothbrush, turned on the water, and blinked against her burning eyes. She inserted the toothbrush into her mouth and furiously scrubbed her teeth until her gums tingled with cinnamon. When she finished the chore, she rinsed her mouth with cool water.

By that point, her eyes' burning had increased beyond the blink management stage. A tear splashed from her lashes and mingled with the water. Amanda dropped her toothbrush, turned off the water, covered her face, and heaved through a storm of emotion.

She fumbled for a towel and buried her damp face in its fresh folds. *Stop crying!* she commanded. *Stop it now!*

Amanda and Haley were meeting Franklyn for lunch today at the mall. The last thing Amanda needed was red-rimmed eyes. Franklyn had actually instigated the meeting. As things had turned out, Mason had given *him* the portrait of Haley since Nate wasn't at church this week. He called Haley with the news and arranged for the three of them to get together.

Given the fact that he and Haley had become fast friends, Amanda was certain he was making up excuses just to be near Haley. Of course, Amanda hadn't even hinted of her suspicions to Haley. This time Amanda watched the swift-moving romance unfold and attributed Haley's cheerful week to the budding relationship. Before long she was certain Haley wouldn't even remember Roger's name.

Having gotten control of her emotions, Amanda rubbed her face with the towel and checked her watch, lying on the countertop.

"Only seven?"

Amanda yawned and looked at the bed. She hadn't fallen asleep until two o'clock. Last night was indicative of every night this week; she hadn't been this sleep-deprived since college. The brass bed beckoned anew. Amanda laid her watch and towel on the countertop, clicked off the light, and padded toward her bed.

Haley stood outside the Italian restaurant and fumbled through her handbag in search of her coin purse. All the while, she scouted the mall traffic flow in search of some sign of Amanda or Franklyn. Haley was certain Franklyn said they would meet outside Mario's at noon. She checked her watch again and acknowledged that, yes, indeed, it was twelve thirty.

Her stomach specifically requested a large serving of the pasta that filled the air with tantalizing fragrance. And as much as Haley wanted to allow the waiter to go ahead and seat her, she needed to connect with Amanda first. However, neither she nor Franklyn had arrived, and this whole lunch was his idea.

I must have gotten mixed up, Haley thought and strode toward the hallway where the public telephones and restrooms were. Amanda had offered to stop by and pick up Haley, but she'd opted for an early drive to the mall and browsing for bargains. This time, Haley had come up empty-handed, but the shopping had proven quite relaxing.

Haley entered the long hallway, and the tap of her low-heeled pumps echoed against the walls and ceiling. A row of telephones claimed the space between two restroom doors, one marked "Men," the other, "Women." Haley noticed a trio of leather-clad young men hovering near one of the phones, and she decided a trip to the ladies room was in order. Hopefully, when she came out, the earringed, tattoo crew would have vanished.

She kept her gaze down, hugged the wall, and passed the three. They smelled of body odor and liquor and seemed to be having problems with cash flow, if the "Please, mom, please, just one hundred more dollars," was anything to go by.

A wave of panic insisted Haley was in no way safe. Her skin crawled along her neck, and she knew they were watching her. She increased her pace and shot a glance toward them just in time to see one of them step toward her.

Before Haley had time to react, the youth snatched her purse like a bird plucking a worm from the ground.

"Aaaahhhh!" Haley gasped and groped for her bag's leather strap, tangled in her fingers. With a final jerk, the teenager yanked the strap from Haley's grasp. Her pinky caught in the strip of leather and protested as the strap ate into her skin.

"I've got some money! Come on!" the purse thief bellowed and sprinted up the hallway.

The kid on the phone dropped the receiver and left it to dangle while he raced after his two friends.

"Help! Help! Somebody help!" Haley's scream bounced off the walls. "W–w–wait! You can't do this!" She cried and lunged after them.

The three teens laughed as they dashed toward the mall traffic. "You can't do this," one of them mocked before running headlong into a tall, blond figure who appeared out of nowhere.

"Haley?" Franklyn hollered while wrestling the purse thief.

"My purse! He's got my purse!" she shrieked and dashed toward Franklyn.

"Let's get out of here!" one of the teens bellowed. And two of them zipped past Franklyn and the youth he was fighting.

Haley's purse dropped between them. Franklyn kicked the purse down the hallway and tried to block the teen from escape. But the young man lowered his head, shoved Franklyn into the wall, and scrambled after his friends.

Franklyn grunted. Arms sprawled, he tried to stop himself from falling, but to no avail. He landed on the concrete floor with a bump and "Umph!"

Panting, Haley retrieved her handbag and collapsed at Franklyn's side. "Oh my word!" she babbled. "You—you fought them! You got my purse!" She held up the leather bag. "You were so brave. I can't believe it. Are you all right?"

Franklyn frowned and stroked his midsection. "Yes, fine," he admitted and rubbed the back of his head.

The pounding of footsteps neared the hallway, and Haley looked up to see Amanda and a security guard.

"Haley," Amanda exclaimed, "are you hurt?"

"N—no!" she shook her head and tried to stand. But she trembled so severely she couldn't support her own weight.

The security guard, dressed in black, helped Franklyn to his feet, and Franklyn and Amanda began fussing over Haley.

"My partner is trying to catch those thieves," the security guard rushed. He glanced over his shoulder and backed away as Haley regained her footing. "I'm going to help him, but we'll need you to make a statement shortly."

"Sure," Haley agreed.

"We'll be in Mario's," Amanda said.

Franklyn placed a supportive arm around Haley. Gripping her purse, Haley didn't reject the kindness. He and she had developed a pleasant friendship since Amanda's corporate party, and his protection and support were welcomed.

"We arrived at the restaurant at about the same time," Amanda explained and caressed Haley's arm. "We thought we heard you yelling. When we saw the guys running out of the hallway, Franklyn ran to help you and I went for the security guards."

"Thanks," Haley rasped and tried to hold back the swell of emotion that threatened to take her down. But her self-control snapped, and a broken cry accompanied a gush of tears.

Franklyn stroked her hair, and Haley buried her face against his chest. "Don't cry, Haley," Franklyn fussed while Amanda patted her back. He smelled of expensive men's fragrance that seemed a bit too much—especially when a young woman is used to a man of simple tastes.

"Sweetie, it's all over," Amanda crooned, and *never* had Haley heard such a satisfied sound. "I'm so sorry I was late," she continued. "I overslept."

"Overslept?" Franklyn asked. "It's after twelve thirty."

Haley raised her head and fished through her purse for a packet of tissue. "She's hardly slept all week."

"How did you know that?" Amanda questioned.

"I could tell." Her hand unsteady, Haley pulled a tissue from the packet and rubbed at her nose. "You start acting like Cuddles."

Franklyn released Haley, raised both hands, and inched away from Amanda. "Back, back," he teased.

"Oh you." Amanda waved him aside and said, "I'll have you *both* know I'm much more cheerful today."

Haley discreetly examined Amanda's eyes while dabbing at her own. Even though Amanda's smile, her rosy cheeks, her immaculate pantsuit all bespoke her claim, her eyes told another story. Haley hadn't pried, but she suspected Amanda's problems involved Nate—or the lack of Nate. He hadn't been around all week. And Amanda looked as miserable as Haley had felt when she was missing Roger.

"Well, now that I've done my Superman act for the day, I'm starved," Franklyn said and rubbed his hands together.

"I *was* starved," Haley admitted. "But after all that, my appetite isn't quite what it was." She managed a nervous laugh.

"Mine's not at its tops," Amanda admitted and observed Franklyn. "Maybe you'll have to eat for all three of us."

"If you insist!" Franklyn held out both his arms like an usher. "Ladies," he invited, "let's eat."

Amanda and Haley each looped their arms through his, and the three friends walked the length of the hallway, only to spot the winded security guard arriving from his chase.

"We lost them," he said.

By the time Haley fully regained her composure, gave her report, and began her meal, she realized that Amanda was up to her usual matchmaking tricks. Except this time, her boss hadn't bothered to inform Haley.

Once the salad was served and devoured, Franklyn excused himself for a bathroom break. And he'd no sooner left their table than Amanda leaned forward and hissed, "I think he likes you!"

"Me?" Haley replied. "I thought he liked *you*. Before he left for London, I thought you and he—"

"No, no, no," Amanda said with a mischievous smile. "He and I just aren't." She wrinkled her nose. "There's no lasting chemistry. But with you!" Amanda widened her eyes. "Did you *see* how he protected you!"

Haley toyed with the remainder of her breadstick. As she'd predicted, her appetite hadn't been the best this meal. Neither had the breadsticks. She stared at the half-eaten, olive-oil soaked specimen and contemplated everything Amanda was saying. While she and Franklyn both enjoyed each other, Haley was too distracted with Roger to notice whether or not he was thinking romance instead of friendship.

"I hope he doesn't think I'm leading him on," Haley worried and nearly blurted something about her commitment to Roger. "I mean, I hope he doesn't think I'm chasing him or anything," she corrected.

"Are you kidding?" Amanda smiled, and the dark circles under her eyes were almost unnoticeable. "At this point, I don't think he'd run very fast." She leaned closer. "I promise, you should have seen him when he realized you were in trouble. He said, 'That's Haley,'" Amanda mimicked his British accent to the syllable and added, "like you were the Queen of England or something."

If what Amanda was saying was true, then Haley had a significant problem. She lowered her gaze, picked up her cola, and sipped at the straw in an attempt to wash the garlic taste from her mouth. Haley gazed across the crowded restaurant, decorated in traditional Italian décor. The jazzy number flowing through the speakers reminded Haley of some of the music at Amanda's party.

After Mason and Sonja had been so rude, Franklyn had taken Haley under his wing. He'd even given her a ride home since her car was in the shop. Haley hadn't viewed the evening as anything more than an outgoing man being kind to a wounded spirit.

But what if Amanda's right? she worried. The last thing Haley needed was Franklyn chasing her when she and Roger were *so close* to becoming engaged. And this time, when he asked, Haley was going to say yes before he even finished the proposal. Let Amanda say what she would, Haley *longed* for farm life and for being a farm wife. She had never been so sure of anything.

"Ssshhh!" Amanda hissed as if Haley had been talking non-stop. "Here he comes."

Haley straightened her shoulders and tried to act as casual as a young woman can who's dreadfully suspicious of a new male suitor.

"Are you going to be okay, now?" Franklyn asked while taking the seat next to Haley.

"Yes, I think so," Haley said and flexed her pinky. "My finger is still attached. It hasn't fallen off yet."

Franklyn touched her finger, and Haley nearly jerked it back.

"I'm afraid my stomach is going to be sore tomorrow," Franklyn said. "That kid really gave me a hard push." He stroked his abdomen, then patted Haley's back. "You were terribly brave, even if I have to say so myself." His kind blue eyes twinkled with admiration, and never had a woman so disliked being admired.

"*You* were the one who was brave," Amanda responded and barely winked at Haley.

"I'm afraid if I hadn't been so late, maybe none of this would have happened. Didn't you say you were trying to phone Amanda and that's why you went down the hallway?"

"Yes." Haley nodded and turned toward Franklyn. "But don't blame yourself for that," she admonished.

"The truth is, it really wasn't my fault." Franklyn rubbed his temple. "I was on the phone with my uncle. You know, he and my aunt raised me after my mom died."

Both Haley and Amanda nodded.

"Well, my aunt's health is atrocious."

Haley caught a doubtful glance from Amanda. She recalled her mentioning that Angie believed the lady was a hypochondriac.

"My uncle's afraid she won't be here much longer. I'm trying to decide whether to go back home for the duration or to stay here awhile longer. I've taken off this semester in my studies. In June, I start my internship, so I'm having a bit of a vacation before I do that. Anyway, I'd planned to spend most of it with my father. Now this. She's not been healthy for quite some time."

"If you really think she might be dying," Haley said and hoped she didn't sound too eager to have him leave the country, "don't you think it's best to be with her?"

Franklyn stared across the room, then snapped his attention to Haley. "If only it were that easy," he mused and gazed out the window. "I haven't been that close to my father. Now we're really becoming great friends. I'm so enjoying it all. And then there's—" He stopped, looked down, and creased the edge of his linen napkin.

Amanda shrugged and widened her eyes. And Haley's mind spun with possibilities. Perhaps Franklyn's "And then there's—" involved his not wanting to return to London because of *her!*

"I guess I forgot to tell you." He looked at Haley. "I do have your portrait out in Angie's car. I didn't want to bring it in. I guess we can just shift it when we leave."

"Thanks," Haley said.

"You did a great job on that piece, Amanda," Franklyn said.

"Thanks."

"But then," he turned his attention to Haley, "you had a beautiful subject."

Haley's face went cold, and she went into a flight mode. "Heaven help me!" she gasped. "I've got to go to the ladies room!"

Amanda looked at her as if she'd broken out in purple hives. "Are you okay, Haley?" she questioned while Franklyn discreetly rose as if women always called upon the heavens when attacked with the need for the ladies room.

Thirty-Two

Amanda, I need to speak with you in person. Can you come over?
Angie's urgent phone call at seven in the morning had driven
Amanda to quickly shower, throw on a pair of sweats, and hustle
to Angie's new home. After a chilling rain, the neighborhood
birds were invigorated and ready to wake the world. Amanda
glanced down at her damp sneakers and wished she'd grabbed a
jacket on the way out.

She shivered, rang the doorbell, awaited an answer, and
expected the worst. Her first thoughts were for Wayne. Months
ago, Angie had confided that he had high blood pressure. As
intense as his job was, Amanda was not surprised. She hoped he
hadn't been hospitalized. Angie had waited so long for a good
husband and a happy life, Amanda cringed to think Wayne's
health might be faltering. She pressed the doorbell again and
breathed a prayer that no ill had befallen him.

When the doorknob turned, she fully expected Joe, the smile-less one. Instead, she encountered Angie, still wearing her satin robe. Her hair was mussed, her face pallid.

"Where's Joe?" Amanda asked and wondered if the emergency might involve him. As cheerless as the fellow was, he'd swiftly become apart of Angie and Wayne's family.

"It's Sunday, his day off. Remember?"

"Oh yes." Yawning, Amanda stepped into the spacious entryway. This time the marble floors posed no threat for a pair of rubber-soled sneakers.

"We've got the place to ourselves," Angie said and fiddled with her robe's tie.

"Is Wayne okay?" Amanda asked, the aroma of gourmet coffee beckoning her further into the room.

"Yes, he's fine." Angie snapped the door shut, rapidly blinked, and gripped Amanda's hand. "We need to talk," she admitted and tugged Amanda across the entryway.

"So I've heard." By the time Angie led Amanda down the hallway and to the breakfast nook, Amanda was nearly as jittery as Angie.

"Here. Sit down." Angie pulled out a wicker chair, picked up a silver-plated urn, and filled a fragile cup with steaming coffee. After sloshing the liquid into the saucer and bumping the cream dish, Angie plunked down the urn and exclaimed, "This is all so dreadful! Just *dreadful!*"

"It's okay, Angie," Amanda said, shaking her head. "It's just cream." She took her seat, grabbed the cotton napkin, and blotted at the white liquid.

"Not the cream, silly," Angie scoffed. "Wayne's sister!"

Amanda stopped blotting. "The sick one?"

"Yes. Except she's not sick any more."

"You mean she—"

"Yes!" Angie said, her lips strained. "I can't believe she was really sick. And here all this time, I thought—" She shook her head. "If I'd known she was really ill…I just have to say I respect her so much more now that…" Angie worked her mouth and plopped into her chair.

"Now that she's dead?" Amanda questioned and couldn't help but feel sorry for Franklyn. She knew he must care for his aunt as much as she cared for Angie.

"Well, it's just that…" Angie fiddled with her half-eaten grapefruit. "I honestly thought she was just putting on an act to keep Franklyn in London. He'd planned this break in his education to spend time with Wayne. And her illness just worsened so…so…*conveniently*—or at least that's what I thought," she admitted.

Amanda picked up her coffee cup and partook of the Hazelnut brew.

"But none of that is the reason you're here," Angie explained.

"It isn't?" Amanda placed the cup back in the pool of coffee claiming the saucer.

"Absolutely not." Angie balled her fists atop the table, leaned forward, and whispered, "You're never going to believe this. Just never! I can't even believe it myself!" Angie's eyes reddened.

Amanda leaned forward and awaited all sorts of horrid news.

"It's *you* I feel so terribly sorry for." She gripped Amanda's arm.

"Me?" Amanda bleated and tried to follow the logic.

"Yes, you, dear." Angie shook her head. "Wayne is taking Franklyn to the airport now. He's catching the first flight back home to London. And he's taking Janet French with him."

"Janet French!" Amanda exclaimed.

"Yes! Can you believe it?"

Amanda blinked and shook her head. "Whatever for?"

"They're engaged," Angie stated.

"Engaged? Janet French and Franklyn West?" Amanda leaned back in her chair and stared at the Monet print claiming the wall. The painting reminded her much of the morning, all gauzy and rainy and hazy gray. Trying to make sense of this news perfectly fit the painting and the morning. The facts were as hard to absorb as the details of a fog-cloaked countryside.

"They've been engaged for months," Angie explained. "They met when Franklyn visited months ago when you were in Paris."

"Poor Haley," Amanda breathed as fresh irritation nibbled at the edge of her spirit.

"Poor Haley?" Angie squeaked. "Poor *you!* You're the one who was falling in love with him."

"No!" Amanda shook her head and relived the times Franklyn had flirted with her. "No. I thought maybe—maybe before he left the second time. But when he came back, I knew. Remember, I told you before the party that I hadn't even thought about his not contacting me?"

"Yes, but I thought you were just being—"

"I was being *honest*," Amanda stated and reflected upon her worries that Franklyn was going to propose that evening Nate came over. Whatever he was trying to tell her, she realized it had nothing to do with her marrying him.

Maybe he wanted to tell me about Janet, she thought. If that was the case, his reaction to Nate's ringing the doorbell made perfect sense. He'd looked upward and said, "Maybe this is Your way of saving me from myself." *Perhaps he wanted to ask my advice,* Amanda deduced, and the whole episode was beginning to make perfect sense.

Angie slumped against her chair. "Well, I guess this changes everything then."

"Actually, I was beginning to think he was interested in *Haley*," Amanda explained.

"No." Angie shook her head. "He told us this morning he'd done his best to keep his cover. He and Janet both agreed it was best for him to seem flirty, rather than anyone suspect the two of them were together."

He used us! He used Haley and me both! Amanda thought. "The piano," she said. "He's the one, isn't he?"

"Positively yes!" Angie said.

"Why all the secrecy?" she raised her hands.

"Because Franklyn is his aunt's sole heir, and she didn't like Janet." Angie laid her hands on the table and patted her fingers against the lace cloth.

"Why not?" Amanda shook her head. "She seems like a terribly sweet woman." And since Janet was no longer a prospect for Nate's mystery lady, she was getting sweeter by the second.

But if she's not the mystery woman, who is? Amanda relived that tumultuous dream, and Nate's mystery lady in the passenger seat remained as elusive as ever.

Angie pushed at her hair and continued, "Franklyn says he thinks his aunt was jealous."

"Of Janet?" Amanda asked and tried not to think about Nate. "Why?"

"Why indeed." Angie's level stare had never been more penetrating.

Amanda looked down. "Okay, maybe I've been tempted there myself," she admitted. "God forgive me. Forgive us all." She paused and recalled all major crimes Janet had committed: great smile, golden skin, thin hips. But none was as wretched as having the audacity to be gorgeous.

"But she's just so beautiful and petite," Amanda defended, "and here I am, looking like a redheaded version of the Jolly Green Giant." She fluffed her hair.

Angie laughed and placed her hands over Amanda's. "You don't have to apologize to *anyone*, darling," she assured. "But I'm afraid my sister-in-law was jealous because she didn't want to share Franklyn. She just knew Janet was going to take him away forever. So," she released Amanda's hands and leaned back, "she threatened to disinherit him if he didn't stop seeing her."

"What?" Amanda gasped.

"Yes, indeed." Angie picked up her coffee cup and shook her head. "Franklyn said that's when he and Janet decided to play it cool. His aunt is worth millions, you know."

"No, I didn't know."

"Of course. She received an equal inheritance with Wayne when their parents died."

"Oh really?" Amanda said and discreetly eyed the plate of croissants sitting in the middle of the table. She'd known Wayne West for many years because he was her banker. She'd also known he had some money. However, Amanda hadn't pried for his level of monetary advantage, even though she'd been dying to know for ages.

Angie giggled.

"What?" Amanda asked and shifted her focus to her maternal friend.

"You're so transparent, Amanda. Don't ever take up lying. No one would ever believe you."

"What?" Amanda repeated.

"I can see it all over you. You've been so curious for so long and now you're trying to hide it."

"Well…" Amanda hedged.

"It's quite all right, dear." Angie patted her knee. "You deserve to know. Wayne is more loaded than *I* even imagined."

"You deserve it, Angie," Amanda breathed and squeezed her governess' hand. "You've been better to me than ten mothers. I can say that you're a major reason for all my successes."

"That, and you have a father who adores you."

"Imagine what *he'd* be like if I ever seriously considered getting married," Amanda said.

"He's so spoiled, he'd have to move in with you. Or you'd have to stay at the villa with your husband."

"On second thought," Amanda picked up a silver teaspoon and stirred her coffee, "awhile ago, he *did* mention my getting married, believe it or not. He hinted that he thought Nate Knighton and I were going to get married," Amanda said and wondered what possessed her to mention the very name she'd cried herself to sleep over. Nevertheless, the idea of her father's imagining something *romantic* between her and Nate still left her befuddled. A deep friendship that promised to last a lifetime could in no way be grounds for a romance! "Isn't that the most ridiculous thing you've ever heard?" Amanda asked.

"Hmmm," Angie mused and stared into the kitchen.

Amanda studied Angie and couldn't fathom what she meant by that "Hmmm." It was as elusive as some of Nate's "Humphs." She put down the spoon, administered a large swallow of coffee to her grumbling stomach, and reached for a croissant. But no sooner had her fingers touched the flaky pastry than she thought of Haley again.

"Oh no, Haley!" Amanda breathed and stood. "I've got to go see her now. She needs to know."

"You mean about Franklyn?" Angie stared up at Amanda.

"Exactly," Amanda affirmed. "I was trying to make a match between them. I hope she won't be too disappointed."

"And all this time, I thought *I* was making a match with you and Franklyn." Angie stood. "It looks as though my stepson was promised in three directions," she said through a dry laugh.

"Yes, but only *one* that he arranged," Amanda added. She picked up the croissant, nibbled the corner, and took a final sip of her coffee to bolster her nerves.

The conversation with Haley could not be postponed.

Thirty-Three

By the time Amanda stood at Haley's door, the irritation that had nibbled at her spirit now implanted itself in the center of her mind.

The nerve of that man! she thought as she rang Haley's doorbell. *He came to my home, brought chocolates and flowers, and even said, "Olé!" to my cat.* Amanda rang the doorbell and ferociously knocked. Her knuckles protested the abuse, and she rubbed them against her other palm.

Then "oléd!" Haley—more or less, she added. *Well, he rescued her and her purse anyway! Of all the nerve!* Amanda fumed.

The doorknob rattled. The door swung inward. Haley leaned her head against the door. She wore her thick glasses. Her hair was frizzed, her makeup gone. She looked more like the old Haley than she had since she was sick, right down to the worn, fuzzy housecoat. Amanda touched her cheek, free of makeup. She probably looked a mess herself.

"What's the matter?" Haley asked. "You don't look so good."

"I'm exasperated beyond belief!" Amanda spewed. "Mind if I come in?"

"No, of course not!" Haley opened the door wider and rubbed at the corner of her eyes. "Sorry to be such a lazy head. What time is it anyway?"

Amanda checked her watch. "Eight o'clock."

Haley shut the door. "We need to get ready for church."

"Not so fast." Amanda strode to the couch and plopped therein. She patted the cushion beside her. "I have some *shocking* news."

"What's the matter?" Her eyes wide, Haley joined Amanda.

Gripping Haley's hands, Amanda looked her in the eyes. "Haley," she began, "brace yourself."

"Okay," Haley agreed and hung on to Amanda's fingers.

"Franklyn West has been secretly engaged to Janet French all this time."

"Oh." Haley blinked. Her fingers relaxed. "Is that all?"

"Is that all?" Amanda repeated. "Haley, he *used* us—both of us—as a cover for the engagement!" After that declaration, Amanda related all the details of his aunt's death and the ramifications of the whole ordeal.

"Well, I hope they'll be happy," Haley said through a yawn. She stood and stretched. "Want some tea?"

"Haley, aren't you the least bit upset? Yesterday at the mall, you acted like you were starting to *like* him."

"No." Haley shook her head. "I was praying you were wrong about his liking me."

Amanda stood and placed her hands on her hips. She eyed Haley, and Haley eyed her right back. A great, unspoken message lay between them. And Amanda decided the time had come for some honesty. She was more certain than ever that Haley had been hiding a Roger revival. Her lack of interest in Franklyn only supported her interpretation of the last weeks.

Just about the time Amanda decided to press for the truth, Haley spoke. "Amanda," she pushed up her glasses and observed her friend, "there's something you need to know."

"Yes, you're right." Amanda flopped back onto the couch, grabbed a pillow, and pulled it to her midsection. "Go ahead and tell me," she said and decided the time had come to accept the inevitable. Haley was going to live in mooville for life.

"I'm sorry I've been hiding it from you, but..." Haley sat on the edge of the coffee table and hunched forward. "It's just that...it's like Nate says, I guess, you just care too much. And sometimes..." Haley shifted back and fidgeted with her glasses. "Sometimes..." She stood and gently patted the sides of her thighs.

The telephone's peel pierced the moment. Haley jumped and stepped toward the cordless phone sitting on the end table.

"Hello," she said as Amanda allowed all her hopes for her friend to unravel. *Oh well, I tried,* she thought and decided the time had come to fully release Project Haley. Amanda had made a complete mess of the Mason ordeal. Only pain had come of her efforts. Then the Franklyn match had been a sham and nothing more. Despite it all, Haley had gone right back to the person Amanda was certain was not right for her.

"Yes, I see," Haley said into the receiver. Her shoulders hunched, her back to Amanda, she faced the hall. "Yes. You're right, of course."

Amanda sat upright. She narrowed her eyes. Something was odd about this conversation.

"I can't really, um..." She stroked her forehead. "Yes! How did you guess?"

Whoever this is, Amanda thought, *Haley's trying to hide his identity.* Then one name stormed her mind: *Roger!* And Amanda decided that when Haley hung up, she would put her dear friend out of her misery. She'd tell her she knew the truth and give her blessing.

There's nothing left to do, she thought as the conversation came to a close.

"Of course. I won't say a word. Yes, the same to you, Nate," Haley finished. When she pulled the receiver away from her ear, she went stone still for a full five seconds. Then she cast a furtive glance toward Amanda before placing the receiver in its cradle. Never had a glance held so much mortification.

Amanda observed her friend's profile while a new series of issues presented themselves. "Was that Nate?" she asked.

Haley nodded.

"Did he know I'm here?" Amanda scooted to the edge of the couch.

"Well, he, uh…" She studied her thumbnail.

"He's still in Brisbane, right?"

"Um…"

"Is he back in town?" Amanda stood and tossed the pillow back onto the sofa.

"Actually, he is," Haley replied with a quick nod. "Yes, he's back in Highland."

"But he hasn't called me." Amanda shook as Nate's departing statement rotated through her mind like a mantra of pain: *Sometimes the death of one relationship has to happen so another can be born.*

"Well, he's…you know," Haley shrugged and mumbled, "busy, I guess." She walked toward the hallway that led to the kitchen and sunroom. "Still want some tea?"

Amanda didn't know if she nodded yes or no and didn't care. She watched Haley disappear into the short hallway. Soon the sounds of tea-making clinked and clattered from her small kitchen. And Amanda began to put together a series of clues that had been so blatant she couldn't believe she had missed them.

The night Haley met Mason at O'Brien's, Nate had been highly impressed with Haley's makeover.

At the villa dinner party, Nate had been furious over Amanda's trying to pair Haley with Mason. He said it had been on Roger's behalf, but was it?

During Janet's "Welcome to Highland" party, Nate had insisted on jumping to Haley's rescue when she spilled the ice. He'd spent much of that party basking in Haley's presence.

The day Haley was late from lunch weeks ago, she mentioned she'd run into Nate Knighton. Nate had also canceled lunch with Amanda that day because he had an "important meeting."

When Mason and Sonja were hateful to Haley, Nate had whisked her away to her office. Upon Amanda's entering the room, he'd been kneeling in front of Haley.

That same evening, Nate had repeatedly frowned at Franklyn when he paid Haley any attention. He'd also said that Haley was so pretty these days she'd look good with anyone.

"Now, he's in town and calling Haley and Haley's trying to hide it," Amanda whispered. *How long has he been in town?* she wondered. *Did he even leave town at all? Maybe the whole story was just a cover to give him time to get closer to Haley and avoid me!* The fact that Haley had been the epitome of happy this whole week validated every thought.

As the facts and worries and suppositions slammed into Amanda, her concerns over Haley being involved with Roger seemed like child's play.

Haley isn't involved with Roger! Amanda thought. *She's Nate's mystery woman! She's the one in the dream!* Amanda closed her eyes and relived that sickening scene, and the ethereal figure sitting in the passenger seat finally materialized.

"Haley Schmitz!" Amanda whispered. She opened her eyes, only to discover the room was spinning. "It's Haley!" she mumbled and swallowed against the nausea creeping up her throat.

My best friend! She balled her fists. *My two best friends! I've lost them both!* She covered her face and groaned.

"Here you are!" Haley said.

Amanda lifted her face. Haley was breezing into the living room wearing a cheerful although strained smile.

"Are you okay?" Haley asked and halted six feet away.

Shaking her head, Amanda gargled out some inane sound.

"Amanda?" Haley gasped and sat the tea mugs on the coffee table. "Are you choking?" She hurried forward.

Holding her throat, Amanda stumbled away from Haley. "Don't touch me!" she gasped.

"Amanda?" Haley stopped.

"You were trying to hide Nate on the phone," Amanda squeezed out.

"Yes." Haley looked at the floor.

"Be honest with me, Haley!" Amanda wheezed. "I've got to know... Do you... Are you... Has there ever been a time when you—you were attracted to—to Nate?"

"Well..." Haley hedged and toyed with her robe's tie. "I guess..." She lifted her head, stammered over several more attempts to communicate, then finally said, "At first, of course. But what single woman wouldn't be at first?"

"Are you involved with—with *someone* now?" Amanda couldn't even bring herself to say Nate's name this time.

"Amanda, I was going to tell you!" Haley said. "I feel so bad and so sneaky. But it's just that I knew you wouldn't be happy. So I—Nate even agreed it was best to keep it quiet this time." She shrugged. "Is there any way you can forgive me?"

"I've got to go," Amanda said. She snatched up her purse from the coffee table and struggled to the door. "I won't be at church today."

"I'm sorry, Amanda!" Haley called.

As hot tears blurred her vision, Amanda slammed the door and ran for her car.

Thirty-Four

Standing at the window, Haley watched Amanda whiz from the drive. She stroked her face, shook her head, and strained for some means to deal with Amanda's reaction. She'd suspected Amanda would be upset over her relationship with Roger, but she never imagined her friend would be so broken.

"She's not even going to church this morning," Haley whispered. "This is bad."

Maybe Nate will know what to do! she thought and swiveled for the phone. When he told her the issues involved Amanda and to keep the conversation confidential, Haley had marveled at the irony of having Amanda sitting in her living room.

Finally Nate detected her awkward responses and said, "Is Amanda there by chance?" Haley had swiftly affirmed his supposition, and Nate said he'd call back later.

"I'll just call him," Haley mumbled as she picked up the receiver. After pulling her address book from the end table drawer and fumbling until she found Nate's number, Haley pressed in the number.

While Haley awaited Nate's answer, she pondered Amanda's question about her ever being attracted to Nate. The unexpected query had nearly struck Haley dumb. She'd never planned to tell Amanda of her initial attraction to the Knighton heir. But Haley had made it clear that her attraction had been at the *first* of her acquaintance with Nate. Then she had shifted to Roger.

"Hello," Nate's weary voice floated over the line.

"Nate, this is Haley," she explained, her voice tight. "Amanda's gone."

"You don't sound very good," Nate replied.

"I'm not. She just found out about Roger and me, and she's taking it really hard." Haley picked at her terrycloth housecoat.

"What do you mean by 'hard'?" Nate questioned.

"Well, she told me not to touch her." Haley squinted. "Then she ran out of here like somebody had died."

"That's odd," Nate said.

"Very." Haley reached for the mug of tea. Cradling the cordless receiver between her ear and shoulder, she picked up the tea bag string and stirred the liquid with the bag.

"Maybe she's having a bad hair day," Nate said with no humor.

"Well, she was actually," Haley replied and considered her own hair. "I think we all are, for that matter."

"This is really odd," Nate repeated. "But then, I'm not sure I can predict Amanda *at all* these days. That's part of the reason I was calling earlier."

"Oh?" Haley sipped the black tea laced with honey.

"You know I've been visiting my brother."

"Yes…"

"But you don't know why." He hesitated and sighed. "Or do you?"

Haley settled onto the love seat and snuggled into the corner. "No, I don't."

"Good," Nate replied. "I was hoping nobody knew. If you don't, then I've done a good job of keeping everything undercover."

"What's going on?" Frowning, Haley attempted to understand Nate's cryptic comments.

"Like I already said, Haley, this is confidential."

"Right." She nodded and sipped her tea.

"I'm in love with Amanda," he blurted.

Haley jumped forward and sloshed tea all over her housecoat. By the time she placed the mug on the coffee table, she marveled at her own surprise. Nate had been Amanda's constant companion ever since Haley started working for Wood-Priebe International. And now that he'd admitted his love, Haley's mind replayed scene after scene in which Nate had come within a breath of flirting with her boss.

No, she amended, *he did flirt with Amanda. All the time, as a matter of fact.*

"Haley?" Nate prompted.

"You meant it at the steakhouse when you said we all love her to pieces. You really meant it!"

"Actually, I said that before I thought," Nate replied. "I assumed you thought I love her like you love her."

"Well, I did." Haley brushed at the droplets of tea dotting her housecoat.

"But I didn't mean it like that." Nate's voice had never been more serious or more distraught. "That's the reason I wanted to talk to you. I've been in Brisbane asking my brother's advice. I needed to get away and decide what to do. I promise, Haley, I'm in so much torment, I'm thinking about just relocating—maybe to the Paris store, even. They need a manager, and—"

"But that would be a huge demotion," Haley said.

"I don't care. I've got to get away from her, or *I am going to die.*"

"Why don't you just tell her how you feel?" Haley stood and padded toward the kitchen.

"That's what Gordon says I should do. But I promise, if she rejects me, I think it would kill me."

Haley retrieved a towel from the kitchen counter and stroked at the spill. She tried to imagine Nate Knighton, strong, sophisticated, self-assured, as vulnerable as he sounded.

Shaking her head, Haley said, "Nate, get a grip on yourself. Listen to what you're saying! You're thinking about moving to another continent without even telling her. What if you told her and she loved the idea…maybe she'd even say she loves you too."

"That's why I'm calling you, Haley," Nate's voice took on an eager edge. "Has she said anything that would make you think I might have a chance?"

"Uh…" Haley leaned against the kitchen counter, covered her face with her hand, and desperately tried to recall anything that might encourage the man.

"There's not anything, is there?" Nate asked, his voice flat.

"There *might be,*" Haley said, "but my brain just won't cooperate. She's been really grouchy all week, if that helps," she said. "It might have been because you were gone."

Nate sighed. "I can only hope."

"I'm sorry I can't be more helpful," Haley said. "But if it's any consolation, I've wondered over and over again why Amanda took you for granted. Maybe it's time for her to wake up." Haley nodded and straightened her shoulders. "I *do* think you should just tell her, Nate. I agree with Gordon."

"All right then, Haley," Nate said. "But if she laughs in my face, I want you to know I'm going to need a psychiatrist. And you'll be it."

Haley laughed. "Oh Nate," she said, "what woman in her right mind would turn you down?"

"You would, wouldn't you?"

"In a heartbeat," Haley quipped and laughed. "But then I'm in love with Roger."

"Ah ha! You said it."

"Yes." Haley sighed and walked back toward the living room. "You're right. I said it. But don't tell Roger."

"Oh, I won't," Nate replied. "That's *your* job, right?"

"Right," Haley said and brainstormed ways she could tell Roger she really did love him.

By the time she hung up with Nate, Haley decided she needed to do something that would really get Roger's attention. During their whole courtship, she had always allowed Roger to make the first move.

Maybe if I made a move, he'd get the hint, she thought and wondered what Roger would think if she just showed up at his country church. To keep up the secrecy, she'd been attending church with Amanda. But now that all was in the open, Haley decided a surprise was in order. And maybe if she hinted of her love strongly enough, Roger would propose again.

The very idea swept aside all her worries about Amanda. Her friend had obviously endured a hard week. She was probably just under stress. *When people are under stress, they always overreact.* Haley decided to call Amanda later this evening.

Amanda sat on the edge of the cliff behind the villa and blindly stared at the ocean pounding the shore. She'd cried until she could cry no more. Her eyes were swollen, her heart shattered. Somewhere between Haley's apartment and her villa, Amanda had realized that Nate was much more to her than a friend or older brother—he was the man she loved.

The cold mist barely lingered, but Amanda was so numb she barely registered the moisture that beaded on her lashes. She pulled the hood of her jacket onto her head, hugged her knees, and rested her forehead on them. She closed her eyes and began to pray as she'd never prayed before.

"Oh God," she whimpered, "it was because of *me* that Mason hurt Haley. I know it was. Is this some kind of punishment? Mason fell for me instead of Haley. Now Nate has fallen for Haley instead of me. Oh, Jesus," Amanda groaned and tightly closed her eyes. "Please tell me this is some nightmare. I just don't think I can live if it's for real."

The smell of saltwater and earth, the cry of seagulls, the cold, autumn wind whipping at her hood did nothing to reassure her. Nothing. And Amanda sank deeper in the mire of despair. She imagined herself in the next few weeks watching Nate and Haley grow more in love as they planned their wedding.

"I can't do it," Amanda pleaded. "Oh, God, please don't make me. Please, please forgive me for ever thinking I could help someone fall in love. Nate was right. I *was* trying to play God. I should have just let Haley marry Roger! Then I wouldn't be in all this pain!"

If Roger really loved Haley, I wonder if this is how he felt? The hard reality of that question made Amanda pity Roger for the first time. *Oh, God,* she pleaded again, *help Roger forgive me.*

Amanda lifted her head and gazed into the gray morning. The water stretched to the horizon, changing from aqua, to dark green, to infinite blue. She could identify with the ocean. That's how large her love stretched for Nate. She felt as if she'd opened a door within her heart where years of adoration had been stored. Now the love rushed through, filling her heart to a depth she never dreamed possible.

She recalled all the years she'd known Nate, all the times she'd depended upon him to be there. He had been like a light switch in her life she'd taken for granted. Amanda had simply flipped him on when she needed his presence and never questioned that he'd be there for her. She'd relied upon him for even the smallest details of her life like Mr. Adair and his dog.

Nate always comes through, even when I'm trying to help someone else, Amanda concluded.

Fresh pain zipped through her heart as she recalled telling him there could *never* be a romance between them. The pain increased as she relived the hug he'd bestowed after her party. He'd even kissed her. Amanda stroked her forehead. She'd been so confused that night, not fully understanding his meaning.

Now his meaning was clear—painfully clear. He was allowing the friendship with her to die so the romance with Haley could flourish. That kiss had been his goodbye kiss, so chaste and simple. The hug had been his way of saying their relationship was forever over.

Even though Amanda thought she couldn't cry any more, new tears filled her eyes. She covered her face with her hands and heaved. Fortunately, when she arrived back at the villa, her father was still in bed, unaware of Amanda's state of emotions. And she had no intention of returning inside until she had fully regained composure.

At this rate, she thought and pulled a damp wad of tissue from her jacket's pocket, *I'll be out here all day!*

"Amanda?" The soft, male voice floated on the breeze, mingled with the swish and rush of the ocean. At first Amanda thought she had imagined the voice. After all, it sounded like Nate. The second time the "Amanda?" resonated with the waves, she swiveled toward it.

Nate Knighton stood 20 feet away, hovering on the edge of the rocks like a shy schoolboy afraid to move. Dark circles marred his eyes. His face was haggard. The wind rumpled his hair. He wore a hesitant smile and the jogging suit Amanda had given him a few years back.

"Nate?" Amanda said and rubbed at her tears with the wet tissue.

Thirty-Five

Haley stepped into the canopy of traditional music that filled the steepled church. The organ wheezed out the melody of "Amazing Grace," while a crowd of 60 Sunday worshipers faithfully sang in sequence with the minister of music. Haley spotted Roger sitting behind his family near the back row. His mother and father, sister and her husband claimed the two rows in front of him. Roger sat all alone.

Her heart pounding, Haley eased down the aisle and relished the scents of old wood and well-used hymnals. She knew she'd always think of this day every time she smelled a hymnal. This was a pivotal day in the life of Haley Schmitz. Today she had reached into the bottom of herself and found some bravery. When Roger pursued Haley before, she would have never dreamed of just showing up at his church without his invitation. Last week either, for that matter.

But what Nate said had given her the courage to drive to the country and somehow let Roger know that she loved him—that she'd never stopped loving him. If only she could wipe the pain from his eyes and win his trust once more, Haley was certain he would propose. And she was equally certain she would say yes.

She stopped at Roger's side and was about to touch his shoulder when he looked up at her. He jerked his head back, gaped a full five seconds, and began juggling his hymnal until he dropped it. His father and mother both looked over their shoulders while Roger scooted over and made room for Haley.

By the time Haley settled on the pew, her spine was stiff. Roger's parents had to know she'd turned down his proposal. And if they knew, she feared their resentment. But their kind glances revealed nothing but acceptance. Roger's sister offered the same as she discreetly turned and grinned at Haley.

Her back relaxed. She smiled into Roger's eyes as he took her hand. Her fingers trembled next to his, and Haley placed her other hand along his forearm. Roger wore a simple plaid shirt, a new pair of jeans, and a clean pair of work boots. Haley had dressed in a denim skirt and loafers and a sweater she bought on last year's clearance rack. While the outfit was far from sophisticated, Haley felt much more comfortable than if she'd been wearing spike heels and a chic suit. Furthermore, she fit Roger and his world, and the fit felt good.

Haley knew beyond all doubt that this was where she belonged—in Roger's life, in his church, on his family pew. She belonged in his tiny, one-bedroom house where she could hang her drawings and make the home hers.

Oh, God, please, she prayed, *please let him ask me again.*

"Amanda," Nate repeated and moved closer. She sat on the edge of the cliff like a hunched-up monkey. Her eyes were red, swollen, and full of sorrow. Trying to fathom how she could have such a strong reaction to Haley's news, Nate wondered where to start.

"Your dad and I couldn't find you," he explained. "He suggested I check out here."

She rubbed her cheeks with the tissue, stroked her disheveled hair, and stood. Haley had been right. Amanda *was* having a bad hair day. But she was so beautiful to Nate, he couldn't have cared less.

"This is where I come when I need to think," she said and walked toward him. Amanda stopped 15 feet away. She looked down and nudged at a rock with the toe of her sneaker.

"Haley told me everything," Amanda choked out. "I...I'm glad for her."

"Me too," Nate replied.

"She deserves the best."

"I agree. Haley's a wonderful lady."

Her face straining, Amanda pressed her lips together.

Nate looked toward the ocean and prayed for divine guidance. *Just tell her,* Gordon's words reverberated through his mind. The seagull's shrill calls took on the rhythm of the words, *Just tell her. Just tell her. Just tell her.*

"Amanda," Nate said and stepped toward her, "there's something I've *got* to tell you."

For every centimeter he neared her, she moved back.

"Amanda," he began again, "I—I need to tell you...uh..." Nate zipped and unzipped the jogging suit jacket. On a whim, he'd placed something in his vehicle that he'd considered clever when he left home. By the time he arrived, Nate decided the idea had been too sappy. But now he was beginning to think he *needed* the item to communicate his love. He didn't seem to be doing a good job on his own.

Given the fact that Amanda's arms were crossed, her face was stiff, and she stepped back every time he stepped forward, Nate didn't know if he even should declare his love. The fear of being rejected nearly sent him running back in the way he came. Nate's heart thrashed his ribs. He broke out in a film of cold sweat. His mouth went so dry he could barely swallow.

This was the same woman he'd flippantly flirted with for years. But now Nate could find no glib remarks, no light teasing, no humorous quips.

"Before I left for Brisbane, you said you wanted to see my mystery woman," Nate managed to say.

"I...I..." Amanda hugged herself and shook her head.

"I've got a...um...picture of her in the car," Nate said and pointed over his shoulder.

"I don't need a picture," Amanda replied. "I already know."

"Y–you do?" Nate stammered. If she did know, then her posture and expression were not good indicators of his success.

"Yes, Haley told me."

His body flashed hot while all his blood felt as if it drained to his feet. "She—she told you? Already?"

Amanda's nod was fierce and sure. "So you don't have to show me her picture. I already *know* what she looks like!"

"Haley told you?" Nate repeated. He shook his head and couldn't believe she had so swiftly broken her vow of silence. Furthermore, he couldn't move to Paris soon enough.

"Yes! She told me!" Amanda cried and ran past him. "Just— just go!" she demanded as she trotted toward the villa.

The shaking started with Nate's lips and vibrated through every joint until it stopped at his ankles. "God, help me!" he groaned and powerlessly watched Amanda dash up the balcony steps and into the villa.

◠ ◡

Haley smiled into Roger's face and clung to his hand as they walked up the winding country lane that led to the Miller farm. "It's only half a mile," Roger had encouraged. "Let's leave your car here and just walk. I'll drive you back to get it after lunch."

She'd gladly agreed, and now couldn't have been happier. The mist had stopped. The gray skies had cleared. The sun spread its warm rays on the whole afternoon. Only the slight chill in the air attested that April was nearing, and with it, the promise of more autumn weather.

The closer they grew to the farm, the more silent Roger became. The amiable banter they'd shared died. A tense silence cloaked them, and Haley began to wonder if she'd made a mistake in coming. She never would have driven to the church if she'd suspected Roger didn't want her there. Now she was beginning to think exactly that.

Haley withdrew her hand from his, tugged her sweater sleeves over her hands, and crossed her arms. Her small, leather purse swung with the rhythm of her steps. Haley was tempted to remove her keys from the purse and develop some well-suited excuse for her departure.

Roger bent, picked up a rock from the dusty road, and tossed it toward the paddock that Haley recognized as his family's estate. He stared straight ahead, fidgeted with nothing, and finally blurted, "Haley, I've got to say it!" He turned toward her, gripped her upper arms, and peered into her eyes. His tormented soul lay bare before her.

"Roger?" Haley gasped.

"I love you, Haley," he groaned. "Please tell me you feel the same before I die."

"I *do!*" Haley whispered. "I *do* love you!" she added.

"You do?" The torment dissolved.

"That's why I came today—to somehow tell you. But I really didn't know how." Haley shook her head. "I wanted to say how sorry I was for turning down your proposal and for—" She stopped and placed both hands over her mouth. Her face warming, she lambasted herself for her unplanned admission. She'd just as good as asked Roger to ask her to marry him.

"Haley, oh Haley," Roger said and wrapped his arms around her. "It nearly killed me when you said no. I was so sure of you...of us."

She rested her head against his chest and slipped her arms around his torso. Haley absorbed the comfort of his embrace, the warmth of his love. "I'm sorry," she breathed against his shirt. "Amanda..."

"I know," Roger replied. "Nate told me everything. And if you want the truth, I've really had to fight an attitude toward her."

"Please don't." Haley lifted her head. "She means well. She really does. She loves me like a sister and just wants what's best for me. The problem is, her ideas of what's best are totally different from mine...and God's."

Roger lowered his lips to Haley's and let her know that his idea of what was best involved her and him and a wedding march. Finally he trailed a row of kisses to her ear and whispered, "Will you marry me?"

"I thought you'd never ask...again," Haley replied and couldn't deny a giggle.

His laughter matched hers as Roger pulled away and said, "I'm taking that as a yes."

No sooner had Haley nodded than he grabbed her hand and pulled her toward a gate. "Come on," he urged and ran across the lane. "There's something you need to see."

"What?" Haley gasped for every breath as she tried to keep up with him. But they didn't stop until they'd run across a paddock full of grass and cattle and oaks and come to a white cottage surrounded by a picket fence.

Haley jostled to a stop and gazed upon the cutest house she'd ever seen. The afternoon sunshine christened it in silver while the cottage seemed to say, "Welcome home."

"I love it," Haley breathed, and Roger slid his arm around her waist.

A golden retriever on the porch lifted her head, wagged her tail, and perked her ears.

"Is that Mr. Adair's dog?" Haley asked.

"Yes. That's Goldie."

"But I thought Nate was going to keep her."

"He was, but I offered to take her. He brought her out last night. She's settled in nicely already."

"Amanda's got a good heart," Haley observed.

Roger sighed. "Maybe you're right," he mumbled. "I just wish she'd cared a little less in our case."

"Nate said something like that," Haley replied and squeezed Roger's hand. "But maybe if the two of you give each other a chance, you'll learn to care about each other."

"I guess I'm willing to give it a try," Roger agreed.

"I have a feeling Amanda will too. She's notorious for doing the right thing when all is settled."

"So you do you like the house?" He waved toward the cottage.

She rubbed her fingers across the top of the gate post and relished the slick feel of new paint. "Like it?" she exclaimed and didn't dare to hope for what she suspected. "I *love* it!" she repeated. "I think it's the prettiest cottage I've ever seen!"

"Do you recognize it?"

"It's your old place, but I'd have never recognized it…except it's in the same place."

"I had it all remodeled and expanded—just for you!"

"For me?"

"Yes. Remember when I was out of town before—before—" He stopped and Haley was humiliated to once again be reminded of his initial proposal. She focused on the stepping-stones that led to the cozy front porch and wished she'd never even considered turning him down.

"I was out of town for a few days. But then I came back home and was working to finish it, especially for you."

"And I turned you down. Oh Roger!" Haley's eyes stung. "I'm so, so sorry!" she repeated, then leaned closer and kissed his cheek. "I didn't deserve all this in the first place. And now a second chance! Is there any way you can ever forgive me?"

Roger's face fell into lines of doubt, and he rubbed his chin before a sly smile claimed his features. "Before I can forgive you, you'll need to kiss this side too." He turned his face so she could reach the other cheek.

"If you insist," Haley said and wasted no time fulfilling his request.

"Then you'll have to promise to marry me this week."

"This week?" Haley exclaimed.

"Yes." He crossed his arms, and even though his stance appeared confident, his eyes remained uncertain. "I figure we would have been married by now. We need to make up for lost time."

"This week?" Haley repeated.

"I believe that's what I said." Roger wrapped his arms around her and rested his forehead on hers. "If I have to, I'll beg," he said. "I can even promise a honeymoon in New Zealand."

"You don't have to beg," Haley said, her heart hammering. "I'll be *glad* to marry you this week—New Zealand or not."

Not since before she'd received the awful news of her parents' fatal boat crash had Haley felt as if she belonged. Now, basking in the warmth of Roger's love and acceptance, Haley once again belonged—really belonged—to someone who loved her more than life.

Thirty-Six

Even though Amanda told her breaking heart it was best to lock herself in her room and not watch Nate leave, she stood at the front door window. Amanda hung on to the curtain rod and watched as Nate dejectedly trudged toward his vehicle. With his shoulders sagging and his head low, Nate looked like a thinning old man rather than the young, virile male that he was.

He's lost some weight, Amanda thought and attributed it to being in love and losing his appetite. *Haley is the luckiest woman in the world!* She wondered how she could have been with Nate all these years without seeing the force of her own love.

"I've been a blind idiot," she whispered as Nate reached his Mercedes. She clutched the curtain rod and told herself not to give in to the urge to run after him. She didn't want to let him go, and especially not like this. When the vehicle rolled forward, Amanda couldn't stay inside another second.

"Nate!" she hollered and flung open the front door. "Nate, wait!" Amanda wildly waved her arms and careened down the yard's pathway. When she emerged onto the circular drive, the vehicle was pulling from the driveway. Winded, Amanda stopped and groped for her next breath.

I waited too long! she thought. Amanda rubbed her upper arms and nursed her wounded emotions. All the while, she gazed after Nate with the longing of a heart captured by love.

When his brake lights flashed and the car backed up, Amanda realized her mission hadn't been in vain. Nate had seen her. He was returning. And now that he'd seen her, Amanda didn't quite know what she should do with him. At the window, she'd thought she should wish him the best in a polite and civilized manner. But now she didn't trust herself not to entrench her body on the hood of his car and beg him not to marry Haley.

The car whizzed to only feet away and stopped. Nate popped open the door and got out. "Were you calling me?" he asked.

"Y–yes!" Amanda said as her vision blurred again. She chastised herself for giving in to tears yet again, but she was powerless to stop the flow. She rubbed at the tears and stumbled toward the man she loved.

"I just wanted to—to tell you that—that—to wish you the best with—with H–H–Haley! And I wanted—I wanted—I just wanted to tell you I think she's the luckiest woman in the world," Amanda blurted before bolting back toward the villa.

"Amanda!" Nate hollered. Once she arrived at the pathway through the yard, he was restraining her. "Amanda!" He repeated and stepped in front of her. "Did you just say what I *think* you said?"

Amanda looked no higher than the neck of his sweatshirt.

"You think I'm in love with Haley?" he asked through an incredulous laugh.

"Well…" She rapidly blinked while fresh confusion swept away the tears. She looked in Nate's eyes and saw a mixture of relief, victory, and the fervency of a man in love.

"Oh Amanda," Nate chuckled. "How could you think…"

She silently observed him, all the while realizing she had made some sort of dreadful mistake. Shafts of sunlight filtered through the thinning clouds as Nate's expression warmed Amanda's heart.

"I'm *not* in love with Haley," Nate said.

"But she said—and you were on the phone this morning—and—and—she apologized and said the two of you had decided—"

Nate shook his head. "I don't know how you and Haley could have gotten your information so mixed. But I can promise you, it's not Haley I'm in love with." He took her hand. "Come on," Nate said and urged her toward the running vehicle. "I told you I wanted to show you a picture of the woman I'm in love with."

Too confused to resist, Amanda followed Nate to the car. He reached inside, pulled out a brass-trimmed frame, and said, "I guess it's not really a picture I have, but I didn't exactly know what else to call it." With an assured smile, Nate held up a mirror to her face.

Amanda blinked at the swollen-eyed, pale woman whose red hair had gone flat from too much mist.

"*This* is the woman I love!" Nate placed his index finger on the mirror.

"Me?" Amanda breathed. "You love me?"

"Yes!" Nate said. "And I've been eaten up with it ever since you blew me that kiss in O'Brien's."

"You love me?" Amanda whimpered and nearly collapsed with the release of all the pent-up tension. "Oh, Nate, I love you too!" Amanda looked from the mirror to the man who held it and was overwhelmed by the power of his love. "I think I have for ages, and I didn't even know it! I couldn't stand the thought of you even looking at another woman. And that mystery woman you talked about at Christmas—"

"That mystery woman was *you*." Nate laughed. "But I couldn't tell you because I didn't think you were in love with me." He chuckled again.

A gust of wind whipped at her hair, blue shone through the breaking clouds, and the sun heated the top of Amanda's head.

"This is not funny, Nate!" Amanda placed her hands on her hips. "I have suffered for months! I've even been having nightmares. How could you do this to me?"

Nate dropped the mirror in the driver's seat, grabbed her arm, pulled her next to him, and said, "I've been a crazy man, and I haven't known what to do or how to handle any of this. When I first realized I was falling in love, I even put all your gifts in my closet. I think Betty Cates thought I was turning into a slob."

"She did." Amanda chuckled. "She told me all about it—including the basketball that nearly hit her on the head. But I thought it was because your mystery woman made you—because she was jealous and didn't want you having any of the things I'd given you."

"Oh Amanda," Nate said, "I'm so sorry. I guess I should have told you sooner."

"I'm not sure I was ready then," she admitted.

"Are you ready now?" he mumbled, his gaze settling upon her lips.

"Absolutely," Amanda replied. "I've never been readier."

He wrapped his arms around her as a tide of magnetism drew Amanda's lips to his for a kiss that had been simmering for ages. Amanda hung on tight and relived the years she'd known Nate Knighton. She'd gone from the hero worship of an early adolescent to the fondness of a collegiate to the friendship of an adult…and now the love of a woman.

With the earth tilting beneath them, Nate pulled away, rested his forehead on hers, looked in her eyes, and said, "You told me you didn't think there could ever be any romance between us. What do you think now?"

"I think I was daft," Amanda said.

Nate kissed the edge of her mouth and said, "Do you think there could ever be any *marriage* between us?"

"Marriage?" Amanda whispered and eased away. "Oh my word! Marriage?"

"Well…" Nate nervously observed her face. "That is usually what people do when they fall in love."

"But what about Daddy?" She rested her forehead on Nate's shoulder. "He's the reason I decided not to ever get married. And now!" She lifted her head and begged for an answer. "What do we do now?"

"I could always move in here." Nate shrugged and motioned toward the villa.

"You'd do that?" Amanda asked. "You'd give up your beach house?"

"Now, I didn't say *that!*" Nate said with a cunning grin. "We could still use it for weekends, but I'd be fine staying here most of the time. I really like your dad. I think he likes me too."

"Yes. I think he'll be fine with our getting married," Amanda replied.

"I know *I'm* fine with it," Nate said. "And it can't happen soon enough."

Thirty-Seven

⌒⌒

Two weeks later, Amanda stood on the porch of a white cottage. Nate knocked on the door, and they waited. Amanda looked up at him and tried to smile. "I'm really nervous," she admitted and toyed with the large solitaire claiming her left ring finger. Ten days ago, she and Nate had taken a special trip to Paris and came back with the ring and many precious memories. Amanda touched the stone, shimmering in the porch light, and wished the bluish diamond could bequeath her some bravery.

"It's going to be fine," Nate said and squeezed her hand. "Roger's a great person. Very easy and forgiving. You'll love him. Just give him a chance." Nate leaned closer and kissed her cheek.

Amanda clung to his arm and relished his support. This was the first time she had spoken with Roger since before Haley broke up with him several months ago. There were no secrets. Roger fully understood the role Amanda played in trying to stop Haley from marrying him.

Now that they were married and settled into the cottage, Roger and Haley had invited Nate and Amanda over as their first guests. Before they arrived, the couple had made a pact never to tell Haley that Amanda had thought she and Nate were engaged. Amanda decided that little piece of embarrassing information should never be aired.

A muffled "woof" from beside the house preceded Goldie's appearance near the porch.

"Goldie!" Amanda cheered. Wagging her tail, the dog trotted up on the porch and absorbed every ounce of affection Amanda offered.

The cottage door opened, and Haley exclaimed, "You're here!"

"We're here! We're here!" Amanda said and wrapped her aproned friend in a hug. The smell of broiling salmon welcomed the guests along with Roger's, "Hullo out there!"

"Hello!" Nate and Amanda called in unison.

Amanda glanced across the cottage's interior. Haley had a way of stretching money as no one Amanda had ever met. The cottage looked like it belonged in a home magazine, but Amanda suspected Haley was in the throes of decorating the whole thing for pennies on each dollar.

"This is *so cute!*" Amanda exclaimed and fell in love with everything from the rock fireplace to the polished wooden walls to the chintz furniture covers.

"We love it," Haley said.

"Nate!" Roger exclaimed from the kitchen's entryway.

Amanda turned to see the two men shake hands and whack each other on the shoulders. "Good to see you," Nate said. "You're looking much more relaxed than the last time I saw you."

"Yes, but was I *married* then?" The two men laughed.

Haley moved to Roger's side, slipped her arm around him, and patted the front of his sweater. "He's fattening up nicely," she said.

Amanda smiled toward Roger, and he nodded. "Amanda, it's good to see you," he said.

"Thanks," Amanda looked at Nate and rubbed her hands along the front of her fur-trimmed jacket.

"Let me take your coats," Haley offered, and Amanda and Nate both relinquished their coats. "I'll put them in the hall closet," Haley offered.

"Here. Let me help," Nate said.

Amanda pressed her lips together and gave Nate a wide-eyed glare. He glared back and jerked his head toward Roger. Tempted to wrap herself around Nate's legs as he left the room, Amanda awkwardly stood near the doorway, toyed with the zipper on her jogging suit, and stared at the flames flickering in the fireplace.

She knew Roger was watching her. She also knew Nate had gone with Haley to give Amanda the space to do what she needed to do. He'd probably ask Haley for a grand tour just to make certain Amanda had plenty of time. She cleared her throat and dared to look at Roger.

Opening her mouth, Amanda planned to begin the rehearsed spiel, but instead said, "Need any help in the kitchen?"

"Oh, uh, sure!" Roger said. "You can butter the bread. It's almost time to put it in the oven."

Amanda followed Roger into the small kitchen and recognized Haley's touch in every corner, right down to the row of ceramic chickens hanging on the wall. She picked up the butter knife lying near a cookie sheet covered in sliced bread.

Roger opened the oven and peered inside. "Salmon's almost done," he declared.

Amanda eyed the tub of whipped butter, scraped the knife over the top, and prayed for an extra boost of courage. The time had come to voice the apology. "Roger..." Amanda pinched at a piece of bread.

"Yes." He turned from the oven.

"I'm s—sorry," she said.

His forehead wrinkled. "Really?"

"Yes. Really." Amanda nodded. "I should have never interfered in your and Haley's lives like I did. If it's any consolation, I thought I was doing the right thing. I just didn't understand that you really loved her and...I guess I didn't understand a lot." She helplessly shrugged.

"It's okay." Roger neared and smiled at her. "Nate thinks you're the best thing in the universe. If he's so sure, then I've decided to give you some grace."

Amanda smiled. "And I guess I'll give you a chance."

"Might as well," he said with a cocky-yet-endearing smile. "Looks like we're in-laws."

Laughing, Amanda nodded. "Yes, looks that way."

"Well now, isn't this cozy," Nate said as he and Haley entered the kitchen.

"We were just discussing our in-law status," Roger said. "I'm married to Haley's adopted sister, and she's about to marry my cousin."

"*About* to?" Nate said and lifted his left hand. A golden wedding band claimed his ring finger.

Roger and Haley silently gaped at the ring for several seconds before looking at Amanda. She raised her left hand to reveal her own wedding band nestled against her engagement ring.

"You aren't the only ones who can be quick and sneaky!" Amanda said with an impish grin.

Haley squealed and lunged at Amanda. The two women fell into a sister hug that left the men laughing. "When did you two do this?" Haley exclaimed and pulled away.

"Well…" Amanda drawled and looked at Nate.

"When you two got married and ran off to New Zealand, we got inspired. "So we had a tiny wedding with just our parents and Bev and Gordon. Then we shut down Amanda's office, sent Harold off to Bev and Gordon's, and flew to Paris. We just got in yesterday."

"Why didn't you *tell* me!" Haley exclaimed and slapped at Amanda.

She shrugged. "We wanted it to be a surprise," Amanda said.

"Well, I'm surprised!" Haley admitted.

"You old goat," Roger said and punched at Nate's arm, "You move fast, don't you?"

"Me?" Nate said. "It took me 15 years to get Amanda to marry me."

She moved to Nate's side, wrapped her arms around him, and kissed his cheek. "But I'm worth waiting for, don't you think?"

"I must admit I had to raise you first," Nate teased and pulled her closer.

"Maybe *I* was raising you," Amanda shot back.

"Ouch!" Roger winced.

"I'm *soooooo* mistreated," Nate complained.

"Yes, we all believe that," Haley mocked. "You already look as spoiled as Mr. Priebe."

"Oh, don't you believe it," Nate replied. "*She's* the one who's spoiled!"

As the group of friends fell into companionable laughter, Amanda observed her husband and relished his admission. She *was* spoiled already. He'd served her breakfast in bed in Paris, massaged her feet in the hot tub, and swept her away to a romantic restaurant where he hired a violinist for their own private serenade. Nate couldn't seem to do enough for Amanda, and Amanda couldn't seem to stop falling in love.

About the Author

Debra White Smith continues to impact and entertain readers with her life-changing books, including *Romancing Your Husband, Romancing Your Wife, Friends for Keeps, More than Rubies, It's a Jungle at Home: Survival for Overwhelmed Moms,* and the *Sister Suspense* series. She has been an award-winning author for years with such honors as Top-10 Reader Favorite, Gold Medallion Finalist *(Romancing Your Husband)* and Retailer's Choice Award Finalist *(First Impressions* and *Reason and Romance).* Debra has more than 40 book sales to her credit and over a million books in print.

The founder of Real Life Ministries, Debra speaks at events across the nation and sings with her husband and children. She has been featured on a variety of media spots, including *The 700 Club, At Home Live, Getting Together, Moody Broadcasting Network, Fox News, Viewpoint,* and *America's Family Coaches.* She holds an M.A. in English.

Debra lives in small-town America with her husband of 23 years, two children, and a herd of cats.

To write Debra or contact her for speaking engagements, check out her website:

www.debrawhitesmith.com

or send mail to

Real Life Ministries
Debra White Smith
P.O. Box 1482
Jacksonville, TX 75766

Great Books by
Debra White Smith

❧ ❧

THE AUSTEN SERIES
First Impressions
Reason and Romance
Central Park
Northpointe Chalet
Amanda

SEVEN SISTERS SERIES/
SISTERS SUSPENSE SERIES
Second Chances
The Awakening/Picture Perfect
A Shelter in the Storm
To Rome with Love
For Your Heart Only
This Time Around
Let's Begin Again

MARRIAGE
101 Ways to Romance Your Marriage
Romancing Your Husband
Romancing Your Wife

MOTHERHOOD
It's a Jungle at Home

ROMANCING YOUR HUSBAND
by *Debra White Smith*

Early days in a relationship are exhilarating, but they can't touch the thrilling love affair you can have now. Cutting through traditional misconceptions and exploring every facet of the Bible's message on marriage, *Romancing Your Husband* reveals how you can create a union others only dream about. From making Jesus an active part of your marriage to arranging fantastic romantic interludes, you'll discover how to—

- make romance a reality
- "knock your husband's socks off"
- become a lover-wife, not a mother-wife
- find freedom in forgiving
- cultivate a sacred romance with God.

Experience fulfillment
through romancing your husband...
and don't be surprised
when he romances you back!

ROMANCING YOUR WIFE
by *Debra White Smith* and *Daniel W. Smith*

Do you want your husband to surprise you and put more romance in your relationship? *Romancing Your Wife* can help! Give this book to your hubby, and he'll discover ways to create an exciting, enthusiastic marriage.

Debra and her husband, Daniel, offer biblical wisdom and helpful advice that when put into practice will help your husband mentally, emotionally, and physically improve his relationship with you. He'll discover tools to build a dynamite marriage, including how to—

- communicate his love more effectively
- make you feel cherished
- better understand your needs and wants
- create a unity of spirit and mind
- increase the passion in your marriage

*From insights on little things
that jazz up a marriage to more than
20 "Endearing Encounters,"
Romancing Your Wife
sets the stage for love and romance.*